The Prince of Rumandy

JOSEPHINE ELI

The Prince of Rumandy

Published by
American Griffin

Copyright © 2015 by Josephine Eli

ISBN: 978-0-9961211-0-1

Contributing editor Janet Swedorske

Cover by Josephine Eli

~Dedicated to Kathleen Rea~

Here's to many more talks and cups of tea!

CHAPTERS

Chapter 1

A Cordial Welcome to Rumandy

*Often a person cannot see where a road is leading until he
has trodden it to its finish. Likewise, some lives travel in
ways unimagined from the start.*

-The Journals of Bengolian

There was once a prince named Percival Cornelius Vladimir
Oswalden Edwalter Ambrogio Reginald Isidore Barnaby IV who
lived, as can be expected of a prince of Rumandy, a refined,
cultured, and very comfortable life. In fact, he had surpassed all
other princes in the whole of Rumandorian history regarding his
wealth, his appeal, his celebrity, and not least to mention, his
immeasurable vanity.

His royal highness possessed one hundred servants awaiting
only the tinkle of a bell (which was tinkled quite often) to attend
to his every desire. He had a plethora of exotic pets, seven
chambers full of the finest clothing acquirable, one hundred and
thirty-seven pairs of shoes, and so many hats I don't think anyone
could ever keep a reliable tally. Hats were his particular forté in
fashion, you see, and although they had been previously

considered outdated, the prince re-established a hat wearing trend among the youth of society. This was, arguably, one of his most noteworthy accomplishments.

Now not only was our prince rich beyond measure or imagination, he was also terrifically famous for it. Consequently, it was only natural that in the springtime before his seventeenth birthday, word reached every regal ear (as well as all the commoners' ears, but they are not nearly as significant in this story) that the prince was soon to throw a magnificent celebration in honor of...well, himself.

Seventeen was then considered to be the ideal age for a prince to begin the formalized process of arranging a suitable match—that is, a marriage which would benefit the kingdoms on both sides of the agreement. Such a union would, above all, ensure prosperous affairs between the two conjoining countries and a valuable alliance in times of warfare. It would be naive to think these sorts of things were about romance and love, you understand. They were, in point of fact, all about money and strategy, which are much more useful.

Typically, a princess would loathe such political grounds of matrimony, but upon receiving the portrait of the prince included in the invitation, and beholding the image of His Highness Prince Percival's stunning, fair face framed by the angelic golden locks of his hair, the princesses all simultaneously decided becoming the future queen of Rumandy was the new all-important competition of the century. Prince Percival was very good looking, after all. And the twenty-seven or so mirrors he kept in his room attested to the fact that he was not shy about it.

The prince realized finding someone fit to share in his magnificence was a difficult task. Naturally, no one could be entirely worthy of him, but on account of his extraordinary altruism and modesty, he was willing to marry a princess of less excellence than himself, provided she was indeed the very best the civilized world could offer him.

Now, as these sorts of occasions often evolved, the term "birthday celebration" was gradually amended to "ball." Hence, all the young princesses and duchesses and otherwise rich and politically significant girls were sure to receive invitations. All throughout the early weeks of August, while summer in the South was in its prime, royalty flocked to the palace at Rumandy. Guests arrived by carriage, horseback, ship, and riverboat. Every pompous, powdered-nosed princess to be found in civilization was expected to attend.

It was a bright afternoon, the last few hours before the ceremonies were to officially begin, and the courtyard was milling with the throngs of newly arriving young ladies—and their luggage, which took up the greater portion of the space. Servants bustled here and there laden with bags to be carried, drinks to be served, royalty to be pampered, and so forth. The day was drenched in August sunlight, and everywhere young ladies flapped large, elegantly feathered fans to cool their rosy cheeks. On the piazza near the broad open doors of the palace, where people scrabbled in and out, musicians played lovely melodies in allegro. Such performances were not actually listened to or appreciated, of course, but they were accepted as a standard background feature for royal gatherings.

Upon the grass, large picnic blankets were laid down for the young ladies to rest from their journeys and relax in the glorious outdoor air. Meanwhile, their luggage was shuffled in through the porticoes and their servants saw to their accommodations. The girls sat upon the decorative little rugs in clusters of three or four, poised and proper, prattling on relentlessly like typical young ladies of society. Their topics covered everything imaginable for girls of their age and state, which unfortunately was not very much: powder and pins, ribbons and rings, hats and hair, pearls and, above all, as you can probably imagine, the prince.

"I myself have never seen him in person, but they say he is *divinely* handsome. Just like his portrait," said a certain Princess Priscilla to her cousin, Brigitte of Rothwel. "And, of course, I am sure he is. Rumandorians are born with it, just like us from Wilporsprings. Those born of the line of Wilporsprings are always born with an incontestably natural beauty and grace. That's what they say, anyway. I wouldn't make such a bold statement myself, though I cannot disagree."

"Oh, Priscilla..." her cousin Brigitte began, cynically. "Why, that statement is nothing more than a fanciful fabrication of your own mind. You're obviously just trying to establish your claim on the prince by boosting your arrogant confidence!"

Priscilla's eyelids closed condescendingly as she exhaled. "Whatever that means, Gitty...Jealousy turns your face a dreadful shade of green, you know, and I can hardly bare to look at it. And besides, that is not my intent at all!"

"Oh, isn't it?"

"I would never establish a claim on a prince I've never even seen before. What if he wasn't even handsome after all? And it's quite possible he isn't as handsome as his portrait paints him to be. That happens often, you know. And none of us can claim to have seen him in person, now can we?"

"I saw him the other day," inserted the third princess on this particular blanket, Cloeneth of Fairbourne. Her voice was considerably softer and more reserved than the voices of the other two. "He was in one of the great halls."

"...You saw him? You really did? In life?" Priscilla of Wilporsprings bounded forward and nearly choked on her own excitement. "Well, for goodness' sake, Cloe! Why on earth haven't you mentioned that before? We were sitting here, talking about him all this time and you don't mention you've seen him till just now! Well, is he as handsome as they say he is?"

"Well, it...it was only a glance," Cloeneth responded. "He was talking, I think, to another prince I didn't know."

"Oh, yes, yes, well we don't presently care about any other prince we don't know, do we? So, come now, get on with it! And you've been talking so unbearably slowly lately, Cloeneth, I can hardly stand it! You must think less and speak more!"

"I...thought he was very handsome," Cloeneth said without expression.

"I knew it! I KNEW it! See! What did I tell you, Gitty? What did I tell you?" Priscilla raised her chin haughtily. "I told you I was sure he was divinely handsome, and now we have an eyewitness account. Oh, do let us visit the galleries now! How I wish to gaze upon his portraits again! Such divine features! And quite similar to those of Wilporsprings. We would make exceptionally fine-looking children."

"Oh, please, Priscilla," Brigitte glowered, "don't recommence your pestering self-praise. Frankly, I am tired of hearing such outrageous assertions."

The three girls on this particular blanket sat silent for a moment and flapped their fans, Brigitte with poorly concealed irritation, Cloeneth with detachment from the scene, and Priscilla with overconfident daydreaming. It was the third at length who broke the silence:

"What do you think of that new girl who arrived today?"

"Well, almost half of the guests are arriving today, I don't know..."

"No, no, Brigitte, the one from the northern kingdom, what's it called..."

"Lordale?" Cloeneth offered.

"Oh yes, that was it. What do you think of her?"

"I haven't met her," said Cloeneth

"Nor have I," added Brigitte.

"Yes. Neither have I." Priscilla yawned and patted her gaping mouth with her fan, "Well, at any rate, she's certainly a perfectly disagreeable and unpleasant person. That's certain."

"Priscilla!" Cloeneth protested. There was a bit of an awkward silence as the fanning continued. Each girl recognized there may have been something a little strange about the princess of Lordale. It was nothing disagreeable perhaps, but it was unquestionably strange. "I do not claim to know her," Cloeneth added at length, "just as you cannot, but by what I have seen, I can only speak well of her."

"Oh, Cloeneth, you kindhearted soul. You would only speak well of a toadfish."

"I will speak well of whatever I wish to speak well of, Priscilla. Whether it is a princess of the North or a toadfish is my own matter."

"Well put, Cloeneth!" Brigitte interjected. "And you, Priscilla, would be best to seal your fat lips and leave the rest of us in peace, as you don't know the least bit on the subject. Your lack of knowledge of such matters vexes me, my dear cousin."

Priscilla stopped flapping her fan momentarily. "Hold on just a moment...Are we talking about the girl from the North or the toadfish? Because I would wager the toadfish has no objection to any accusations I may make."

"What I am talking about, my dear cousin," Brigitte persisted, "is how arrogant and self-infatuated you are. You incessantly overestimate yourself, Priscilla! Why, I don't think you're even any more extraordinary looking than the girl from Lordale!"

Priscilla's mouth dropped open at the insult. The fan fluttering began over again. Then, after a seething silence, the conversation resumed from its intermission:

"That's utter nonsense," Priscilla insisted. "The girl is entirely loutish and mundane. And her wardrobe is so peculiarly outdated.

I was almost embarrassed for her. Quite an awkward-looking and repulsive thing. . .I saw her this morning, you know, and she just looked so entirely uncouth. Quite like a toadfish! It is a splendid comparison, indeed."

"Why are we mentioning toadfish again?"

"Because...I can't remember. That's beside the point, Brig— ouch!"

Priscilla was cut short by a sudden slap on the knuckles from Brigitte's fan. Brigitte directed the group's attention ahead. Walking near to the courtyard's central fountain was the princess of Lordale herself, hardly ten feet from where they sat. She could not have been there long before they noticed her, and from her unaffected and rather oblivious expression she did not seemed to have overheard their conversation. Instead, she appeared to be fascinated with some modest little flowers mingled in with the bushes of the fountain.

"Do you think she heard us, Priscilla?" Brigitte asked.

"No, I don't think so."

"We were talking rather loudly."

Fanning themselves in pretended insouciance, the three slipped curious little glances at the strange girl now and again. She actually didn't look all that horrific—just perhaps a little misplaced and overly-simplified. Her hair was not curled or arranged but falling in a simple, dark brown braid; she was not wearing so much as a crumb of jewelry; and most noticeably, she had no stiffened bodice, no whalebone corset, and no full skirts exaggerated with a hoop or panniers. Instead, her dress was simple and a bit peasant-like.

"She's nothing like I've ever seen before," remarked Brigitte.

"And nothing of which I'd care to see more of," Priscilla added.

"Priscilla, hush!"

"She can't hear us, Brigitte," Priscilla flapped her fan with casual disdain, pensive and judgmental. "Hm," she muttered. "Lackluster. Her entire outfit. But then again she is far too scrawny to wear anything that would flatter a woman's form."

Brigitte rolled her eyes, "Just because your corset is bursting at the seams doesn't mean everyone else is too thin."

"I am NOT bursting at the seams, ninny!" Priscilla pursed her lips threateningly, then felt over her waist for reassurance. She grumbled as she mentally compared waists between herself and the two other girls on the blanket. "You're fatter than I am, Gitty! You're just jealous, aren't you? Isn't she, Cloe?"

Cloeneth didn't answer.

"She does have, indeed, the strangest nose I think I have ever seen," Priscilla continued, dropping the previous subject abruptly.

"Who?" Brigitte inquired

"The northern princess, idiot!"

"What are you talking about, Priscilla? Don't be stupid. It's a perfectly fine nose. Yours isn't any better."

"I didn't say hers was repulsive. On the contrary I think there is nothing particularly unattractive about her features. With some tending to, she could even prove to be rather pretty. But, she's far from that now. Look at her, slouching! Did you see her lifting up her skirt as she dashed across the grass earlier today? Apparently they have yet to invent walkways in the North. How unrefined for a lady to scramble across the grass! Why, with her mannerisms I would hardly be surprised if she were a common country milkmaid. Not that there is much of a difference in Lordale between princesses and milkmaids. Have you heard what they say about that country? The place is entirely primeval. All forests, nothing civilized. Dirty roads, dirty animals, dirty people, dirty everything." Priscilla fluttered her eyelids in rhythm with the flapping of her fan, "Some even say the land is crawling with sorcery from influence of the savages north of the border. I wouldn't be surprised. Look at her! Slouching again."

"Oh, Priscilla, for heaven's sake!" Brigitte clasped Priscilla's fan and the three froze suddenly. It looked almost as if the princess from the North was approaching them.

"Wait a minute; is she coming this way?" Brigitte asked.

"Of course she isn't coming—wait. Oh dear, look what you've done!"

"Is she coming over here?"

"Hush up, Brigitte!"

"Don't tell me to hush up! You're the one with fat lips you can't keep shut!"

"I most certainly do not have—"

The three quickly thrust their gaze to the opposite direction and pretended to be preoccupied in something else; there was not enough time to decide what. The fans fluttered more violently now, poorly concealing the princesses' tension.

"Excuse me," came the northern princess, "I'm sorry to interrupt."

"Oh, no, no, not at all!" said Priscilla and Brigitte, nearly in unison.

"All of the other blankets are filled, it seems. Might I sit here for a moment?"

There was an awkward pause. "Well...certainly!" said Priscilla with pretentious charm.

Priscilla and Brigitte each bore a synthetically beaming, puffed up smile, as though they had not noticed her till that very moment and were fully delighted to make the acquaintance. This was a usual habit of royalty, you see—to gossip ruthlessly of one another one moment and then appear of the highest degree of amiability to each other the next. Cloeneth of Fairbourne had, however, some true sentiment of kindliness, and her civility needed less inflation than that of Priscilla and Brigitte.

There were a few moments of awkward silence. The new guest seemed to be neither very shy nor very sociable. She was not entirely shy for she herself approached the party and yet not entirely sociable for she spoke no word to the company till Priscilla broke the silence out of strained courtesy.

"You are from the...North?" she inquired, as though she hadn't already known.

"Yes. Lordale."

The girls eyed each other, each waiting to see who would be first to imperil her reputation with an introduction. Priscilla cleared her throat insinuatingly and glared at Brigitte with an exaggerated smile, but Brigitte only battered her eyes coyly, refusing her cousin's wordless request. At last an arm was extended:

"I'm Cloeneth of Fairbourne," said the third princess.

Brigitte and Priscilla stared a moment in astonishment of their third member, fan flutters suddenly coming to another halt.

"...Brigitte of Rothwel," added the one.

"Priscilla of Wilporsprings," added the other.

"Delighted," the northerner said with a smile. "I'm Frayda...Oh. Of Lordale, but I guess I said that already," she laughed a little awkwardly.

"Hmph," Priscilla muttered beneath her breath. The fan flapping started up again with another gap in the conversation.

"You've arrived just today, then, Frayda?" asked Cloeneth.

"Yes, only a few hours ago. It's a long ways between Lordale and Rumandy."

"Yes. Apparently it is," said Priscilla.

Frayda of Lordale, seemingly unconscious of their scrutinizing eyes, ripped out a little tuft of grass and began to fiddle with it.

"Have your mother and father come with you, then?" asked Priscilla.

"No. My mother is expecting a child soon. My parents are both at home."

Priscilla grimaced. "Of course. Ah, well. What a shame; having a sibling. You probably won't receive half as much attention once another child is born, especially if it happens to be a boy. I am an only child, you see, and my parents are now too old to have others. I do relish the position greatly."

"Oh. Well, actually I have five in my family already."

"Five what?"

"Siblings, of course."

"...Siblings?"

"Yes. Brothers and sisters."

"Five!"

"Well, this will be the sixth."

"Sixth!"

"Yes. That makes seven, all together."

"Seven!"

"How do you all function in such a large pack?" Brigitte asked.

"What do you mean?" the northerner asked.

"How do you decide who is going to marry whom? And when?"

"I'm...not quite sure that we answered all of that yet."

"Good heavens, that sounds horrible..." Priscilla added.

"It's...really not that bad," Frayda said, a little shyly. "I don't think..."

"At any rate, how was your journey to Rumandy?" Priscilla said, changing the subject.

"Not all bad. I enjoy riding."

Another halt of fan flaps. "You rode from Lordale to Rumandy? On horseback?" said Priscilla.

"Well, yes. Just me and a few servants." Frayda of Lordale smiled sweetly. "It took almost three full days, including the stops and all, but I enjoy the countrysides."

Priscilla's face seemed to curdle with surprise. "Were all of the palace carriages being used up by your family members when you left?"

Frayda laughed again, her dark eyes glittering like black marble and her unpainted face reddening prettily like a peasant. "Oh, no, you must forgive my northern simplicity. I'm actually more used to a horse's back than a cushioned carriage. Lordale is not as refined a culture as Wilporsprings or Rothwel, I am afraid."

"That's true," said Brigitte.

"Such elegance and sophistication is incontestably only found in the South," added Priscilla.

"...Right." said Frayda.

"I'm surprised you even received an invitation," said Brigitte, rather bluntly.

"Oh. Yes, well, I..."

"And I mean, of course, we're not saying that to offend you in any way," Priscilla added. "I think they were right to send you an invitation. I mean, you know, I think you're perfectly lovely."

"Or at least, there's nothing seriously wrong with the way you look," said Brigitte.

"Oh...Thank you."

"You wouldn't stand out in a crowd as being particularly stunning, but you're not ugly. And you have a sweet sort of nature about you," said Priscilla.

"...Thank you."

During a short pause in the conversation, Priscilla and Brigitte both began to consider the possibility of forming a social alliance with Frayda, who was clearly not a serious threat in the competition for the prince's hand but could prove to be useful somehow in the scheme of things. Cloeneth, inserting herself rather suddenly into the picture, addressed Frayda quietly with a kind and almost apologetic smile. Cloeneth, it seemed, spoke only in sincerity, and only when the scene required a sincere word. "It's wonderful to have you," she said.

"Thank you," Frayda replied again.

Priscilla cracked her neck to get out a kink. It was a bad habit she had acquired, but she never apologized for it because she believed it lengthened her neck and made her taller. She drew her head upward proudly, a contented smile of crimson painted lips stretching across her face. "You know, my dear," she said to Frayda, "I think I am actually going to like you. I can hardly believe I'm hearing this from my own lips, but I think that I will take you under my wing this week. You could use some direction on how to behave, I am sure."

"And I'll assist in the undertaking," Brigitte added.

"Oh. That's not necessary, but thank you," Frayda replied with an embarrassed laugh.

"No, no, I insist," said Priscilla.

"So do I," said Brigitte. "I insist on helping."

"It's settled," Priscilla concluded.

Frayda, at that moment, couldn't possibly decline the offer as she had no excuse, knew no one else there, and was trying her best not to purposefully be the outcast of society.

The afternoon was slowly waning as the four girls on the

blanket continued a conversation which was not altogether dull. In fact, even though they deviated from talking about the prince for almost a full quarter of an hour, the girls hardly noticed anything lacking in their discussion. The courtyard's bustle and noise had been dying down slowly, till a sudden fanfare rose above the music.

A herald stood at the door of the palace and said, after a priggish clearing of his throat: "Four hours till the great banquet feast of the prince! Four hours, my lords and ladies!"

At this, a thunderous commotion arose in the courtyard.

"For heaven's sake," said Priscilla, "why didn't they make an announcement sooner? Three hours! Where did the time go to? One can hardly prepare for such a ceremony in three hours!" She began to rise to her feet arduously. The fluff and bone and hoops and whatever other sorts of contraptions were layered beneath ladies' skirts were obviously not made for a convenient shift from a sitting to a standing position.

"Oh. It takes four hours?" said Frayda of Lordale, standing as well.

"That is barely enough time!" Priscilla exclaimed. "How many balls have you attended, my dear?"

"I...well, I suppose this is my first, really."

"Oh, dear..."

"What?"

"Oh, you have much to learn. Don't worry, I'm sure you'll be lovely. And we'll help you. Now, excuse me, I have to get ready immediately. It was indeed a pleasure meeting you, Frayda,"

Priscilla replied cordially and with some surprisingly truthful fondness. If truth be told, Frayda of Lordale was quite difficult to dislike. Even if Priscilla saw her only as a sort of peculiar and awkward pet, there was something about this Frayda of Lordale that was subliminally attractive and demanding of a liking. Of course, Priscilla would not have admitted to all of that, as it might have lowered her confidence in winning over the prince for herself.

"It was...nice meeting all of you as well," the northerner said shyly. She watched them bustle into the palace, took a deep breath as she pulled a little white flower out of the garden for good luck, and made her way into the palace as well.

JOSEPHINE ELI

Chapter 2

A Wash and a Wager

*There are two kinds of people in the world: those who
think themselves very foolish, and those who ought to.*
-The Journals of Bengolian

Now, as all of this was occurring, the prince was busy in his
rooms being groomed and pampered for the evening. You are
probably aware that neither fairy-tales nor historical records
usually express the common infatuation people of royalty have in
themselves, but in this story, I fear I must convey this horrible
truth of our Prince Percival of Rumandy: he was self-absorbed,
snobbish, bad-tempered, and all together spoiled to a rot. He did,
however, have several affable qualities, or at least he thought so,
and no one dared to tell him otherwise for fear of banishment or
imprisonment or the like. Percival fancied himself splendidly
talented in arts and performance, musically gifted, very
courageous, extraordinarily charming, and remarkably generous
to his pets, admirers, and servants. Usually, in that order.

On this particular morning, or afternoon, rather, as the prince
was not accustomed to waking in the wee morning hours, Percival

firstly enjoyed a wondrous bath. Note that a bath at the royal palace of Rumandy was not at all like those of the common bathing system of those countries, where one simply scrubs his hide with a thick bristle-brush while sitting in a cramped wooden tub of sudsy water. Oh, no. Here a bath was of the highest degree of delight. The prince's bathtub itself was five feet in length on all sides and three feet in depth. It was a passable volume for his approval. Of course, a bath of that size takes great effort to keep at the perfect temperature, and servants had to rush in and out regularly with pails of steamy water.

That day the bubbles were six inches high from the pool, and the prince sat propelling his bath-toy ships through the foamy seas. He would never have admitted to playing with toys in the bathtub, as he was now quite old for that. Therefore, he would have described this as early and elaborate scheming for an immense naval battle.

An old, bony servant, who had been a nursemaid to the prince from the days he was a very young child, arrived with a fresh pail of hot water.

"I say, Mourha, what time will my breakfast be served?" inquired the prince. The maid began to slowly pour the water into the tub.

"Well, yer the late one today, young master," the maid said. She had been raised in a small, rural, uneducated area and retained most of her peasant's accent. "It's well past breakfast, Yer Highness, but luncheon will be served within the hour, I'd say."

"Well, do see to it the kitchen makes haste. I'm simply

famished. And I trust their service won't be as poor as it has been of late. Kindly inform them that yesterday's breakfast was deplorable. Tell them my supposed 'soft-boiled egg' was nearly solid, and the charcoal slab they called a piece of toast was drenched. Tell them I prefer to have more toast than butter. And the pepper shaker was all but empty, make sure it's refilled today —oh, and tell that turnip of a pastry chef Fritz the lemon cake was positively stomach-churning. Have him make an apple cake today."

He sank one of his toy ships in his bathtub-battle, and it bubbled out from underneath the waves confirming defeat.

"Aye-aye, captain!" The maid saluted. She was the only servant in the palace who dared to jest with the prince, for she had known him too long to be taken aback at his airs, and he had known her too long to see her in the stocks.

"Fetch my robe, Mourha. If I linger in this sod-water any longer I'm sure to prune. I hate it when that happens. And someone find Bromley; he will be dining here at noon with me, and I need to talk to him, so I don't want him to be late again."

"Yes, Yer Highness. I heard yer cousin has been in the stables since the morn."

"Bromley is always in the stables since the morn...And see to it the kitchen serves to my own dining room. I wish to eat in my own quarters today."

"Yes, Yer Highness."

For his luncheon, Percival donned an elaborate morning-robe with blue leggings, golden slippers, and an ostentatious feathered hat. His ensemble would, of course, be changed soon after the meal in preparation for the ball, but princes rarely dress in smocks as they eat, and this particular prince enjoyed being fashionable on even the most trivial of occasions. His dining room was a glorious, mahogany space dressed with rich, carmine curtains, golden candelabras, a harpsichord in the corner (a stunning instrument which was often polished and seldom played), and a beautiful, ornately designed rug covering most of the floor. Far too many chairs lined the long breakfast table, which had far too much food laid out upon it. Percival had just sat to table when Bromley burst through the door.

Now, Bromley Duccorio had no significant royal position besides his relation to the prince. He had lived in the palace for as long as Percival could remember. The two had, therefore, spent nearly all their time together from the outset of boyhood. Bromley was of the prince's age but had no other resemblance. He had an inexhaustibly ludicrous smile which spoiled his otherwise handsome face. He was a little taller and a bit thinner than the prince, his lanky posture at times mimicking that of a lolloping clown. However, there was a certain look about him which was curiously irreplaceable—like a mutt so motley in its breeding as to make it adorably unique. His head was an extraordinary stock of tittering, red-orange tufts which sprung out capriciously in every direction. He had rather pale skin which reddened when he laughed, and glassy eyes the color of a stormy sea. That afternoon, Bromley wore his usual disposition, a gleeful, impishly charming smirk, as he swung the prince's chamber door wide and said:

"Hullo, Percy! Starting without me again, I see!"

"I believe it is you who is late."

"Of course. My apologies, Highness. My own most grievous fault." The boy sat down with a thud and immediately swung his leg over the armrest of the chair. He gulped down a glass of pulpy orange juice, licked his lips and tried to heave down a giant muffin.

"Bromley, I haven't called you in here to stuff your face," the prince said, yanking the food from Bromley's mouth.

"Hey, that's mine—"

"Now," Percival lifted his chin with an air of absolute authority. "I have a most vital decision to make before this evening in preparation for the banquet feast and I have so stressed myself at the struggle that I've stooped as to query your assistance."

"...Alright then." Bromley replied.

"Now, at the banquet, shall I don my crimson beret with the ostrich feather, or the indigo one with the silver pendant from Nenchester?"

"I don't know, Percy. How about...the blue one."

"I was leaning towards the red one. Yes. Red it is. I've decided. Thank you." Percival took a sip of his wine, "That means I ought to have something crimson laid out to complement. Two waistcoats were tailored for the occasion, but I'm not particularly fond of either of them. Perhaps the one I bought in Hastineve last month will do. I haven't worn that yet."

"You're nothing but a fig-muffin, Percy; you know that? Can't you think of anything but your apparel at a time like this?" Bromley stuffed in as much food as he could between his words. "Can I have my muffin back, please? It's the last blueberry."

"Or maybe I should have someone sent out to buy something new. I also need a new cravat."

Bromley stared, silently, until Percival was forced to notice his numbed expression. "You know what," he swallowed down the soggy heap of food in his mouth, "this could very well be the night you discover the princess of your dreams and sweep her off her toes and ride her away into the sunset and all that other stuff that comes along with that damn romanticism." Bromley had the unique gift of making anything sound unromantic. "I mean it is going to be your choice isn't it? The girl?"

"Well, of course it's going to be my choice, you idiot."

"Right, so you see, the way that I see it, and this is just untainted and effortless genius coming from the expansive imagination of my head...Look, here's the plan. You may pick one of the girls...and then *I* will get the rest of the bunch. Hey?"

"I'm really not sure that you could succeed in captivating any *one* female, let alone a group of them."

"What are you talking about? All the kitchen-maids are mad about me...the whole slew of them."

"Really?" the prince said, disbelievingly.

"Yeah, who's that one...Antoinette? No. Amelia? I forget; that adorable little ginger with the accent that I can hardly understand...I swear, she does nothing all day but sit around and daydream about me. And then there's what's her name...Miss Blue-Eyes over in the muffin house...I swear, best damn muffins in the universe."

"There's absolutely no reason one of the princesses coming to meet me would fall in love with you instead."

"Blueberry. Muffins. So good..."

"Princesses are a different breed than kitchen-maids."

"Oh, no they're not. They just wear more layers. And I just bet you you're wrong. I bet you I'll find one."

"Is that a wager?" inquired the prince with a laugh.

"A wager indeed!" Bromley declared, suddenly overly theatrical, "I shall venture to wager thee, Percival of Rumandy, that I'll find a girl who is charmed and smitten, hooked and besotted in love...with me. And not even remotely interested in you. Some girls must prefer redheads to blondes."

Taking a sip of his drink, which was immediately spat back after hearing Bromley's gamble, the prince let out a roaring, arrogantly thunderous laugh, clapping his hands. "Bromley you incorrigible fool. Really, what? Are you auditioning for the part of court jester again?"

"Do I look like I'm joking? Why, look at this face! Does this look like a joking face? I mean compared to my usual face."

Percival raised his brows and laughed again. "I have but to pick and choose one of these princesses, any of whom would grovel at my feet to be my consort. And you, Bromley. . . How would you attract them?"

"How would I attract them? You talk about them as if they

were bees, Percy!"

"Well, they sort of are. Buzzing around all the time."

"Oh, well, maybe you're right..." a puckish and cocksure grin slithered into Bromley's expression. "At any rate, I think we should bet on it. I'll find a girl before you find yours."

"And with what would you wager?" added Percival. "You have nothing to persuade me."

"That is probably true. But what fun is there to decline an honest bet, brother to brother? Come on, Percy, you can't lose!"

"And you can't win."

"Well, then, there is no need to hesitate in accepting the challenge! Come now, be a good gentleman and pander to my whimsical fancy just this once. I love these sorts of games, and I'm terribly deprived of them. I'll have nothing to do this entire week if I don't have any mischief to make."

The prince was caught between amusement and irritation. He breathed an exasperated sigh. "You want something from me," he recognized wryly.

"Well! How bold of you to make such an assertion..." Bromley smiled, brazenly. "Alcides."

"Alcides?"

"Wager Alcides."

The prince laughed snobbishly. "And why should I wager with my best horse and you with nothing?"

"Well, a true gentleman like yourself can never decline a bet; and besides, if you are so assured that I cannot win, why should you decline?" Bromley crossed his arms and dropped his elbows on the table, leaning in on the prince. "Unless... perhaps there is fear of humiliation in that regal eye! Oh, and I would not blame you for it. What a fantastic story that would make! The fairest maiden in the court... falls head over heels... not for Percival... not for the prince whom the world revolves around...but for his darling little cousin." Bromley batted his eyes and grinned.

"Amusing," said the prince, dryly.

"Yes, *I* think it is. Haha! I make myself laugh sometimes."

"You are only trying to humble me into cowardice. And for that reason, I shall wager Alcides. But if you should lose, which, of course, you will, you must procure for me another horse...and maybe a new pair of shoes."

"For you or for the horse?"

"Both."

"Oh my." Bromley sighed and leaned back into his chair, slinging his elbow over the headboard, "You drive a hard bargain. But, if those are your terms, then those are my terms."

"Now remember, I do not wager for your sake, but for mine. I do it solely to prove that I always win."

"Well, alright! I'll drink to that! To the superiority of Prince Percival of Rumandy!"

"And to my victory in your wager."

"Come now, how terribly un-gentlemanlike of you, Percy! To declare victory before the game has begun!"

"Then, let it begin now," the prince replied as the boys clanked goblets and drank, each with an equally satisfied smirk.

Now it was well past noon, and beams of sunlight illuminated the space, gold shining upon garish gold and warming the wood of the walls, floor, and furniture. The tall, paneled windows gazed toward a corner of the courtyard, and, from below, the guests made a muffled clamor. Bromley leisurely drifted to the window ledge of one of the room's oriels, his goblet still in hand, to get a glance at the scene.

"Damn," he muttered, wide-eyed. "Have you spotted any to your liking yet?"

"Any what?"

Bromley dropped his head across his shoulder and rolled his eyes, "Percy, really, there's a flock of gorgeous females beneath your window...what else would I be talking about?"

"Knowing you, Bromley," Percival laughed, "I wouldn't be surprised if you were talking about buttered croissants for the banquet tonight."

Bromley fell backwards in laughter onto the cushioned oriel, "Oh Percy, how you slash my poetic veins and let them bleed so. Even though I have the unfortunate tendency to butcher the very idealism of romance and mock its very quintessence, it doesn't mean I'd prefer buttery biscuits to beautiful women...not all of the time, anyway. You know, sometimes, I even think that starry-eyed sensation doesn't sound entirely dreadful."

The prince put his feet up on the empty chair next to him and took another drink. "Sometimes, Bromley, I think you must have had an orangutan for a father."

A short, huff of laughter spurted out from Bromley's mouth, but his humor at the prince's quip seemed to dry curiously fast.

"Hey, me too." He traced the rim of his cup with his finger and looked out the window. "I don't think I'd ever be able to choose just one," he said, "Blonde...brunette...it all just depends on the current state of my fickle disposition. But then there's you, Your Highness. You will not tolerate any but the best. Too high standards for beauty and too low for personality; that's what I think is your problem, Percy."

"And your problem, Bromley," replied the prince with half-amused mockery, "is that you have *no* standards for either beauty *or* personality."

Bromley pressed his lips together, crinkled his nose, and raised the wrinkles in his forehead as if taking great effort to evaluate the statement. "...Hm," he muttered, "You're probably right. But when you're only the cousin to the prince and not the prince himself, you have to take anything you can get."

The prince laughed with a slightly scornful air as he picked up a cluster of grapes. "Don't you ever get tired of being such a useless shadow to a prince, Bromley?"

Bromley's grin remained plastered on his face. He raised his cup out in front of himself as if to make a toast. "God save us all if there should ever come such a day, Your Highness," he said.

JOSEPHINE ELI

Chapter 3
Frivol and Fairytales

*A person is rather like a good painting. In time, it
cracks and wears but every stroke the artist has set
down is there for a reason. And you can never
understand a painting at your first fleeting look.*
-The Journals of Bengolian

Now Frayda of Lordale was not as fastidious as the other
princesses, and she had finished preparing for the evening far
sooner than anyone else. After a minute of impatient dawdling
and pacing the room from windows to mirror to bedpost to
windows again, she slipped silently out of her room and into the
narrow passage lined with guest-room doors. She now had two
and a quarter hours before the ball, and she was certainly not
going to spend it in front of the mirror. She could not understand
how some girls were capable of gawking at themselves for such a
prolonged lapse of time, and found it to be a very exhausting
activity for herself.

From within the rooms, sounds of grooming and bustling and
yelling at servants echoed out, but the hall itself was entirely still.

The floor was silent beneath her feet as her steps fell lightly upon the rug, extending through the corridor into the vacant darkness. The hall was lit only by the soft radiance of tallow candles fixed in golden sconces protruding from the walls on either side. Frayda's curious eyes scanned the paintings which usually went unnoticed.

She was not a great connoisseur of art herself, but she thought some of these paintings were rather interesting. They were not so inflated with fluff and trills and all of the refined and sophisticated dross of the South. The candlelight sparsely lit the painted scenes of dueling knights in torn and bloodstained mail, turreted castles that climbed to pale clouds, and misty falls amid green forests. These pictures seemed too primeval, too simple and lovely to be seen in the South at all.

Suddenly the handle of one of the doors beside her rattled, and a sliver of light appeared. There was a dainty little whimper from within the room, followed by a surge of driveling nonsense typical of princesses.

Frayda turned around the corner at the end of the first corridor and pressed herself up against the wall to hide herself. "Where are zhe hair-ribbons? Noh! Not zhose ones; zhe other ones, lummox! Where is Dolce? Dolce! Did you take my ribbons?"

"Noh, styupid!" an identical voice replied. "Zhese are mine! Simona, give me back my pearls!"

More royal babbling in a nearly incomprehensible accent was heard, and quavering voices of servants following in reply. Frayda had to let a tiny bit of laughter slip from pressed lips as she listened. Southern girls were very odd from a northern girl's perspective.

Suddenly, Frayda's eyes fell upon a painting on the wall in front of her.

"*Eh!* Zhis looks dreadful!" came another pout from within the room. "Must zhe Borinoccian princesses arrange our hair ourselves?"

The door slammed closed once more and two maid servants scurrying off in the opposite direction with baskets of linens and a tray of half eaten refreshments.

"Twins..." one of the maids remarked with an exasperated sigh.

"As if one of them isn't bad enough!" added the other.

Frayda watched the maids disappear down the hallway, then returned her attention to the painting in front of her. Again there was silence but for the whining of girls from behind the walls. Frayda narrowed her eyes, taking her back from the wall and drawing closer to the painting in front of her. She tucked under her bottom lip and pinched a smile into the side of her mouth, a pretty little expression she often had when a playful curiosity got the better part of her.

The ill-lit hallway revealed the image only dimly, but even the glimmering patterns of light and shadow added to Frayda's captivation. The painting was of two women, one of which held a crown of silver and the other a golden chalice. The former of these two, the lady that held the crown, was exceedingly beautiful —almost celestial. Her black hair fell in a long braid and her face was very fair. The woman who held the cup was hooded, however, and she had a silvery mantle around her. Her face was almost entirely hidden by the shadow of her veil.

Suddenly, the creak of a heavy door shattered the stillness, and Frayda started and drew away from the image.

"Bless me, m'lady, ye wouldn't be ready for the ball, would ye so soon?" said an old maid. She somehow managed to close the door behind her while carrying a wicker basket with bundles of linens towering almost to her head.

"Yes, ma'am."

"Well, ye'd be about the strangest princess I've ever heard of. Can't say as I've ever seen a princess who didn't spend as much time as she possibly could in front of her mirror before a great ball."

Frayda smiled and laughed a little, "Well, I actually tried, ma'am. But I felt like it was a very strange waste. I'm not going to make myself any more or less attractive with the time I spend gawking at my reflection."

The maid, looking rather surprised, paused for a moment. She laughed, raising the wrinkles around her eyes. "Well, m'lady, that's the most sense I've heard from a princess all day! Where ye from, m'lady?"

"Lordale."

"Ah! Quite northerly, aren't ye then?"

"Yes, ma'am."

"It's good to know they've got some sense up there! What will you do till the ball tonight, then, m'lady?"

"Oh, I just...Well, I had hoped no one would mind my walking about."

"I can't say that I mind, deary, not that I'm queen of the palace. Though I wouldn't want to go lurking about through these dreary passages if I was ye, too gloomy for my tastes, no windows and all."

"It's a shame these pictures cannot be seen in better light."

The maid puffed out a short burst of laughter. "Ah, well, some nice ones here and there, I suppose."

"Can you tell me anything about this one?" Frayda turned back towards the picture of the two women. "Do you know what this picture is about? It seems so strange but so beautiful as well."

The maid looked thoughtfully at the picture. She set down her basket, which seemed to be increasingly heavy and awkward. "Well, now," she said unhurriedly, "That one...I do happen to know about that one, m'lady. It was a present to his highness, in fact!"

"A present to the prince?"

"Aye."

"From whom?"

"Oh, just a strange sort of old man...a long time ago, it was. But that's another story for another day. The picture itself as I believe is from one of those old stories—if ye know. The sort they say is from the Northern Wilds."

"Northern Wilds!"

"Aye. Past the border. My memory has raisined some, old as I am. I've never been one for long names, either way, but I think that picture has something to do with the . . .oh, what was it now?

It was some sort of...what do they call it...tribe or realm or kingdom from the Northern Wilds. Oh, it's, Arm...Arm-something."

"Armidia!" Frayda declared.

The maid put her hands on her hips in surprise. "Well! Ye're as strange a princess as I've ever met! That's not the average fairy-tale to have heard of in these parts, m'lady!"

"Well, my country is much closer to the Northern Wilds than Rumandy. We hear about those stories every now and again."

"Ah, I see, m'lady...Well, all I can tell ye is that they're nothing but distant northern gibberish in these parts, that's if anyone has ever heard of them at all. It certainly won't be any time soon that this picture is moved out of this dingy hallway. No place for it but here in the dark." The maid picked up her basket. "And I suppose, m'lady, I should be on the double to get back to my work."

"Could I help you in anyway? I don't have anything to do till the ball starts," Frayda said, innocently.

"My, my!" the maid laughed, surprised but pleasant in her tone. "Ye surely are the most unnatural princess I've met in years! *Could I be of some help*, she says! Well, a princess thinking of helping an old servant! How wonderfully silly, you are, deary! Thank ye kindly but no thank ye. We'd both get in trouble for it, I'd be afraid. What's yer name, by the way, m'lady?"

"Frayda."

"Well, Frayda. It is indeed a pleasure to make yer acquaintance. I'm Mourha. And ye can call on me any time of day that ye want to talk about old paintings in hallways or girls who gawk at their reflections."

Frayda laughed. "I certainly will."

The maid bowed her head with a smile and entered another room a little ways down the hallway. There was something very pleasant in the way that she walked, Frayda thought. It was delightfully energetic and untailored.

Frayda thought for a moment. Although she was dressed for the ball already and was afraid an adventure outside the palace would end in a stain or a tear, she simply could not ignore the urge to be out-of-doors. She quickly returned to her room and grabbed her riding cloak, hoping wearing it outside might ensure the preservation of her neatness. She knew at the ball she would be rather simply designed in comparison to the other girls anyway, but she preferred walking and breathing to hoop-skirts and corsets. And so, simply clad and covered by her cloak, she made her way out into the palace gardens.

Outside, the skies were turning lavender as wind whistled through the bushes. The courtyard of Rumandy was well-kept, the flower beds weeded and trimmed, and the walkways smooth and clean-edged. A marble fountain stood at the center of the garden with water rippling down in a near rhythmic pattern. There, all the walking paths met in a perfectly geometric design, and beside the fountain were marble benches. Frayda sank down on one of these benches and rocked her feet gently back and forth beneath her for a while.

There were no trees as far as the eye could see. Or at least nothing Frayda thought worthy to be called a tree. There were lines of priggish little shrubs, but nothing a person could climb. For Frayda, that was the deciding factors. If it had roots in the ground and branches that reached towards the sun—and you can climb it, it was a tree. Everything else was simply a plant.

Now Frayda wasn't forced into coming to Rumandy, per se. Or at least, not officially. Her parents certainly were not the type of people who would have made their daughter travel across the world just for the sake of formality, and there wasn't really anyone who cared whether she was there or not. It wasn't as if she had felt going to the ball would gain her anything. In fact, on receiving the invitation, complete with the portrait of the prince, her immediate reaction was to throw it all on her bed, run outside into the wooded glades of Lordale, become enveloped with the soft breezes of fresh forest air, and cringe at the thought of being away from home for an entire week, not including the time it would take to travel back and forth.

But when she later returned to her room, and returned to the invitation lying on her bed, an interesting thought began to creep into her mind. She stared blankly at the invitation, turned quickly aside to the window, looked back at the invitation, paced back and forth at the foot of her bed for a while, looked back at the invitation again and thought...maybe she was just afraid. Maybe that was the only reason she was so eager to refuse. The fear of new things. The fear of open doors. Of adventure. Of new people. Of not knowing what the next day would bring. The fear of falling in love. The fear of growing up.

Those thoughts pressed in on her and choked her until she

felt her life collapse into an abominable pit of blackness. At that moment, she simultaneously dared herself to accept the invitation, and accepted the invitation. And the decision was made. She would go to Rumandy. She would be a lady. She would be socially acceptable. She would be Frayda of Lordale, proper and prim and not awkward and certainly not uncivilized. She would fit in. She would be just like the other young ladies. And she would have as grand a time as ever she could have.

...So, anyway, now she sat there on the bench in Rumandy and saw how ridiculously stupid those thoughts had been, and she completely regretted her decision.

Her feet became restless once more and she meandered away from the bench. Beside the palace wall, she managed to find a little path which looked somewhat less artificial than the main paths in the gardens. This path was a narrow walkway walled by the palace on one side and a tall brick partition on the other. It was probably intended for the gardeners' use in scurrying around the fields, for it was not well-kept, and most likely not often walked by guests. Her fingertips slid along the bricks as the path stretched on beside the palace wall.

After a time, she reached what appeared to be the end of her road. A weather-beaten door stood before her, rust biting at its hinges and moss draping its boards. Frayda, being the sort of person whose curiosity occasionally got the better of her timidity, immediately began to creak the door open. It was heavy and attached by moss and vines to the ground, but she managed to make just enough of an opening to slip herself through. As she did so, she found herself in an open field of tall yellow grass swaying in the wind. The sun, setting across the field, shone out just above the tips of the distant trees, streaming in golden rays across the yellow grass. She breathed a great sigh of satisfaction and stood for a moment transfixed.

Now, Frayda knew it would be completely unacceptable for a girl of her age to step into the freedom of the wild grass. She was well on her way to adulthood. Something as childish as frolicking in a meadow is no longer a possibility for a sixteen year old girl, especially one who happened to be a princess...But just as soon as the thoughts of frolicking in a meadow crossed her mind, a torrent of joy rushed over her and flooded out all good and proper sense. She first ran to the center of the field, then spun and twirled and laughed, lifting her skirt above her knees in quite a deliciously liberated and improper manner. Suddenly a rafter of turkeys sprang out of hiding, gobbling and gurgling away as Frayda shrieked, tumbling to the ground. She lay there, out of breath but laughing softly, then tucked her arm comfortably between her head and the grass.

Beside her, there was a brown feather ribbed with gray which one of the turkeys had left behind. Sitting up, she grabbed it and twisted it into her hair, letting it trail down with her dark locks. It didn't look all bad, she thought. She had seen in a book of northern lore once, a picture of a sylvan woman with feathers strung into her hair, and she thought it looked just positively enchanting.

She remembered picking up the same picture book, seeing

the dark complexion of the sylvan peoples, and then spending the entire day in the sun hoping a tan would make her appear more northern. Instead, she developed a rather painful burn. Then, on another occasion, she picked up a different book of sylvan stories and saw a picture in which the people had very fair skin. This created a terrible dilemma in her mind as she did not know which the more accurate representation was.

Frayda lay back into the field once more and gazed up at the blankness of the cloudless sky. She bundled up part of her cloak to make a sort of pillow beneath her head and situated herself to be perfectly snug and comfortable.

It was not till then that she realized how deprived of good clean air she had been. She yawned a wide, satisfying yawn which extended over her entire face, and then stretched herself out, rather unprincessly. Fatigued by new sights, travel, and displays of appropriate mannerisms, she closed her eyes for a moment or two. A moment or two, however, turned into a minute or two, and a minute or two turned into an hour. And then an hour turned into dusk, and she still lay sleeping contentedly amid the tall yellow grass.

JOSEPHINE ELI

Chapter 4

A First Impression of Feathers and Turkeys

The only difference between a prince and a duck is that, generally, princes don't taste delicious roasted in cranberry glaze.

-The Journals of Bengolian

Frayda opened her eyes suddenly and was shocked to see that the sun had progressed on its course to beneath the horizon. She quickly picked up her skirts and raced back to the gate, down the passage way, and through the dewy grass.

She tromped up the steps of the palace till she reached the vestibule. Her brow was clammy, her face flushed, her hair a mess, and the hem of her dress soiled in two inches of mud. She beat off the dirt as much as she could and made a quick endeavor to tame her hair by combing through it with her fingers. Then she threw her cloak ungracefully into a pampering room beside the hall's entrance.

The echoes of music rang out from the banquet hall ahead, and a warm, golden light gleamed through the crack between the two enormous doors. Promptly, Frayda hastened across the airy marble vestibule, her feet pattering lightly, and she gripped one of the door handles. The door was heavy and difficult to open, especially for someone who was arriving late and not particularly fond of the idea of entering anyway. She was rather thin at least and managed to pinch herself through easily.

Suddenly, the music stifled her hearing with trumpets and cymbals and strings, and the smells of foppish perfumes became nearly pungent enough to suffocate her. She could not see much of anything but the backs of people's heads—the prodigious conglomerations of curls and ornaments or the powdered wigs of her fellow princesses. Everyone's gaze was tied to the open floor area where a single couple were dancing. Frayda could just barely see them through cracks between the crowds, but she presumed it was the prince and one of the guest princesses. To the far wall sat the king and queen, and standing on a platform was a pretentious looking herald holding a long paper scroll. The herald called someone's name, but it was difficult to hear any distinct words in that corner of the room. Another girl stepped out from the crowd to dance as the previous one was escorted back.

Frayda tried to get a look at the prince, but it seemed no matter where she turned, some shoulder or head or fan was in the way. It wasn't any use. She gave up the attempt to at least find an area in which she could breathe with less difficulty.

Now, jostling through any crowd is rather difficult, but making one's way through a ballroom with drape after drape of fabric barricading any steady movement and fans beating convulsively at every turn and frightfully large wigs shielding any hope of perceptibility is truly a great feat. She tried to stay as close as possible to the wall to avoid any serious injury in the expedition, but after her initial few minutes of meticulous evading, she could not help but shove her way through with many terse apologies. Suddenly she crashed, quite literally, into a familiar face.

"Oh! There you are," came a voice which sounded somewhat in between kindness and condescendence. Frayda turned to see that it was one of the princesses she had met earlier in the day.

"Priscilla of Wilporsprings, in case you have forgotten," the princess re-introduced herself.

"And Brigitte of Rothwel," said the girl standing beside her.

"Oh, hello," said Frayda. "Oh...uh, Frayda of Lor—"

"Yes, we know," Priscilla clipped her short, "Where have you been? You really shouldn't hide in crowds, you know. I haven't seen you at all the last twelve dances."

"*Twelve dances?*" Frayda repeated, rather disgruntled.

"No, no, no," broke in Brigitte, "This is the thirteenth, Priscilla. You can't count past your fingers."

"But...will the prince have to dance with every girl here before dinner?" Frayda inquired, her stomach suddenly feeling unbearably empty. "I already feel tired of watching."

"Tired of watching! *Pah!* Don't be silly," said Priscilla. "Brigitte, is Cloeneth done dancing yet? She seems to move at half the pace as the other dancers, somehow...I can't imagine she would have anything interesting to say to the prince, anyway. They must be feeling rather awkward by now. Brigitte, what comes after Fairbourne?"

"F…Um….F…Felsacci."

"*Felsacci!* You ninny! There's no princess from Felsacci, Brigitte! Only that prince what's-his-name. And it's fortunate that there isn't a princess too; a prosperous land like Felsacci could spoil my chances. Now what comes after Felsacci, Gitty? Think!"

"Hm, um…Florenth, I believe."

"Florenth," Priscilla repeated with a laugh and gave a sigh of relief. "*Hah!* That shouldn't pose a problem; Ida of Florenth has a snout like a warthog and she laughs like a parakeet."

A tiresome conversation followed between Priscilla and Brigitte to which Frayda could find less and less to add as it progressed. Her contributions became nothing more than a few "hm"s and "ah"s and then finally she gave up all together. She strained to keep a polite (but rather insipid) smile pasted on her face, but her eyes wandered about the room hoping to find rest from the exhausting superfluousness.

"Well, anyway, Gretel of Irvinghurst said that everybody who is anybody of southern fashion is wearing cerulean-dyed ostrich plumes in their hair but everyone knows that the prince's favorite color is red. One has to be more strategic than to simply follow the base fashions of the times." (We may safely enter the conversation in the midpoint, for neither the beginning nor the middle nor the end had any real substance.) Suddenly Priscilla gasped, "Oh! Brigitte! Did you see that? He *looked* at me! *He* looked at me! I'm sure of it! He looked right this way! Oh, Gitty, look how close he is to us now! I can almost make out his face!

Oh my! Never has there ever been a prince with such a luminance, such a courtliness, such a godlike hue and complexion..."

"I don't think he looked at you," Brigitte argued. "Why would you say that? Maybe he was looking at *me*."

"At you! Hah! You're just jealous, Gitty—as usual! Besides, you don't know half as much as *I* know about him. What's his favorite breakfast food? Hm? Don't bother guessing; it's gingerbread-raisin cake with sugar-crème. His favorite wine? Sauvignon Rouge Cheval! His characteristic cologne? Patchouli-sandalwood and frankincense!"

Quite frankly, Frayda thought that it was a little odd that Priscilla of Wilporsprings knew exactly what scent the prince would be wearing, but she kept her uneducated and uncultured opinion to herself.

"The name of his best hunting eagle?" Priscilla continued, "Hm? Galiano! The dimensions of his royal bathtub? His most accomplished sonnet? His current number of royal hats?" she wisped her fan, chin raised in pride of her own range of information.

"...Does *anybody* know his number of hats?" asked Brigitte, after a pause.

"*You* certainly don't! Anyway, I'm terribly hot. It's stuffy over here. Brigitte if you would stop gabbling for once, let's move to a better spot. I can't see an inch of the prince from here anymore anyway."

Presently as the girls turned to leave, a new head burst into the circle without warning.

"Hold my ladies! Hold, hold! Tarry a bit longer in your little circle if you will, my loves," came the rather curious looking dandy of a figure. He was colorfully dressed, almost to the point of absurdity, but he supported it well enough with an immediately charismatic stance and persona. It was quite as if some resplendent actor—whether of romance or of drollery it was hard to tell—had just stepped from the stage and was not quite out of character yet. "Allow me first, won't you, to simply state that you're looking positively delicious this evening!" he said, "Forgive my intrusion, but I saw you from across the room and had to find my way here. Might a poor, admiring lad inquire the names which come along with the three fairest faces in the room tonight?"

"You may, good sir." Priscilla raised her chin and grinned at the flattery. She extended her hand. "Priscilla of Wilporsprings."

"Wilporsprings! My, my my! Very nice," he said, taking and kissing her hand.

"And Brigitte of Rothwel," inserted the ostensibly second fairest lady.

"Brrri-gee-ta!" the boy repeated with flourish, a shamelessly flirtatious grin lining his lips as he kissed her hand next. "That poor prince. He is going to be in such a fine fettle making his decision this week. Can a body withstand such cruel torment? If I were he, dare I say, I'd go absolutely mad with the selection. Of course, when the prince is accustomed to decisions of selection— say there are seven pairs of shoes in a shop, or ten hats or three puppies—it's almost always his solution to bring them all home with him. I find that method to be the most sensible."

Frayda was beginning to notice how decorated speech became during balls. "Well," she added quietly, trying not to sound out of place, "the prince must truly be in a quandary, then."

"Most definitely!" said the fellow. "Something tells me that the method will fall flat if he tries to employ it on women."

"It would, but I was referring mostly to the problem of space," said Frayda. "With the number of girls present and the amount of baggage they each have collected, I'm afraid the prince would either have to reduce his accumulated possessions or expand the palace."

The boy paused for a moment looking with sudden astonishment at Frayda of Lordale. Then he unleashed an intensely gleeful laugh which reddened his entire face.

"Well, what a marvelous way of reasoning you have, my lady! So direct to the point! I love it! But now...I asked for the three fairest in the room and as of yet am only formally introduced to two! May I, my dear lady, have the pleasure of your name?"

"If you ask for the three fairest in the room I fear I must withdraw from your presence."

"*Agh!* Don't be so modest! I abhor modesty!" The boy crossed his arms and leaned in toward Frayda with examining eyes. "Hm, let's see...Hair like a smooth river of chocolate. Eyes like brown gems. A fair, darling face and..." he snatched her hand and kissed it, breathing in the scent of her skin, "Mhm...pine. How fiery and aphrodisiacal! Surely, one of the three fairest in all the land! And trust me, I have a keen eye for beauty!"

Frayda raised a brow and grinned doubtfully, withdrawing her hand from his and clasping her other behind her back. "And, my lord, how many others have you declared the three fairest in all the land tonight?"

The boy hesitated and read Frayda's expression. "Why, every lady from this corner of the room to that corner there, of course!" he said spryly, bearing the most boyishly mischievous smile Frayda had ever seen. "A keen eye for beauty can't be hampered by quantitative limitations, my lady! But now, I am forgetting myself!" He removed his hat with a deeply dramatic bow, revealing a head of peculiar, whimsical red hair. "If you refuse to give me your fair name, my lady, I shall at least give you mine: Bromley Duccorio of Brushpool; Prince Percival's third cousin and incessant shadow."

"Incessant shadow?" questioned Brigitte with a flirtatious laugh.

"Yes, my lady. See, they were going to order him a jester, but after taking one look at my face, they figured they couldn't do any better and told me on my first visit here that I'd be staying in Rumandy for the rest of my driveling life."

Priscilla and Brigitte giggled.

"Yes, indeed!" the boy continued. "Incessant shadow, loyal companion, jester, page, or idiot. Whichever one he prefers for the day. I know all his likes and dislikes and enough details to make a princess flush and faint. I also know where he sleeps and I have unlimited access to his private chambers. If I were a female that sort of thing would be very exciting for me, but as I am male, it really isn't."

The girls continued their silly laughter behind their fans, except Frayda who was not very much amused and…had no fan, besides. She began to lose interest and attention as the superficial conversation continued. It seemed not a single southern soul had any inclination to converse about anything of value…or anything at all except the prince. As she turned to scan the room again for some liberation, her eyes fell upon the face of an approaching princess.

"Cloeneth!" called Priscilla, "Oh, Cloe, there you are! When did your turn end? Oh, do tell us all about it!"

"My turn has been over for some time now," said Cloeneth.

"Who's dancing with him now? I can't see. Oh, I do wish the twins from Borinoccio would move their fluffed up heads out of my view! Anyway, come here, dear Cloe, tell me all about him!" Priscilla snatched Cloeneth by the forearm and drew her into the circle. "Does he dance well? What does he look like up close? What did he say? Well? Come now, tell us everything!"

Cloeneth's bright but indifferent eyes widened as she looked to be gathering words beneath them; a few times, she opened her lips as if to speak, but said nothing.

"Well, well," laughed the prince's cousin, "Me thinks the lady is lost in love and words have found her not!"

Cloeneth dropped her gaze downward and laughed quietly, "Oh, no, my lord."

"Well, what is it then? Spit it out, Cloe!" urged Priscilla.

"I just dislike speaking when there is no need. The prince is all that you have expected; I am sure you will not be dissatisfied."

"Not be *dissatisfied*!" laughed Bromley, "I should think not! My lady must be very frugal with words indeed if she can find nothing to say of even the most excellent and illustrious prince of all civilization!"

Cloeneth of Fairbourne again said nothing.

"Tell me, my lady," the prince's cousin continued when he saw that the princess would not, "did you find nothing extraordinary in him?"

Cloeneth paused a moment then said quietly, "There are extraordinary things to be found in everyone. What can be said of the dignity of a man who would be king is no less true of a prisoner who refuses to renounce him."

Bromley's forehead creased. It was obviously not the attitude he was accustomed to when he questioned ladies about the prince. He laughed with uncertainty and shook his head. "My lady speaks of things far beyond my sphere of conversation," he said. "I have no jests for that."

Suddenly, a call rang out from the herald.

"The Princess Frayda of Lordale, Daughter of King Corinth and Queen Cybele."

It seemed the music had stopped and all Frayda could hear was the echo of her name. Priscilla gasped. "Are we at Lordale, already? Brigitte? What number is that?"

"I don't know, I lost count."

"Frayda! What are you standing there for? It's your turn! Well, go!" Priscilla commanded.

"Right now?"

"Of course, right now!"

Bromley smiled with flirtation and foolishness once again. "Ah-ha!" he exclaimed, "Frayda of Lordale, is it? Well, adieu to you, fair Lady Frost-Tempered! And good luck."

As he bowed and turned from the group of girls, Frayda also left them. The hall felt miles long while she waded through the billows of fabric towards the open floor.

"*Ahem. The Princess Frayda of Lordale, Daughter of King Corinth and Queen Cybele,*" repeated the orator. As Frayda broke through the crowds and inched her way to the center of the empty floor, the prince gave a refined bow to his former partner and turned to his new one. He had on a rather snobbish grin, and was dressed appropriately to match. He took her hand and bowed.

"And how has your stay been thus far?" he said after a few mechanic turns in the dance. The question sounded as if it were growing a bit old for him, though his face beamed with self-contentment.

"I have only arrived today, my lord."

"Oh. Then I presume you have not had the chance to browse the galleries?"

"Galleries?"

"The art galleries, that is."

"Oh, no but I—"

"Of course I never like to boast of my own skill, but I do seem to have a special knack for fine arts. Though, I apologize, I'm sure you already were aware of that."

"I...actually, I don't think I was."

"...Well, that's certainly very odd you didn't know that."

"I did get the chance to see some paintings in the hallway."

"Oh. Yes, but all of my compositions are in the East Gallery."

"Oh. I...I see."

"Do you draw?"

"Oh. No," Frayda laughed awkwardly. "No. Well, a little. Well, no, not really, actually. I'm afraid my art tutor always says that I'm too...uh...I don't know, too..."

"Oh, well, not everyone is fit for the arts I suppose. I would certainly never show condescension towards any person who is of lesser artistic prowess. After all, I was blessed with the innate gift of artistic talent and had marvelous opportunities to develop my skill throughout my early years. Anyway, enough about myself. I'm sure you already know the majority of what there is to know about me. This time is all about me getting the chance to learn about you. Tell me what your interests are, my lady."

"Um..." Frayda could hardly think, trying to follow the priggish steps of the dance, the music trumpeting in her ear, and all the while being latched to a supercilious turkey dressed in full-feathered finery. He must have, Frayda figured, gone swimming in perfumes. Probably patchouli-sandalwood and frankincense, to be specific.

"I...like the outdoors," she said, hesitantly.

"Oh really?"

"Yes. I always think an outdoor adventure is much more

interesting than staying cramped behind walls."

The prince paused. "How fascinating."

"Yes." Frayda put on an unconvincing smile to match his artificial, perfectly situated, and constantly self-gratifying grin. When she was in the crowd, it seemed each girl had spent no more than a minute or two dancing, but Frayda's own term seemed to tarry on unendingly. She began to grow conscious of the fact that her own moves were less graceful than the music demanded.

"Dancing truly is among the greatest forms of civility when it is done right," the prince said. "There are few with greater regard for the eloquence of dancing than myself..."

We will cut off from the prince's monologue for a moment here, as it would exhaust you to hear it in its entirety. All you need to know is that he gabbled on and on as Frayda tried to pay attention, and everything he said somehow managed to get back on topic to himself. It was actually quite astounding that someone could be so self-involved. Frayda hadn't the slightest idea such a thing was even possible.

"...And since then, archery has been among my most celebrated abilities," the prince continued on. "I believe the festival's archery tournament will be held tomorrow afternoon, a chance for me to demonstrate my skill. I would be content to desist from such glory, naturally. I am a poor, humble soul and embarrass easily when praised for my skills. But, I'm sure it would dismay the guests to have traveled all this way without being given the chance to witness for themselves my renowned dexterity."

Frayda felt a bout of nausea coming on.

"Is your country literate of the arts?" he reverted the subject abruptly.

"Oh. Well...um..."

"Of course, the barbaric northern lands are said to be less modernized, I know."

"...What do you mean by barbaric?"

"I have heard the northerly lands are flooded with all sorts of ancient conjury and necromancy and the like. Being so closely seated to the Northern Wilds."

"Well, you have heard wrong," she looked at the herald hoping her turn was soon over. "My lord," she added, remembering to speak properly.

"Oh, don't think that I would charge it, what's it—Lordale—of being ill-natured without reasonable evidence. I certainly am not so improper."

"Good," she said curtly.

"A most fascinating ornamentation," said the prince, at length.

Frayda slipped her eyes downward to follow his, and her feet almost lost balance entirely. The silky, brown turkey feather which she had strung into her hair was still dangling there amid her loose tresses. She blanched and looked abruptly back to the prince.

"A northern fashion?" he inquired with unhidden condescension.

Frayda's breath came hotly through her nose and she

brazened a stubborn smile, "Actually I acquired it locally, Your Highness."

Percival laughed, unconvinced. "You know, a most peculiar incident occurred just before the ball began."

Frayda put the stale smile back on her face and tried to guess what aspect of himself he was going to elaborate on next.

"As I was in one of my rooms on an upper floor, just ready to make my way down the stairs to the banquet hall, I happened to take a look out of a little window facing the sunset. There is usually nothing to see behind the castle, but today there was an odd little spectacle of a figure...skipping about in the grass."

Frayda reddened at least three shades. The prince raised his chin a little and widened his smile. He was just tall enough to look down at the northerner. "It was rather droll, I admit. But at least it proved you have some sort of dancing capability."

"The Princess Amarídi of Marazinople, daughter of King Bordel and Queen Petunia" called the orator.

"My lord."

"My lady." The prince was as buoyant and pretentious as when he had greeted her. Frayda made her way quickly back to the crowd without even the faintest glance behind her.

"Frayda!" came a voice. It was Priscilla. She beckoned Frayda to come back towards herself and Brigitte.

"What was he like?"

"Hm? Who?"

"Very funny."

"Well, if I must tell you, he was a perfect baboon. He had

nothing to talk about but himself, and his—"

"Well yes, but how handsome was he?"

Frayda wrinkled her nose. She re-hid the feather in the folds of her hair, as inconspicuously as possible. "Frankly, I hadn't noticed if he was handsome or not. I was too distracted by the depth of his character."

"Really?"

"No."

"You didn't notice if he was handsome or not?"

"No."

"WHAT!" Priscilla peaked her head over the crowd, determined to get a look for herself. It was a vain effort. "Well he's rich at any rate, to be sure."

"Priscilla, really, are those the only two things you ever think about? Beauty and wealth?" Brigitte chided.

"Oh, of course not, Gitty, you're just wallowing in self-pity like you usually do."

"Self-pity? Why, my dear cousin, if I was from Wilporsprings I'd have much more reason to be wallowing in self-pity right now."

"And just what pray tell do you mean by that?"

Brigitte grinned competitively, "I'm sure the prince will be fatigued and uninterested by the time he hits the Ws. It'll be so late in the game when he finally gets to you, you won't have a fool's chance to impress him."

"Well!" Priscilla protested. "It just so happens that girls from Wilporsprings have the gift of rekindling interest, even after Rothwel girls have stepped in to dull the scene."

The girls continued with their flummeries of irrelevant nattering back and forth, other princesses joining into the circle occasionally to reinforce the senseless frivolity. Frayda stayed silent for most of the conversations, as she was unknowledgeable in these matters and feared speaking might condemn her to social clumsiness even more so. Suddenly, she noticed an absent detail.

"Where's Cloeneth?" she asked, interrupting Priscilla and Brigitte's current argument. The two princesses took a brief look around them. Frayda had not seen Cloeneth of Fairbourne for most of the conversation, she thought, but she was not sure exactly when the girl had left.

"Hm," shrugged Brigitte. "Perhaps she stepped out for a bit of fresh air. Conversations on Wilporsprings can be such a bore."

"Or perhaps she was growing nauseous of the cheap scent of Rothwel perfumes," added Priscilla.

"But could she really be feeling poorly?" asked Frayda.

"Oh, heavens no," Priscilla replied. "Don't let it upset you, Frayda dear. She's been dallying off by herself since arriving in Rumandy. The poor girl gets terribly unsocial at parties, now and then. She does seem extraordinarily out of sorts this week."

"She thinks too much. Thinking never helped anybody. Actions are what advances one's position in society," said Brigitte.

Frayda pressed her lips lightly together and scanned the room once more, but there was no sign of Cloeneth of Fairbourne.

Eventually, each of the girls was given her chance to dance with the prince, and the feast began at last. Guests of lesser importance were seated in the outer rooms, but the eligible princesses were managed into the main hall with the king, queen, and prince at the head. Frayda seated herself and was greatly surprised when Cloeneth emerged from the crowd and sat, with a somewhat broken smile, directly to her right. Brigitte and Priscilla scrambled through the crowds and were able to find seats a little closer to the prince.

"Welcome, welcome, welcome!" came the magpie voice of the queen, taking the focus of the room, "To all you beautiful, darling, *scrumptious* girls!" She sported every bit the flamboyance of her son, plus pearls enough to buy a quarter of the kingdom. She had a long, lean face, which had been extraordinarily beautiful in her youthful days, and was well-preserved now. She had large eyes, a delicate nose, heavily powdered cheeks, and a very large mouth. "I hope you've all enjoyed the night thus far on this paramount occasion of my son's seventeenth birthday!"

A giggle and flippant accolade from the girls rushed through the room.

"Of course, occasions like these are always so exciting. I remember back to the day I was in a situation quite like this, and oh, what times those were! I couldn't possibly resist ordering red roses for the tables this evening, for I always remember, when I was chosen queen of Rumandy—oh, what a night that was—I had red roses arranged in my hair, and all the girls could only simper regrets of not donning the fashion—Do you remember, that Lionel, dear?" she called to her husband who grinned and waved from his seat. The queen turned back to the girls. "From plain little Faussie with little more than roses to the Queen of Rumandy donned in gold and pearls..."

A priggish and affected round of laughter followed.

"It makes me tear up every time I think of those days....Oh, well, enough about me! May I introduce, my darling son, Percival Cornelius Vladimir Oswalden Edwalter Ambrogio Reginald Isidore Barnaby!" The queen exclaimed his name, and an explosion of boisterous enthusiasm immediately followed. The prince stood and took a flaunting bow as the guests presented him with thunderous applause and giggles, whispering frothy words of admiration among themselves. The queen made some bubbly noises in her throat, which Frayda guessed where signs of delight, and smiled almost as if the guests in the room were admiring her. The king, meanwhile, applauded apathetically from his throne and looked somewhat tetchily around the room, as if he felt idle minutes slipping away. Frayda even thought she caught a yawn escape his lips while his wife went into raptures over their son's flawless character.

The queen babbled on for a time promoting her peachick's celebrity, finishing her monologue at last with, "And now—oh, this is so exciting, I can hardly restrain myself—let the banquet begin!" Suddenly the music came thundering out once more and at least a dozen servants barged through the doors with trays of fruit and meat and dinner rolls and cakes, and so forth. There was a roasted egret, a swan and a crane, a hog-roast, boiled oysters and lobster and everything else you could imagine (plus, some you probably cannot), all smelling of the most expensive herbs and spices.

Accompanied with these came a round of fruits and cheeses and every kind of exotic entity underneath the sun. Then came the desserts, and these were too many and too peculiar to name.

Frayda was attempting to conjure up courage enough to try one of these odd and allegedly edible items set before her, when she noticed Bromley Duccorio plop himself down in a chair next to the prince. The two boys began discussing something quite jauntily, and were almost in range for audibility, but the room was too flippantly aflutter with separate conversations to hear. In fact, from her position, all Frayda could hear was a pair of twins seated to her left, arguing briskly in an elegant, poshly broken, and slightly nauseating accent about whether the boar's head was taken from a bear or a little elephant.

"Noh, noh! But an elephant has a longer snout, Simona!"

"Well, what if zhey cut it off before zhey cooked it, styupid? Besides, Dolce, bears have fur."

Frayda sat stiffly in her chair and scratched the nape of her neck. If they had only removed the brains of the poor animal, they would have matched the intellect of a princess, she thought. She knew it was not a very courteous reflection, so she quickly banished it from her mind.

"Only a few? *Only a few of the ladies catch his eye*, he says!" Frayda caught Bromley Duccorio's laughing voice above the surrounding noise for a moment. It was quickly suppressed again by the boisterousness of the princesses.

Frayda didn't hear the prince's responding comment but decided it wasn't worth overhearing anyway. She was normally adept in holding in her disapproval, but there are certain moments any female cannot help but vent her repulsion to the next female sitting beside her.

"The prince seems quite happy with himself tonight," she said to Cloeneth of Fairbourne. "I'm not sure he could stoop so low this week as to pick any of the princesses at all."

Cloeneth turned towards Frayda, looking intently for a very brief moment and then back towards her food. "Does it matter to you whether he does or not?"

"No. Well, no, I suppose it doesn't."

Cloeneth took a small handful of pistachios from a dish and set them on her plate. She took one into her rather delicate fingers and cracked it open. She then set the shell halves on one side of her plate and the nut on the other with almost strategic care. The action was meticulously repeated with another pistachio. "Then there isn't a need to speak of it."

Frayda bit her lip. She felt a slight pang of guilt for her impetuousness and complaining tone, feeling very unladylike all of the sudden. It was most likely not an impression Cloeneth meant to unearth, and yet, Cloeneth's cool indifference to the matters that irked Frayda made her feel a bit childish.

"Unless you're hoping he will chose you?" said Cloeneth.

Frayda laughed. "I wouldn't count on that happening."

Suddenly, as she turned her attention back towards the area of the prince, she caught the eye of Bromley Duccorio, who grinned somewhat mischievously at her and raised his glass to his eye as if to offer a toast. Frayda squinted back at him, smiling, and shook her head, a little ashamed to be taken in by his comedic insincerity. "And I should hope not, as well," she added, turning back to Cloeneth.

Chapter 5

The Archery Contest

*I've always wondered why they think of love as being
shot into the heart by an arrow; in most cases, it's hand
to hand combat.*

-The Journals of Bengolian

The following morning broke with a sunny quality, and Prince Percival awoke in an equally buoyant mood. This was fortunate for his servants, who could at any moment be disposed of when the prince felt the slightest fraction of irritation. He once condemned one poor, elderly servant to an afternoon in the stocks for dropping a biscuit. But this occurred on a particularly irritable day, and it was the prince's favorite kind of biscuit, so that, of course, justified the sentence.

The first night of the festival left Percival in an ecstasy of blissfully divine vanity, and he was beginning to see the advantages of admiration given from an entire throng over the quaint affection of a single enthusiast. He almost fancied the idea of living as a bachelor indefinitely and holding annual balls like this just for the purpose of taking in such idolization from the world's female population. The only thing holding him back was the wager with Bromley. Percival had already set the pieces in motion, and if he had no other authentically noble qualities, he at least kept his word when concerning such grave matters as wagers about women.

At breakfast, he called his cousin in, having thought up many new discouragements and mockeries for the imbecile since the evening. Bromley naturally responded to the prince's scoffing with cockamamie confidence, his usual attitude towards just about everything in life. He knew his chances were slim if existent, but, frankly, he wasn't set on winning. He hence had every self-assurance that the game was going splendidly. Percival and Bromley were both rather vain and foolish boys, you see, but at least it may be said of the latter that he acknowledged the fact.

Just south of the palace of Rumandy, there was a great field with arenas and stages and tournament grounds. This place was not used often, except privately by the prince and his cousin for training on leisurely afternoons when Percival would tire of his studies and dismiss his tutors. This day the fields were teeming with a lively circus of knights, clowns, wild animals, flame throwers, dancers, acrobats, minstrels, servants, and, of course, the grandiloquent group of royals demanding entertainment. The day was, like the previous, blindingly sunny. Under the shaded portion of the seating, onlooking a jousting tournament, sat the dignified royal family, sheltered from the sweltering sun. All of the guests attending the tournament were either seated around them or on the opposite side of the playing field. Percival sat sinking into a very comfortable cushioned chair. His ankles were crossed priggishly as he lazily stirred his cup of wine with his wrist, having very little interest in the games in front of him.

The jousters were merely actors, hired especially for the occasion, and there was no chance of any real danger for any of them. They did play their parts quite convincingly at times. For instance, when one was pricked with a lance he would make a grand endeavor to appear hurt, waddling about clutching his shoulder and making a show of panting and swooning. The "victor" would then remove his helmet and orate some or other rehearsed and over-dramatized statement praising the royal family and welcoming the guests to the festival. Practices of knighthood and ideas of chivalrous knights in glittering armor were long outdated in Rumandy, so no one came with expectations of authentic jousting tournaments.

Percival was not very much amused, to tell the truth. The spectacle began to get rather dull after the third or fourth run. Therefore, he kept himself occupied with nearer-sighted and more imperative matters, like examining his fingernails. His concentration could not seem to be kept, however. To his left, Bromley sat noisily munching a succulent apple, taking enormous bites which barely fit into his mouth. For a royal, Bromley certainly had a remarkable deficiency in courtliness. On Percival's right sat his mother jabbering to the king on some irrelevant affair, to which the only responses she received from her husband were a few apathetic "Yes, my dear"s and "Of course, my dear"s. Behind Percival stood two fanning servants muttering inaudible gibberish and servants' gossip, for which the prince discharged them but later called them back when he began to get hot.

During a particularly uninteresting scene in the performance below, Percival began to toy with the ring on his right hand. Every heir to the throne of Rumandy, going back to the kingdom's foundations, had a ring such as this to identify himself. Percival's ring had four diamond studs to pronounce him Percival the Fourth, and a marquis faceted ruby at the center for no really substantial or symbolic reason other than being a thing of beauty. There were also two golden magnolias and two golden birch leaves, both symbols of the kingdom, woven into the ring's braided band. The prince put his glass of wine down and fiddled more with the ring, slipping it on and off casually as if it were but a trifle.

Percival glanced up at the king. The man was sitting in his usual manner of disinterest. The prince couldn't imagine himself like his father. Or at least, he had no present aspiration to end up like the dull monarch. In fact, some days he didn't quite feel like he wanted to be king at all. He was having far too much fun being a prince to surrender the position. His life had a blissful lack of gravity as it was, and the title *Prince Percival* had such a charming ring. At any rate, Percival was beyond the age at which a boy tries to be a duplicate of his father, and not yet at the age when he becomes one.

"So, have you figured out any way of winning the wager yet?" Percival turned his head dispassionately towards his cousin, who was sitting beside him in a noticeably less resplendent chair.

Bromley snickered, "Oh, I've got it, alright."

"Got what?"

"I've got it!"

"Well, what have you got? The plague?"

"I've got the most intricate plot known to my glorious history of scheming up my sleeve right now."

"Right," the prince shrugged doubtfully and yawned as he turned to glance back onto the playing field. "You had best keep it secret then. You don't want it to spoil."

"Oh, I know how much you want to hear it, so I'll tell it to you anyway. Being as kind and generous as I am. Look now, realistically, Percy, there's no way I could win the wager, right?"

"Right."

"Wrong!" A smile squirmed impishly ear to ear on Bromley's face. "You see, a little birdie, that is, a little birdie in the form of hundreds of princesses, has whispered in my ear that you already have things very well ordered to your advantage. You are, after all, what they all have come here for."

"Of course."

"Last night I came to the conclusion that under no conditions am I even remotely close to grasping at your heels on this bet."

"That's correct."

"But then, you see, I've been brooding over this all night and doing real torture to my mental capabilities to devise a plan...till I finally got it. Just now. You see, the key is...poetry."

"What?"

"That's all that's required nowadays with these modern girls!

Draw out some spoony metaphors and similes and they go positively mad for you."

"I'd like to see you demonstrate that, Bromley."

"Well, you know, I'm quite a humble soul, but listen here—this is pure spontaneity, as all good poetry is, you know—listen here: *Oh, thou beauteous rose of mine with eyes like stars and lips like wine...Oh, my fair princess divine....You are graceful as a...as a...*" Bromley snapped his fingers a few times, racking his brain for phrases. "I'm thinking *herd of swine*, but that doesn't really sound quite as congenial as it could."

"If I were you, I'd stick to bribery," the prince said. "It'll serve you farther in life than poetry."

"Bribery? What a terrible business to suggest! You are a scoundrel indeed, Your Highness."

"I wasn't suggesting I would employ it, myself, of course. You might find it useful, though. Since you haven't anything else going for you."

"Oh fig-muffins, Percy. How you pierce my poetic heart to its very core. That's a foul thing to say to anybody and it's dreadfully unromantic of you."

"Bromley, have you ever considered what you would actually do with a girl if you ever found one deranged enough to be taken by you?"

Bromley slung one leg over the arm of his chair. "Why, of course I have. What a silly question. I'd ride my fair lady into the sunset on your horse."

"Oh, yes?"

"It'd be just like a fairy-tale. Fireworks and everything."

"How funny."

"Well, *I* think it's funny."

"If there is one thing you must learn, Bromley, it is that the reason poets sit around all day and talk of idealistic love is because they cannot see it, and the reason they cannot see it is because it does not exist."

Bromley laughed. "Oh, Percy! That's a terrible thing for you to say!" He threw the core of his apple into the dirt of the tournament ground to be trampled on by the next faux knight. "Do you think everything that is invisible doesn't exist?"

"Well, of course things exist that are invisible...but they're all things of the mind, you see. Like jealousy or hatred."

"Or being feverishly in love with a beautiful red-head with cherry-tinted lips—look at that one, Percy! Do you see her? Three o'clock!"

"Things that are invisible are only as real as we make them to be. And when we surrender our reality of what actually exists before us for some fantastic emotions or imaginings of our mind, we create for ourselves an entirely new world in contrast to this."

"Percy," Bromley sighed, "you are a philosopher and a poet. Where is the mystical spring from which you draw such wisdom?"

"It comes naturally."

"Indeed. But, I'm afraid I have to disagree."

"Oh?"

"I do!"

"...How so?"

Bromley chuckled. "Well, I don't agree that the only real invisible things are things that we've made up in our heads. That's silly."

"...It is not."

"It is."

"You're disagreeing with me?"

"Has their been a proclamation issued against disagreeing with the Prince of Rumandy?"

"No, but I'm amused at you playing philosopher."

"Oh, I'm no philosopher, Percy."

"Glad you're aware."

"All I'm saying is that for some reason, I'm stuck with the notion that some things are beyond my philosophical grasp. Visible and invisible."

The prince slouched comfortably in his chair, as if preparing himself for a nap. "Everything is beyond your philosophical grasp, Bromley."

Bromley laughed. "Perhaps you're right, Your Highness," he said. "I do believe you are quite right."

After the jousting acts were over, the arena was quickly transformed into an archery ground. There were several other acts buzzing round the fields that afternoon, but all events came to a halt to illuminate the archery contest. A stream of new arrivals flooded into the tournament grounds, and Percival looked them over, scrutinizing fashion details and the like. One young lady caught his eye, one who was especially familiar.

"Why, is that our friend, the little meadow pixie?" asked

Bromley, following the prince's gaze towards the girl. "The one prancing about behind the palace the other day?"

"I believe it is, indeed. That's right, I did tell you about her, last night, didn't I?"

"That you did, indeed. She's actually quite good looking, you know."

Percival scratched his chin. "Hm. Well, she's not all bad looking," he mused. She was a little scrawny perhaps. A little on the lackluster side, or overly simple to say the least. Then again, those were details which could be corrected in time. Percival was willing to forgive her for being rather unstylish as one can never expect much refinement from the North, anyway.

"What was her name? Do you remember?" asked Bromley.

"I don't know. Something with an *S*, I think."

"No…"

"Or…another letter. I don't know."

"*S*…hm…Sara, Sandra, Sonya; I think you're thinking of Simona. I don't think it's an *S* at all…"

"Sophia…Sahara…"

"Sephora."

"Saphraya."

"Safrayda."

"Safrayda?"

"Frayda!" Bromley proclaimed.

"Oh yes," the prince concurred. "That was it."

"That definitely doesn't start with an *S*."

"Well, it's difficult to keep all of the names straight."

"I never forget a name!" Bromley said.

"It took you long enough to remember it."

"I remembered it before you did!"

"You've spoken to less of the girls than I have, Bromley, and therefore you have less names to remember than I do."

The two boys continued to watch as the princess took a seat by another girl she seemed to recognize. Percival believed it was Priscilla of Wilporsprings. Priscilla looked aghast at the northerner, and then handed over her fan. She began explaining something proudly, and the northern princess, rather self-consciously, began an attempt at using the fan. At first she flapped too vigorously, and when reprimanded by the princess of Wilporsprings, began to flap it too loosely. It flopped clumsily from her hand all of the sudden and fell onto the ground. Percival chuckled. Bromley, on the other hand, was watching her with far less condescending amusement.

After the knights were all spent, either from boasting of triumph or from wallowing in pretend pain, the orator of the games came forward. He was a man which demanded immediate attention the moment he stepped into view, as is fitting for an orator and for any person of notability in Rumandy. He signaled a trumpet fanfare and then explained the details of the archery tournament as a way of introducing the scene. This speech was filled with all sorts of bodacious frills which would be tiring to repeat. Therefore, you need only know that the audience was kept wide-eyed and riveted, their anticipations rising to a boiling point. When at last, the introduction to the games was concluded, a thunderous commotion of approvals and praises suddenly arose. The princesses turned to each other with gasps and squeals and shrieks and any other kind of absurd noises a crowd of young girls could make, waving to the prince and trying to draw his focus to themselves. Percival stood up proudly from his chair and gave a pretentious waving gesture back to his devotees, then strutted down to the center of the tournament ground.

As the prince was having a love affair with his adoring audience, a wooden target was being set up in the center of the playing field. Painted on it were rings of gold and red. It was a magnificent piece of artwork, never before violated by any arrowheads; a target fit for a prince of Rumandy. A small table with a collection of bows and arrows was also brought out. The orator then called forth any courageous boy or man of royal lineage to step forward to challenge the prince's skill.

A surge of anticipation, not short in some trepidation, hushed the crowd to silence. Face met face in the crowd as the royals turned to challenge each other. There were many other princes in attendance, and it is probable that they each felt a shock of inferiority running through them at the thought of being compared to Percival of Rumandy. It was also a stab at their pride to admit they were too fearful to take up the challenge. Finally, Otto of Capris stood and stepped forward, hailed by a generous applaud. He was followed by Alfonso of Felsacci and a few other princes the girls eyed coyly as a secondary option to Percival of Rumandy. One thing that can be certain, however, was that Percival outshone every other contestant in appearance, charm, and grace, and as they all gathered at the center to shake hands, all eyes were riveted on Percival.

The prince removed his hat, and a servant stepped forward with a pillow for it to rest upon. Another servant took the prince's jacket, and another gave him a glass of wine, while two more stepped out to fan him, and another came with a delightful little box of cherry cordials. Finally the prince's bow was brought, a magnificent bow carved intricately and marvelously and decorated with silver trim. Percival took it up with one hand from a case carried out by two servants, and handled it with much style and ceremony. Meanwhile, the other contenders selected their bows and arrows with significantly less pageantry. It was decided each archer would take their turn with a single shot, and Percival's shot would be the finale.

The first arrow fell blankly without hitting the target, and the second bounced off the edging. The third hit but far from the center, and the fourth skimmed the left side of the board and flew on past the target another fifteen feet. None of the archers, in fact, seemed to be having any luck, and Percival stood behind the lines contently eating his chocolates. The ninth...or tenth (no one was keeping a sure count on the numbers) came fairly close, a few rings out from the center but far more successful than the others. Some of the final shots were reasonably near to the center as well.

Finally, it was time that Percival step forward. He showily sauntered to the firing line and drew his bow adroitly as the crowd ogled his every move, though they had just seen a dozen archers perform the same routine moments ago. Percival closed his eyes, turned in a half-circle, breathed a deep breath of self-assurance, and began to set the arrow to the bow. He halted suddenly, had a servant bring out another chocolate, and then continued. Silence came to perfection; breathing stopped. One princess almost fainted in her seat, but was revived by a maid attending her. Percival readied the arrow, pulled back on the bowstring, and released the shaft into the air. The crowd gasped in unison, and the arrow wisped and struck.

The center ring! Silence, then uncontrollable shouts and applaud and laughter and tears! The prince flipped back his golden hair with a vain jerk of his head, turned to his audience, and flattered them with a grandiloquent bow. The orator announced bombastically, "His Royal Highness Prince Percival of Rumandy triumphs!"

And what a splendid victory it was! The crowds were now entirely on their feet, girls hanging over the railings with arms extended pathetically and blubbering tears streaming down their faces. From the balcony, the prince's mother could be heard all throughout the arena, screeching like a magpie and rapidly slapping her hands together in enthusiasm. A few girls tossed roses to the prince's feet, and Percival showily picked one up and kissed it, eyeing one particular admirer with a flirtatious pucker. Jaquetta of Delamúre was the fortunate young lady on this occasion.

Keeping his flaunty atmosphere high as before, with dramatic bows and quaint gestures, the prince scanned the faces of the swarm. All of them were tied to him and his stupendous victory, of course, and he sighed a long, happy sigh of self-gratification. The world was his, and he was the supreme deity of all those noblest of creatures wearing powdered wigs and corsets.

But the interesting thing about such a feeling of euphoria, even for a prince of Rumandy, is that sooner or later it must come to an end. Unfortunately, this one ended quite suddenly. As Percival was scanning the crowds, you see, he happened to get a glimpse of that peculiar northern princess. He couldn't believe his eyes at first. She was still fiddling with that preposterous fan, and seemed so intently focused on the methods and formulas of proper fan beating, that she was hardly paying attention at all. The prince wondered if she had even bothered to watch the arrow hit its mark!

In a few moments, the orator revealed the act the prince would be attending next, and bid the crowd make their way to the spot while the prince collected himself here. This instruction was not easily carried out however, as each princess thought she might stay behind to talk singularly to the prince for just a moment. As a result, the entire crowd began flocking to him like flies to a single morsel of fruit cake. With some effort, the servants managed to detach them and send them on their way.

As the girls were departing, Bromley came swaggering onto the scene. "Well, well, Your Highness," he tipped his hat with an exaggerated and slightly parodying gesture of tribute.

"Well, well, what?'

"I needn't say it! You don't gain anything from the congratulations given by a poor, hapless relative like me."

"Naturally," the prince replied. He glanced back at the mob, and happened to spot the northerner.

"Bromley. Do you see that girl? The northerner, if you recall."

"Huh? Who, the red-hair?"

"No"

"Blonde?"

"No, no. The raven with the listless brow."

"Um...?"

"The meadow-pixie."

"Oh, that one," he twisted his head to see more clearly through the people. "Oh Yes! I quite like her."

"Is that so," the prince muttered. "I think she's quite a plain thing."

"Well, I think she's lovely!"

"Oh, is that right?"

"You had better whimper your farewells to that bonny steed Alcides as soon as possible, Your Highness!"

"What?"

"Well, look at her! She doesn't care much about you, that's apparent...I've got much more of a chance with her than you do...and I'd be willing to wager she'll fall head over heels for me before the end of the week."

"Really now, since I know you cannot be serious," Percival began with his usual manner of conceit, "don't you think she's rather odd?"

"Oh, I don't know; a little standoffish, maybe. But not in a terribly unattractive way. She's not like the others; not so cheeky.

And frankly, I think she's much more beautiful."

The prince raised his chin and pushed out his lips to a sort of vain pucker. He thundered out an order to a servant close by, and the page marched off immediately after the northern princess.

From where Percival stood, he could hardly see any change of emotion on the princess's face when approached by the page. He saw her barely glance his direction, a little puzzled and perhaps a little annoyed. She gave a slight gesture of compliance, then followed the servant through the remaining crowd to where Bromley and the prince were standing.

"The Lady Frayda of Lordale," introduced the servant. She curtsied passively, or rather gave a quick bob, like an apple dropped into a pail of water. Percival tilted his head and made a condescending bow—a slight cock of the head really, still keeping his chin high, as if his gesture was essentially meant to acknowledge one's veneration for him.

"Tell me, my lady, how have you been enjoying yourself, this afternoon?"

"Very well, thank you, Your Highness." Her answer was polite and rather stiff.

Percival seemed to be waiting for something else, and the princess stood blankly for a few awkward moments. She eventually caught on.

"Your...skill with the bow...is very impressive," she said.

"Yes, it was rather a good day for my aim, wasn't it?" the prince said with some satisfaction. "It is truly my delight to shower upon my guests such demonstrations which would easily please them; many delicate flatteries I gladly present from time to time. But in the area of archery, I'm afraid I hardly ever meet with any contender bearing enough agility to be a challenge to me."

Percival thought he caught Frayda roll her eyes slightly, but he might have been mistaken. "Well," she said, "then I suppose the luminance of your victory is dimmed, my lord."

"...Oh? How do you mean?"

"If you have never been beaten before, then I would hardly expect you to be beaten today so easily...It's not very exciting, is it?"

"Oooh, Percy, she's good." Bromley crossed his arms, already finding himself entertained.

"I see, my lady," Percival replied without reference to his cousin's insertion. "And might I ask what *will* win your sanction of entertainment? Perhaps archery is not appreciated in less cultured society?"

Frayda stood for a moment with an ineffable expression, grinning stubbornly. "It is a magnificent bow," she said. Her eyes shot to the bow in the princes' hand, but her expression remained unmoved.

"Is it not?"

"Yew wood, I presume?" the princess said.

"Indeed, my lady, the finest obtainable material for archery."

"And does it not grow most prosperously in the North?"

Percival laughed through his nose. "I see you are very knowledgeable of your country's exports. I believe the materials did indeed come from that area, though I presume mostly your country finds little craft in the wood itself. Rumandy often receives raw materials from the less cultured countries."

The table standing next to them still had a few spare arrows for the contestants (besides the prince, who carried his own). Frayda picked one up suddenly and began to examine it with unusual aggression, turning this way and that, fingering every part, and peering down its length. Bromley looked nervously to his cousin, as if slightly fearing Frayda's plan was to run both of them through with an arrowhead.

"These are poorly made," said the princess. "Their weight is imbalanced and the shafts are not very straight. The fletching isn't done correctly either, see? Two feathers were taken from the right wing and the third is from the left; you can tell because they curve differently. An arrow's fletching should be taken from a single wing, otherwise the arrow will fly with difficulty, and its accuracy will most certainly be deferred. These feathers are soft and worn too; probably from a hen. Tom feathers are preferred. They're a lot stiffer."

"Oh, she's *very* good, Percy!" said Bromley.

"Indeed; so it would seem," Percival laughed a little, still wearing his well-recognized patronizing grin, which seemed to grow in vanity as time went on. "In speech at least you seem to know much of this subject, my lady. Not remarkable, even for a young woman of high rank seeing as that she lives in indelicate society. But if another contestant's arrow was inferior, he should have recognized this and exchanged it before the contest began. Therefore their fault was in their wit not their ability. And, if I may compliment you, my lady, the combination of their skills and your intellect would perhaps merit my equal concerning archery."

The princess raised an eyebrow. She let a huff of laughter out from her throat. "Well, that is definitely a compliment," she said, sounding a bit sarcastic. "I'll return the favor by praising your accuracy as being unfathomably close to perfection."

"Ah, yes, well, thank you, my lady..." The prince paused and reassessed the northerner's compliment. "What do you mean *unfathomably close* to perfection?"

"I'm afraid your arrow is not precisely in the center, Your Highness."

Percival and Bromley both jerked their attention to the target for a thorough examination. It was not at all hard to distinguish the prince's arrow; not only was it a great deal better made than the others, but it was also the only one in the center ring.

"Well, well, Percy," Bromley laughed after some scrutiny of the arrow's position, "unless my eyes deceive me, it looks as though your arrow may be a little to the left of the center of the bull's eye. Just by a hair's breadth, mind you...or maybe a... thumb's."

The prince was quite lost for words for the moment, and his patience was being drawn to its utmost limits.

"But of course, you still won, Your Highness," said Frayda of Lordale, with ever so subtle mockery. "Whatever imperfections your shot may have had are easily overlooked...no one else noticed, I'm sure."

"Very well, my lady," Percival said, with a smug pretense of courtesy and a bit of irritability and embarrassment, "And how is your own aim?"

"...I'm sorry?"

Bromley swallowed his impending guffaw. The whole scene was playing out almost too delightfully in his eyes for him to believe it was reality. "Percy, now really, you can't be suggesting to challenge a young lady to—"

"A young lady who has been so generous as to bestow on us her knowledge of archery but has not yet proven if she indeed possesses any tangible skill with a bow, which I cannot help but doubt."

"She's a girl, Percy..." Bromley protested.

"I have never claimed to possess any skill at the bow, Your Highness," the princess said.

"Yet it seems evident by your air that you have some confidence of the sport, and it would please me greatly for you to present what skill you have."

"Don't let him shock you, my lady;" Bromley interrupted, laughing. "He's just practicing being a tyrant for the day he inherits the crown."

"I accept," said Frayda abruptly.

Both the prince and Bromley froze in astonishment and exchanged furtive looks.

"If I may use your own bow and one of your own arrows, Your Highness," Frayda added.

Percival regained his inflated confidence and handed her the bow and an arrow from the case. He cocked his head and leisurely propped himself against the table next to him to enjoy the demonstration. Frayda did not take her eyes off the target while she strung the arrow, raising it deftly to position. The air was sweltering, static, and intensely quiet. The arrow wisped and struck. All was quiet for a moment between the three.

"Hot-muffins," Bromley muttered. He then began to keel over, laughing. "*Ha!* Percy! She's as good as you are!"

"Her arrow is a little to the right."

"And yours is a little to the left."

"My arrow is clearly closer to the center than hers."

"I don't know about that; what say we measure them! Just to make sure!"

"No need to bother, Bromley; it's quite evident."

"My lord," came the girl, who had been listening quite contently to their argument, "You shoot very well. I cannot easily claim to equal you, but I would be content to win your regard as possessing skill at least not far below your own."

The prince raised his eyebrows with snobbish amusement at her words. "Very well. Then, you have won my regard, my lady."

"May I go?" she requested, as passionless as possible, but not fully concealing a fleck of victorious dignity.

He nodded, and she returned his bow and then turned briskly away to wander off. The two boys eyed her silently till she was out of audible range, then Bromley let loose another torrent of laughter.

"Say what you like, Percy..."

"I always say what I like, Bromley."

"If I know you, you'll deny it till you lie old and feeble on your death bed ready to relinquish your soul to the devil, but Percy...she beat you!"

"She did not beat me."

"What did I just say? What did I JUST SAY?"

"If anything, it was a tie. The arrows are about the same distance from the center."

"I'm not talking about the arrows, Percy."

"Well then, whatever are you talking about?"

"Oh, you know what I'm talking about!"

"I really don't."

"I've never seen a girl quite so rich-humored in my life. What a fantastic creature. She's a honeybee, Percy. A sweet little honeybee that stung the hell out of you."

"If she is a bee, Bromley, then you are a gadfly. Would you kindly refrain from talking for the next two or three minutes while I clear my mind of insects?"

"As your tyrannical lordship, commands!" Bromley said with a mocking bow.

But Bromley did not quite stop talking at that point. In fact, if anything, he probably began to pester the prince more. It was quite impressive how many of the prince's orders he could circumvent. Bromley knew he had a special privilege; possibly a position no one else in the world could claim to have. I suppose you might even say there was something like a friendship between the two sapheads. But in the eyes of royalty, friendship is nothing exceptionally cherished.

Chapter 6

Ladies of Society

*I've never seen anything more ridiculous or amusing
than a young girl trying to catch a lad's eye; except,
perhaps, the look of the lad who has been caught.*

-The Journals of Bengolian

The days passed blissfully for most of the princesses, for there
was nothing in the world more entrancing than a pleasantly warm
summer week of festivities in the palace of a handsome,
charming, and deliciously wealthy prince...I do say, "most"
princesses, for there were some who considered their stay to be
less than enthralling.

Frayda spent most days in the company of Priscilla, Brigitte,
and Cloeneth. With Priscilla's exceedingly extroverted personality,
however, she was soon introduced to nearly the entire population
of royal guests in the palace. Most received her with a
mendaciously warm salutation and tried with ill-concealed
impertinence to pry out evidence of crudity in Lordale. Fiamette
of Veracci, for example, after an inflated introduction, asked
Frayda in the most properly condescending tone if she milked her

own cows at home and fed the chickens herself. "I've heard that the roads are seldom cared for in the North, is that true?" Fiamette said. "And they say pigs just wander about encroaching upon the passages, even up to the very gates of the castle! Although I'm sure that can't be true...is it true? I would hope not. It would be difficult indeed to bring up ladies of society in such a crude environment. I don't wonder why the hems of your dresses are often stained...It's not true, is it?"

Frayda smiled civilly as possible and tried with all her capacity to remain polite.

Something fresh and exciting was planned for every day of the festival, but each day was the same when it all came down to it; or so it seemed to Frayda. They all feasted on exotic foods and delicacies and rare meats and cheeses; they socialized and danced like superbly civilized nudnicks; and of course, they squealed and swooned over the prince whenever he was present. He performed a harpsichord concert day, which dragged on until it nearly put Frayda to sleep, after which he was given a profuse accolade by his mob of unconditional admirers. The next day was less formal. An outdoor picnic was conducted, during which the princesses all hoped to get more individual time with the prince. He dangled and dallied with every girl as if she was his favorite, and of course, they were all taken in, being as flighty and feather-brained as a drove of dodos.

At one time during the picnic, he delighted his guests with a performance on his whistle. He lay charmingly informal on a blanket covering the grass of the courtyard with a pretty little cluster of girls laughing around him.

Frayda had followed Priscilla and Brigitte there. Cloeneth, however, must have drifted elsewhere. Closest to the prince sat some of the most prominent and the most powdered girls— Fiamette of Veracci, Amarídi of Marazinople, Jaquetta of Delamúre, and Priscilla of Wilporsprings, of course, who managed to advance a few inches closer to the prince every few minutes by distracting other girls with chatter. In the group was also a pair of lovely little twins from Borinoccio, Simona and Dolce, to whom the prince was particularly partial. We have met them briefly before, if you remember, astutely discussing the origins of a boar's head. You see, when they were not arguing, the twins were known to complete the half of the other's thought, which was a good thing considering each had only half the brain that any half-baked ninny should have.

Frayda was whispering a little to Brigitte, and the prince took notice.

"Whatever does the lady of Lordale have to say, I wonder?" he said, purposefully drawing attention to the matter.

She was startled to hear her name and see that all eyes were now suddenly fixed on her. "I was…just talking about the condition of the weather—"

"Do you play the whistle, my lady?"

"No, my lord."

"Really? My, my! Not even a lady of such wide-ranging talent as you?"

Either she was the next victim the prince chose to dote upon, or he was mocking her. The latter seemed to be the more likely idea, and the one which Frayda would have preferred.

"My lord, forgive me, but I never said I possessed any—"

"Oh, you must all hear of Lady Frayda's delightful little game of archery she played with me a few days ago; quite charming! She almost came close to my skill at the bow. I would have thought you were as deft in all areas of sport and art, my lady, but perhaps in Lordale, girls are only accomplished in unwomanly matters such as outdoor games."

The girls giggled and turned haughty eyes again towards the northerner.

"Now, girls, really! Must you giggle so?" began Amarídi of Marazinople with mock civility, "I for one adore Frayda's mode of fashion! In fact, I think I shall visit the poultry-yard this very afternoon to acquire one of those darling turkey feathers she wore the first evening here."

The party's laughter rose again, and Prince Percival led them this time with barefaced approval.

"I thank you all for your kind compliments," Frayda said, turning back to the prince with a crusty smile, "May I be excused?"

"Why not sit awhile and enjoy the music, my lady?"

"I'd rather not, my lord."

"Why ever not?"

She raised her chin to vie his vanity, "In Lordale, my lord, such a whistle is considered to be a very trite sort of instrument, and when it is played with less than perfection, I tend to find the tones a little irritating. Frankly, I'd rather not waste my time listening to such a mediocre performance when it would only serve to give me a headache...my lord." She caught the prince's eyes flare with astonishment, and then, hiding a tiny smirk, she rose and walked away without waiting for his permission.

The next morning was her seventh day in Rumandy and already she was terribly weary of the thought of another day-long formal gathering. Happily, it would only be that day and the next till the festival was officially over. The prince would at last choose a princess to be his betrothed, and Frayda would be free to leave. Many of the guest parties were expected to linger around the castle until their welcomes were unmistakably worn out. Not Frayda. She was invited out of cordiality and nothing more, and she would return it with nothing more than attendance, escaping faster than a rabbit from a hare's trap and with the same excitement of freedom.

But presently, it was dreary outside that morning. The sun was too exhausted to climb out of bed with any vigor, the morning fog was late in departing, and Frayda was no less reluctant to start the day. If nothing else could be said of Rumandy's hospitality, the bedding was certainly quite comfortable. If it had not been for the birds outside her window, she could have been content to stay wrapped up and cosseted till noon like the rest of the pampered visitors.

She yawned out the idea and rose from the pillows, stretched her arms languorously, and scratched through tangled hair to her scalp. She wondered why she had even been invited to the ball. Not only was Lordale of no particular military or political benefit to southern countries, it was also, apparently, not generally among their favorite places in the world. Frayda couldn't guess the reason for this, for she could think of nothing very odd or unusual about her country.

The rumors she had heard had no truth in them, and, frankly, she almost wished they did. Lordale had little connection to the High North, or the Barbaric North or the Northern Wilds or whatever it was they called the lands past the upper rims of civilization. Lordale's people knew nothing more of northern barbarians than Rumandorians did, and yet somehow "royalty from Lordale", "northerners", and "barbarians" had become interchangeable terms in the South.

If there were any genuine savages in the High North, Frayda would have happily been the first to meet them. But as of yet, the wilderness which bordered her country was silent and forsaken. Most people figured there must have been someone living up there, probably some primeval and rustic race of men. But no one cared to gain knowledge of those people.

You see, the High North was forbidden. It was an unspoken rule of society that everyone accepted without question. The Barrier Forests, those woods which barred civilization from the wilderness, were always as far to the North and East that respectable maps were made to chart. Decent persons said the woods were the edge of society, and the peasantry folk said they were bewitched by evil spirits and devilish creatures. That was enough to squelch any interest of traveling past the borders. Except Frayda's.

She was one of the rare breeds of civilized character who was not nearly civilized enough to turn down an adventure. Not that she had ever actually been *on* an adventure, but, if she had been born a boy, she figured she would have already accomplished several daring feats by now. She would have been too busy with a gallant escapade to dawdle at a ball, and no one would have ever questioned her lack of hoop-skirts or corsets or three-foot high powdered wig.

Torment. That's what being a girl was. It was graceful and delicate and charming and insufferably uneventful torment. Torment so dull that it wasn't even *worth* the title of torment. The drawing lessons, the poetry studies, the grooming, the etiquette, and the sewing. The sewing was indubitably the most heinous part of all of it. Frayda had concluded that the thread would knot itself into a fancy predicament just to spite her, and the needle would prick her just because it was the most maddening and obstinate invention in the history of mankind.

At any rate, there was exactly one person in her sad life as a female who Frayda threw her complaints upon, who daily saw her swelling infuriation, and who couldn't seem to care less. That person was her older brother, six years her senior.

"Well, Frayda," he would say with a laugh, *"You're a girl. Girls do things like sew and draw and wear corsets, and they don't do things like go on adventures. It's a timeless certainty of life, I'm afraid. Sooner you get used to it, the better."*

She would simply never forgive him for it; not for his teasing but for the fact that he had been born a boy and she had been born a girl.

At any rate, that morning in Rumandy, Frayda exhaled heavily and slid out of the bed. Today would be a tour of the prince's art gallery, and her stomach churned at the very thought of it. Collections of portraits and busts and statues all in Prince Percival's transcendent and unequaled and positively nauseating rendering. She had seen quite too much of him in the flesh during the past few days to be charmed by the idea. The tour was scheduled to begin at two o'clock in the afternoon, leaving her a decent portion of the day to do something of real interest before being bound up in society. She figured she might visit the stables that morning. She had heard tell of the horses of Rumandy and had some interest in seeing them for herself.

After quickly dressing, she slipped out of her room as quietly as a mouse, being careful not to make a sound in shutting the door behind her. The last thing she needed was a princess waking up and complaining that the crude and clumsy northerner was disturbing her beauty sleep.

No sooner did the door handle clamp shut did another noise startle her.

"Frayda?"

She whirled around with a shriek, as anyone would have done when hearing her name breathed upon the hairs of her neck in the shadows of a strange hallway. Shrieking like that was a terribly ungraceful thing for a princess to do, and when she saw the face to which the voice belonged, she felt even more embarrassed. It was Cloeneth of Fairbourne.

Frayda hardly recognized the girl at first. Her hair was flowing loosely, handsome golden curls rippling down her shoulders. She looked quite unprepared for the day, in fact, bear faced with no added rouge or paint, and a simple dress which was noticeably less constricting than the dresses customarily worn to formal events.

"Oh. Good morning," said Frayda.

"Good morning," said Cloeneth.

There was a pause. "I thought I would be the only royal body out of bed this early in the morning," said Frayda.

"Yes. I had thought the same myself," said Cloeneth.

"I like to get up with the birds."

"So do I."

Another pause occurred, followed by a series of typical, stale inquiries and responses. Their conversation was the kind of which both speakers are eager to change the subject, but neither can think of anything interesting to say. Finally Cloeneth broke the pattern. "Anyway," she said, "I was going to visit the palace stables this morning."

"The what?"

"The stables."

"Why, that's curious! I was just going there myself."

"Really?"

"Yes!"

"How funny."

"Yes." Another pause. Frayda cleared her throat. "Well, um...should we just go there together then?"

"Oh, yes. We could."

"Yes."

"Alright..."

To tell the truth, I don't think either girl was particularly excited about going together with the other at first. They were both looking forward to some solitude and time to think. But a joint adventure was almost inevitable if the two girls had planned the same starting point and destination. So, they set out.

There were no restrictions or locked gates to the stable, as the entire location was within the palace walls, and only royalty and royalty's servants would have the chance to come near it. Rumandorians were very trusting of themselves. A few wranglers, stable-men, and farriers bid the girls terse good mornings, otherwise paying them little heed. The neighing and whinnying of horses was the most dynamic welcome.

Like every other part of Rumandy, the stables were grandiose and ostentatious to the point of absurdity. They were emblazoned on all sides with finery fit for a king, and trilled with a plethora of equestrian embellishments. The largest and most impressive of these decorations was at the stable's entrance. It was a life-size, marble statue of a great horse rearing on its hind legs, its proud neck curving elegantly as the action of shaking its mane was frozen eternally in stone. Beneath the statue's hooves was a plague which read *"Alcides, the Prince of Horses."*

Inside, the two girls made their way through the rows of magnificent animals. Each horse looked bred for perfection, trained in excellence, and, of course, keeping with the popular theme of Rumandy, exceedingly spoiled.

Of course, animals, and horses none the least, have personalities as distinct and recognizable as those of human beings if one knows how to see them. It's mostly in the way they stomp their hooves; the way they swat flies from their backsides with their tails; how they twitch their standing ears, nodding and nickering and shaking their manes. Flickers of light in these horses' ink-black eyes said very clearly, *"Yes. Indeed, we are the finest horses in the world. I'm sure you've heard as much; and now you can see for yourself that it isn't an overstatement!"*

The girls were conversing quietly as they walked, half of their attention drawn to the animals and the other half simply taking in the glorious morning atmosphere as the fog was beginning to lift and the sun beginning to stream in through the windows. They had just stepped two strides passed a particularly proud and bodacious beast when the animal started a loud ruckus of neighing and sneering and stomping and blowing and huffing, as if it was insulted they did not stop to admire him.

"Well, you are a squawker for attention, aren't you?" said Frayda, turning back across her shoulder.

The horse nodded and nickered boisterously.

Frayda stepped closer to the animal, cupped his muzzle within her palm, and ran her fingers down his white forelock. "Does he look familiar to you, Cloeneth?" she said softly.

"What do you mean?" the other princess asked.

"He looks just like the statue outside, doesn't he?"

"Oh," Cloeneth approached the horse herself with some

hesitation. "Yes, he does." She reached up, stretching her arm up to scratch the animal's ear, as Frayda copied the horse's conversational noises in the back of her throat.

"Does the stall have his name anywhere? Seems like it should," said Frayda.

"I don't see one."

"Maybe one of the workers can tell us."

Frayda and Cloeneth turned to scan the stable. There was only one sight of a stableboy, whom Frayda had just noticed busily grooming an animal towards the end of the line of stalls. "Excuse me?" she called out.

The boy didn't seem to hear. He was tucked under the belly of the horse and only his arm and shoulder revealed him. Frayda thought that his position looked rather precarious beneath the animal, but there was seemingly a trust between the boy and the beast which transcended technicalities and safety precautions. "Pardon me?" Frayda said again, this time making her way towards them.

The boy was whistling a tune cheerfully as he brushed the horse, till suddenly, his head popped out into view. Frayda was about to inquire about the horse she and Cloeneth had just left, but was cut short by the surprise of a startlingly familiar face. Carroty-red hair jutted out in messy tufts, and his eyes beamed with curious playfulness. It was the prince's cousin. His face, normally quite fair in color, was now darkened with smears of reddish dust. "Well, hullo-hullo!" he said with a chuckle. He straightened himself, scuffling his head with a dusty hand and throwing his scrub brush into a pale of suds behind him. "What a pleasant surprise! Now, don't tell me," he said with a laugh, holding up his finger to assure the girls' silence. He squinted his eyes at Frayda and made a show of racking his memory. "Don't tell me...it's...Lordale, isn't it? Frayda of Lordale?"

Frayda pressed her lips into a humored but rather tart grin. "Apparently it's not difficult to remember."

"Well, of course it isn't! Could I forget your name?" Bromley replied with his usual act of dangleation. "I just couldn't! Not in all eternity, my lady! From the exact moment I heard your name spoken, I took that name in and kept it tight inside a little box, right here," he pointed to his chest and grinned flirtatiously. "Under lock and key."

"It must be a pretty large box," Frayda answered with a stubborn smirk.

"Excuse me?"

"I'd be willing to wager you say that to most girls you meet. Are you keeping all of their names in one box?"

Bromley let a smile ease over his face, and the mischievous but rather handsome smile grew until it was just wide enough for a little chuckle to slip out from the boy's lips. "Well, you certainly aren't one to wrangle with, are you?"

"I'm certainly not one to try to flatter, anyway. I don't take well to it."

"Good! I despise a coquette...But I'm sorry, ladies, I forget my manners," he added, acknowledging Cloeneth and all of the sudden realizing he was being rather bold in his fixed attention towards the princess of Lordale.

"What was your name, my lady?" he said to the pretty blonde from Fairbourne, "If I recall correctly, I don't believe we have ever been formally introduced!"

"Cloeneth," answered the princess.

"Cloeneth? That's a lovely name. Rather uncommon!"

"It is."

"Bromley Duccorio at your service, my ladies!"

"Bromley Duccorio," Frayda repeated with a nod.

"Of Brushpool. It's a small country not far from here. Not nearly as illustrious as Rumandy, I'd say, but a fine little hamlet to visit now and then."

"I had thought this country was your home," said Frayda.

"Indeed it is! I do live here, you see. Quite perpetually. Brushpool is a fine little place to visit, as I said; that's why I visit there and *live* here. There's nothing to do living in fine little places like that. They get so dreadfully dull. And everyone goes to bed at such a ghastly respectable hour that there's positively no trouble to be seen." Bromley leaned back as he reached a hand across the horse beside him to smooth the hairs of its withers. "Anyway, now, what brings you ladies to the stables so early in the day?"

"It isn't that early," said Frayda.

"Oh, for a princess it is! For a princess this is very, very early…Or is the sun just rising late this morning? She does that, you know, every so often in Rumandy."

"Does she?" asked Frayda, with a doubtful smile.

"And I don't blame her, either. Look around the palace...
what is there but snoring, snoring, all morning! The sun shouldn't
have to toil up in the sky just to shine on bed-ridden beauty-
sleepers!"

"There are plenty of other things that need the sun besides
princesses in palace beds," said Frayda, matter-of-factly.

"Well, naturally...but that's no motivation for the sun to get
up! I'll tell you why, it is, though...."

"Why is it?"

"You can't tell anyone else; it's a secret."

Frayda raised an eyebrow and smiled.

"Promise you won't tell!"

"I promise."

"It's because," Bromley checked the corners of his eyes and
drew closer to the girls, his voice quieting to just above a whisper
and his eye sparkling with playfulness as he prepared to unveil his
secret. "She's really very jealous when she sees beautiful girls out
walking in the morning. So, she pops out of bed with all her
energy and starts being her glorious self! If it gets around that
there are more beautiful faces than the sun gracing the stables,
you see...well, hell on earth, we may end up with some rather
unmanageably jealous weather!"

Frayda narrowed her eyes a little. "I do believe you are trying
to flirt with us."

"Me? I wouldn't do such a base and atrocious thing..."

"And it's not working."

"Fig-muffins." He made a pouting, playfully disappointed face and diverted the attention back to the grooming of the horse.

"To answer your earlier question," Frayda continued, "about why we are here so early, we both decided we'd like to spend some time discovering what Rumandy has in store besides its prince..." Her last words were muffled by a sound of neighing and stomping which arose from back down the line of stalls.

"Hey, pipe down over there! There's a lady speaking!" Bromley called back. The boisterous horse was the same that had caught Frayda and Cloeneth's attention earlier. Bromley turned back to the princesses, "Alcides over there is pretty much the ideal embodiment of equine grace to descend to the earth, but that doesn't stop him from being a real jackass sometimes."

"So, that is Alcides, then!" said Frayda. "We thought it must have been him when we walked past him!"

"Oh, that's him alright. It's hard not to notice him."

"You know, I actually have never heard of him until this morning when we read the plaque underneath his statue."

"What?"

"It's true."

"Well, you can't be serious; you've never heard of Alcides? That's...that's terrible! He's much more worth talking about than Percy is...Don't tell anyone I said that."

Frayda laughed, "That doesn't sound too surprising to me."

"You're not very taken by the prince, are you?"

"He hasn't taken me anywhere, I'm happy to say."

Bromley laughed, a good boyish laugh which shook his shoulders and made his eyes sparkle with glee. An idea popped into his head suddenly.

"My ladies, it's already starting to be such a lovely day because of meeting you here. But, would you allow me to introduce you to Alcides? I promise you couldn't get a better escort to meet him. I know him better than anyone else ho rides him."

"You ride the prince's horse?" Frayda asked, disbelieving.

"Oh, I get away with a lot around here, you know. You'd be surprised! Let's go meet him! What do you say?" Bromley turned towards Cloeneth, whose eyes were already drawn back to the horse. "How about you, my lady?"

"Yes. I would like to." Cloeneth's tone of voice had a surprising stubbornness to it that Bromley didn't quite expect. It wasn't unpleasant, but it was almost as if she had been waiting for the invitation, and finally, on its arrival, she pounced immediately at the chance to answer in the affirmative.

"Are you a horse-lover, yourself?" Bromley asked.

"I'm curious about this one."

"As well you should be!" The boy slapped his hands together to pat off the dust, then smeared a patch of dirt from his brow. "He is famous, after all. And besides, I just can't let you come all this way to Rumandy to meet only one of the two most conceited animals in the kingdom...they both have a very fine collection of shoes, I might add."

They walked back to Alcides, who stood tall and proud, his entire body a sleek, milky color and his build commanding a presence of strength as well as rare beauty. He was probably aware they had been talking about him. He was used to the attention but seemed extraordinarily delighted about it this day. Bromley approached the animal first and began to scratch it just above the nostrils. "There's a good boy; there's a pretty boy...He's very keen on flattery. If you tell him how spectacular he looks, he'll like you more."

"I think you spoil him too much," Frayda protested.

"Oh, I know I do...There's no doubt I do. But there's no horse to deserve better, right boy?" Bromley began to make nickering noises in his throat as he continued to scratch and rub the horse down. "So, Alcides here was Percival's birthday present four years back. He was a wild ass of a horse back then. Well, he still is, I suppose. Makes the other horses spinach green with jealousy sometimes."

"He is beautiful," Frayda acknowledged with a smile, running her hand across the animal's side.

"He's alright, I guess."

"There's something different about him," Cloeneth put in.

Bromley turned to the girls and leaned his elbows comfortably against the stall behind him. "I should certainly think there is...I haven't mentioned the juiciest detail about him." A smile stretched across Bromley's face as he caught Frayda's eye.

"You'll like this, my lady. They all tease you quite a bit for being from the North, don't they?"

"I suppose they do. Why?"

"Do you know what breed Alcides here is?"

Frayda shook her head and Bromley amused himself with retaining the answer for himself a moment. "He's a Rantipole. At least that's what they call him here. That's not the breed's original name though."

There was a pause in which Bromley seemed to tease the princesses with silence.

"I don't quite think I understand your meaning," said Frayda.

"I'll give you a hint...anyone who dares to make fun of you for being too northern is entirely hypocritical while they celebrate Alcides, here."

"He's an Ohonko, isn't he?" Cloeneth asked suddenly, and Bromley and Frayda both turned towards her in surprise.

"What'd you just say?" Bromley asked.

"He's one of the Ohonko Katori."

A look of wonder crossed over Frayda's face. "What? How on earth did he end up as a present to the prince?"

"One of the only few traders who crosses the border of the Barrier Forests brought him here," Bromley explained. "He's worth a fortune."

"I'd imagine."

Bromley turned to Cloeneth, "But I'm surprised you'd know that, to tell the truth. Hardly anybody knows the northern name. I barely remember it."

Cloeneth's smile lit up as she lightly touched the horse's face. "I've never seen one before, but I've read about them, sometimes."

"Have you really? My goodness...you ladies both are odd, aren't you?" Bromley laughed. "Not that I hold that against you. I'm so delighted to meet peculiar girls that read something besides reports on what the prince is wearing."

"Oh, I can guarantee I've never read such a thing in my life," said Frayda, appalled at the very idea of it.

"Good," said Bromley. "Keep up the habit of avoiding it."

Frayda and Bromley both laughed for a moment, and their eyes met in a curious sort of manner that neither one of them fully expected. Whatever the reason for this, Frayda cut it off abruptly by turning her head away with the slightest bit of blush sneaking into her cheeks.

Chapter 7

The Prince's Choice

In the course of a man's life, he makes billions upon
billions of choices. Such as what foods to eat and what
words to say. And each choice changes him in some
little way. He can get fatter or thinner by choices of
foods, and he can get smarter or stupider by choices of
words.

-The Journals of Bengolian

Now, in the latter half of the morning, the prince awoke and
was promptly taken through the usual process of pampering. He
was feeling rather irritable and distracted since he got out of bed
that morning. More than usual, that is. After some time, he called
for his brunch to be served in one of his own drawing rooms.
Bromley was late.

The door was swung open with less enthusiasm than usual,
but the same waggish character promenaded through the entry
way with his usual "Hullo." Percival had his feet propped up on
the table, one arm behind his head and the other bringing a cup
of wine to his lips.

"Bromley, do you know why they call them the Barrier Forests?" he asked.

Bromley stood a moment quite baffled at the question. He followed the prince's direction of vision to mark the enormous map hanging on the wall behind him. The Barrier Forests on the map ran all along the northern border and down the eastern border to Rumandy. Bromley shrugged. "Because they're *berrier* than any other?"

"No." Percival sat his cup down, unamused. "It is because they bar the civilized world from the wild and archaic lands beyond them. Without them and the mountains, we would surely be overrun by savages. "

"Ah." Bromley sat down over-sophisticatedly, mocking the prince's courtliness. "I can see that this conversation is of the utmost importance, Your Highness." He put his feet on the table, crossing his ankles delicately, "My ears are ready channels awaiting to carry the wisdom from your mouth to my poor, little brain."

"Naturally. Allow me to explain," said the prince. "Now, if you will, turn your attention to the northern section of the map." Bromley jerked his head backwards. "And what do you see, Bromley? Why! Lo and behold! The forests stop at Lordale, the mountains trail off further to the East, and that miserable country is left susceptible to the influence of barbarianism!"

Bromley raised an eyebrow and let his mouth dangle open absently.

"Following?" asked the prince.

"Not really."

"Bromley, have you never heard of the rumors of the Barrier Forest?"

"Uh…"

"They say the forest is haunted; infested with fiends and impish creatures and all sorts of ridiculous figments of the imagination."

"Uh-huh."

"That's why nobody wants to go near it. Because unintelligent peasants are easily convinced and controlled if you put silly ideas of monsters in their heads. But how do you suppose these stories originated? There had to be some liable support, don't you think?"

"I…maybe?"

"And it surely must have been from countries in the North. Even the filth of the streets in Rumandy are more intelligent than most anybody in the northern countries."

Bromley continued chewing his breakfast, completely gone astray. Percival exhaled an irritated puff of air. "The point is this: geography clearly supports my belief of northern countries' coarseness and lack of cultivation."

Bromley chewed for another moment, then a thought struck him suddenly. He thrust his head backwards with a loud laugh. "So you're still distraught about being out-shot by that coarse, little uncivilized princess, are you?"

"I figured you'd bring it to that," Percival glowered. "Be it known, therefore, that my opinion of her—Princess Whats-Her-Name—is not so favorable as to ensnare my resentment." He took another sip of his wine, his mouth suddenly parched. "I really have no opinion of her at all."

Bromley chuckled, "It's Frayda,"

"What?"

"Her name is Frayda." Bromley grabbed a breakfast roll, a little slower than his usual way of doing so, and slopped it over with billows of butter. Certainly he had the same repulsive eating habits, but something in his movements caused Percival to wonder at him. He was unusually apathetic towards his meal, it seemed. The food rolled around in his mouth like a cud of grass in the mouth of a cow, as usual, but nothing seemed to pass his taste buds. He would look to the corners of the ceiling then stare lazily out the window then come back to his food uninterested. But he was far from melancholy. He might even have been happy. But a very peculiar happiness which somehow didn't relate to his meal. It wasn't normal.

A preposterous thought struck Percival suddenly. "Bromley," he said with an ill-humored stare crusted over with suspicion.

Bromley didn't seem to hear him.

"Bromley?" he repeated and waved his arm in front of his cousin's face. "Hello?"

"What?" Bromley looked up with eyes innocently widening.

Percival's smile sat rigid but growing stale. "If I didn't know any better, Bromley," he said, "I'd think you were in love."

Bromley sat silent a minute, then laughed. "Ha-ha-ho. That's funny. Ha! No," he mumbled, shaking his head and bringing it downward as if to hide the smile sneaking into his face. He stuck his finger into the center of a cinnamon roll sitting on his plate.

"Oh, no?"

"No, yeah. Really, no," he laughed.

"Hm," grinned the prince, doubtfully. "Well, I suppose it is time I come to making my final choice, anyway," he sighed casually.

Bromley shook off his daydreamy state for a moment to scavenge through a basket of rolls and muffins and pastries, "Any blueberry left? Oh, yes! Here's one!"

"The twins from Borinoccio catch my eye in particular."

"Simona and Dolce? Those bone-headed bunnies?" Bromley whistled sourly and rolled his eyes. "Which one are you thinking of?"

"Well, it wouldn't matter, really. Eeny-meeny-miny-mo. They're both the same when it comes down to it. I can't understand a thing they're saying most of the time, but that doubtlessly is nothing unusual in a marriage. Also under my consideration... Fiamette of Veracci."

"Hm." Bromley did not seem to be interested.

"Priscilla of Wilporsprings, Isolde of Hastineve, Gretel of Irvinghurst, Amarídi of wherever she is princess of..." Percival scratched his chin in minor reflection as his cousin reached over the table and snagged a cluster of grapes from the fruit display. "Hm... The princess of Fairbourne," he added.

Bromley raised his eyes with a slight contort of his smile, "Cloeneth?"

"Yes, I think that's her name. Unusual."

"*Pah!* I never would have thought you'd be interested in a girl like her. I mean, she's so...so...."

"Fairbourne is as fine a country as there is, at least in the southwestern region; besides Rumandy. And Felsacci which has no princess, unfortunately."

Bromley blew out a short puff of laughter but lowered his eyes, toying with the grapes on his plate.

Percival patted his lips with his finger and looked ponderously to the ceiling. It really did seem like a very good choice. "In point of fact, she does seem quite like everything that a queen of Rumandy should be."

"What's that? Blonde, blue-eyed? Thirty-six-twenty-four-thirty-six?"

"She is a little bit odd though, now that I consider it. Very...I don't know. Different."

"Indeed. I think I know exactly what you mean, Your Highness. Sort of mysterious, I think."

"Perhaps, in her oddness, she is too much like the person of Frayda of Lordale."

"Frayda of Lordale!" Bromley laughed and shook his head. "Hot-muffins, yes, they do have something in common, don't they? I'm surprised you noticed."

Percival sighed irritably and set his drink down on the table. "Why are you always talking about muffins, Bromley?"

"I like muffins."

"I can see that." The prince leaned back comfortably into his chair and raised his chin. "So, you've been getting to know the northerner quite well, then?"

"Oh, we run into each other here and there." Bromley swallowed the rest of his incompletely chewed food. His usual, weaselish grin returned, and all of a sudden he nearly choked in laughter.

"Is something funny?"

Bromley clapped his hands together and made an unsuccessful attempt to stop his laughter. "No, no, Your Highness, nothing. I was just thinking about if….ha! Never mind."

"I see." Percival grinned coldly and brought his cup to his lips again. He was quite done with the conversation, so turned the subject to the weather for the remainder of their breakfast.

Later in the day, at the prince's art display, Percival noticed something most intriguing. He was sitting on a burnished chair on the dais of the room. Beside him was perched the queen babbling to the king who, as usual, was not really listening. Bromley was losing himself within the crowd, his orange head popping out obtrusively every now and again. Through the entry came a small crowd of girls, within which Percival could easily recognize the princess of Lordale, dressed more commonly than the rest. Bromley greeted the girls. The crowd was so dense that Percival found himself impatiently shifting his weight to get a better look, straightening and sitting properly, slouching this way and that in his chair, ducking and raising his head, straightening himself again in the chair, and repeating the routine. The northerner was especially articulate towards Bromley, it seemed. The two were speaking to each other, and the rest of the little party all laughed with them between their words.

Percival noticed he was leaning rather far to his left in his chair again, so he straightened himself. He knew Bromley too well to not recognize the absurd act of flirtation. But of all the girls invited to the ball, he never would have suspected Frayda of Lordale to be the little minx that would be taken by it.

Percival scratched his chin. He scanned the room, scrutinizing with a little desperation for the most attractive face in the court. His eyes accidentally fell on Frayda, who was obviously not the most attractive, so he decided to try again. Why did the girls suddenly all appear so dull and indistinguishable? So puffed up and porcelain; so artificial and uninteresting? How could he possibly pick one to be above the rest when they were all equally lackluster? Frayda of Lordale laughed again from a distance, but Percival was not nearly so far away as to overlook her effortless, unceremonious, and magnetic mannerisms. He continued his search with little success and many inadvertent glances back at the northerner. At last, Bromley bowed drolly, Frayda curtsied with a playful smile, and the two parted.

I can only pretend to know what Percival's actual motive was. What sorts of subconscious jealousies or suspicions or imaginations were festering in his mind. Perhaps it was only the mere idea of seeing something which was not his that prompted him. Or perhaps it was a hidden and involuntary allure for a creature so distinct and foreign and somehow suddenly majestic. I will only say this as certain: after several moments of acute contemplation and awkward configurations in his chair, Percival straightened once again and put his cup to his lips with a smug grin. He had made his final choice.

JOSEPHINE ELI

Chapter 8

Viam Siti

It would be a mistake to measure a road by its length alone. Some roads are flat and smooth, others have rocks and steep inclines. Sometimes, the shortest roads can be the most difficult.

-The Journals of Bengolian

Beneath a canopy of branches, through which cracks of hoary moonlight found their way sparsely, a cobblestone path wended its way through slender beams of white aspens. The forests of Fairbourne were said often to shimmer like silver at night, but now the air whispered threats of a storm, and the light was tainted. Down the broken and overgrown trail a cloaked figure swavered; the sounds of uneven footsteps, laughter, and a few incongruous sentences broke the quiet of night. Little creatures, whose eyes glinted yellow-green in the darkness, hid themselves as the figure approached along the pathway.

"What an absolutely lovely night. Glorious night! Hello; you're beautiful. How are you?" the man tipped his hat to a tree. "...What? You're not even going to answer? Well, you stingy trollop, you're too skinny, anyway." He tripped and fell backwards in wheezing laughter into the middle of the stone pathway. He bought a jug of ale to his lips and sung a few lines from a tavern song, the words broken with uncontrollable titters. The velvet hat he had been wearing, which looked far too expensive for a common drunkard's, fell from his head, revealing a face which might have been youthful and handsome had it not been spoiled with sweat, mud, and liquor. He laid his head back onto the road, his loose, dark hair falling indifferently into the dirt. He stared lazily past the overhanging branches and stayed there for some time, as lifeless and inert as a rodent's corpse along the wayside.

At length, the rim of the bottle found its way to the young man's lips once more, the last drizzles running down his chin. When he was quite sure the last drop had reached his mouth, he hurled the bottle at the trunk of a birch tree and rose arduously to a slouched sitting position.

Laughing grimly, he glared upward towards the moon. "Can't anybody get any privacy beneath the sky these days? No, sir. There's always some bloody thing watching. It's like there's a watchtower perched at day in the sun and at night in the moon… and there's nothing any goddamn soul can do to get away from it when he doesn't want to be seen." He laughed and waved absurdly to the dark sky. "Hello, up there!" he yelled, "Hello! Can you see me?...Is this amusing?"

He paused, and his laughter faded into light coughs. "Hello?" he said again, this time between mockery and irritation, as if he had half expected an answer back. "That's the problem isn't it?" he muttered. "You only look and never answer. Or is all of your watch-guarding just to preserve the good virtue of your privileged, spotless ones. Like her."

A darkness dimmed the young man's reddened and watery eyes. He took several slow and languid movements to raise himself to his feet. His unsteady form again walked the pathway, and he continued to snicker and cough. "I never thought I could hate someone so much as her. Leastways, hate someone for no apparent reason. There are so many other people I hate, but all of them I can at least think of some basis for it. I mean, I hate my mother for dying, my brother for living. You know, I hate every woman I've had for not satisfying me, and I hate every idiot I've ever fought for not killing me. Those are all pretty good reasons." His steps grew more precarious, till at last he collapsed again and sat upon the ground. But this time he turned silent. He raised his knees and leaned back, spitting over his shoulder. "Damn the girl," he said.

He was silent for a long while, and the night noises whispered with maddening repetition around his head. He swatted at his thoughts, murmuring round him like hornets. "God damn you!" he shouted suddenly through the blackness. "I hate you!" He pulled at his dark and clammy hair and beat the sides of his head with clenched fists. The spasm ended abruptly and he returned to hard laughter. "And yet, what is any of it worth in the end? If I were to tell her, she probably wouldn't take any offense at it since I'm far too beneath her for her to care about it. There's no pleasure in hating someone that doesn't hate you back; it's like drinking from rum bottles filled with water."

The man stood up once more and dusted off his backside. "No. She wouldn't trouble her damned spotless mind on what I think of her. She'd probably even go straight and pardon me for it, so it's not worth saying to begin with." He made a disgusted choking sound in his throat, coughed, and spit again. "There it stands, then; the two things I hate more than anything else in the world: forgiveness and Cloeneth of Fairbourne."

And he continued down the eerie walkway.

Now, in a tavern on the docks of the River Sontani, which runs along Fairbourne's eastern rim, the dealings of the world beyond the hostelry walls were seldom mentioned. It was an unusual thing, therefore, when upon that night, affairs of the nobility of Fairbourne were the main topic of conversation.

It was far into the night now, some hours past our last account. The moon had sunk beneath blackened clouds and a drizzling rain brought a raucous mob from the docks to within the tavern.

"Oh, come now, gentlemen, we all know she's not what she makes herself out to be," said one of the tavern's wenches. "Take my word for it. White lace has always been the best way to hide red deeds."

"Take your word for it?" a grubby fellow contested as he dealt a round of playing cards, "Abilene, what idiot would take the word of a woman with your face? Nothing but trouble comes from a gorgeous face like that, every honest man knows."

"Or every man whose ever been with a trollop, at any rate,"

another man remarked.

"Well!" said the wench, "Better my word than some of them girls that call themselves *fine ladies*. Rich, is all that. Pretending to be all proper-like. No one's really that pious. Why, I'd like to find out what sort of kitten she really is behind them fancy closed doors of her boudoir."

"Abilene, really...are we all talking about the same girl? She's as chaste and modest as a saint."

"Sure about that, sir? I heard she's got it sweet with her father's chancellor," the wench put forward. "I'd believe it."

"Ormont De Mourté?" asked another of the wastrels.

"The very one!"

"Naugh! I heard it was with Ormont's brother!"

"I heard it was with both!"

"Both?"

"I heard the same!"

"What did I tell you?" said Abilene. "Fine ladies aren't any much better than the rest of us, when it comes straight down to it. Take off the white lace and them prissy little gloves and what you got then? Just another trollop."

The doorway to this tavern was old and rusted, and the men of regular attendance there were so used to its customary creaking noise that it was almost inaudible. When the heavy door was opened at that moment therefore, no one halted in the conversation nor glanced towards the tavern's entry. Instead, the man who opened it, hooded and stumbling, entered silently and seated himself in a reclusive corner, unobserved.

"Aye. I suppose that's true, Abilene."

"It is true…or they're the worse ones, I'd bet." Abilene set a tray filled with mugs onto the table. "Look here! I don't have to put on airs and act like a lady to get attention like her highness does, is there any man here that would prefer me otherwise? I'd wager not…Another mug for you, Brendan? How about you? Let me take that empty one from you, Ned…"

"Another here, Abilene!"

"You've had four already, Tom!"

"Six, darling. You've been getting more beautiful with every drink."

"Well, you little bastard!"

"I paid for you tonight, you know, Abilene. You shouldn't call me names"

"Well, I better start up on the drinks myself so I won't be so repulsed by you then. Excuse me, gents, while I get another round."

She began to make her way through the crowded spaces between the tables, bumping flirtatiously into the costumers. When she crossed to the corner of the room, she noticed one man sitting there alone and hooded. She paused before him and a coquettish smirk appeared on her face. "Well, well…"

The man made no response, and for his stillness looked as if he had drifted off to sleep. Abilene set down her tray and leaned in towards him. "What have we here? A poor little stranger brought in from the rain? Is he too shy to join the rest of us, tonight?" When the man again gave her no reply, she sat down at the empty chair across his table and crossed her arms. "Now, I know you better than that. Neither sleep nor ale were ever able to get the better of you. I've missed you, you know. That's the truth." She paused. The man continued to sit motionlessly.

"I know love is beyond you," the wench continued. "You feel nothing. Your heart is black and cold; so different from your hands. But, I've missed your hands if not your heart...You listening to me? Terence?"

She leaned forward to touch his face gently, and her fingers ventured to remove the hood from his head. His skin was a pale, sickly color and his eyes were reddened and glazed as he looked through rather than at the girl before him.

"Terence..."

He suddenly stirred, as if woken from a stupor, and began to rise from his seat. His body leaned forward weakly as though he hadn't the strength to stand erect.

"Terence...what's going on with you?" Abilene's voice was angered but frightful and her words came out with shaken defense as the man seemed to tower in above her. He stood, supported by the edge of the table, and then immediately collapsed into the girl. She screamed and pushed him aside, and at once the attention of the rest of the tavern was drawn towards them.

The young man fell backwards, dazed and hardly conscious. A silver sliver fell from his hand; a knife he had been concealing beneath his cloak. Abilene screamed again as she saw him lying on the floor. His hands and shirt were covered in blood.

Several men rushed forward, yelling and swearing. Abilene, still screaming and beginning to weep for fright, refusing to be comforted, pushed aside the men who came towards her.

The dark blood bathed the young man's silken shirt so that it clung to his body as he lie on the floor, all but unconscious. The men circled him, some astonished and dazed, others with angry, suspicious looks.

"Who is it, Abilene?" They yelled, but Abilene could only weep. She pinned herself in a corner of the room and stared wide-eyed and terrified at the man on the floor.

"Do you know? Abilene! Tell us!" the men ordered.

She clenched her eyes shut. "I don't know him! I don't know him!"

"That's a lie, Abilene! I've seen you with this man before!"

"Damn you, Tom, I don't know him!"

"Abilene!"

"Is he dead?" one of the men asked.

"No. It's not his blood!" said another who stepped out to examine him.

"Abilene, tell us who this man is, or you'll be soaking your sores tomorrow, I swear."

The girl softened her sobs, but her body shook as she spoke and her words came out trembling. "He's Terence De Mourté. He's the brother to the king's advisor."

"Hey!" called out the man who examine him. "Look here!" He brought out two objects from within the man's jacket.

"My God," said one of the men, his voice barely above a

whisper. "The crowns of the king and queen."

Chapter 9

Happily Never After

Come to think of it, I suppose I myself have never tasted a roasted prince in cranberry glaze. I take back my proposition; perhaps there is no difference between a prince and a duck after all.

-The Journals of Bengolian

The final day of the festivities in Rumandy arrived, and Frayda woke up with a sigh of relief at that thought. She was tired of the frivolities of the South by now, and was entirely fatigued of trying to assimilate herself into the southern mode.

When the daylight began to fade and make way for the night to sweep in, the castle was lit more brilliantly than Frayda had ever seen—golden and dazzling and flagrantly excessive. The ballroom was lined with twenty-two chandeliers on the North and South sides (Frayda counted during one of the prince's speeches), and ten on the East and West sides. Furthermore, the walls were lined with golden candelabras standing between each window, thirty-two in the whole of the room. Why anyone could possibly need that amount of light, Frayda did not try to imagine, though doubtless it had something to do with creating utmost visibility for the prince's godlike hue and complexion.

If the banquet hall alone had not been decorated expensively enough, the guests surely would have made up for it. Every princess was intent on exceeding the extravagance of her initial appearance, succumbing to the extreme level of flamboyance. Priscilla of Wilporsprings, being one of the major contenders for the prince's hand, had one of the most spectacular appearances in the room. Her hair was puffed up and jumbled in such an agglomeration of ornaments it almost made Frayda lose her balance just looking at her.

Though many of the girls went to great lengths in their attempts to single out the prince for attention throughout the night, Percival assumed a lofty banquet temperament, hardly paying them any heed. He was perched like a peacock on his throne, with gaudy dyed red and yellow ostrich feathers protruding from the side of his satin hat, tilted complacently over his ear. His waistcoat was royal blue and richly embroidered, and a golden cravat was tied beautiful around his neck.

In one corner of the room, Frayda stood with a group of some of the girls she had gotten to know. They were discussing something about the prince, but Frayda found it more interesting to count chandeliers at that moment and was not paying much attention.

"What do you think, Frayda?" Priscilla said, suddenly jolting the northern princess back into the conversation.

"...What do I think about what?"

Behind enormous, ostrich feather fans, the Borinoccian twins giggled.

"Would it be more appropriate for the prince to choose a princess from within the general area of the South, or to set an alliance elsewhere?" demanded Jaquetta of Delamúre.

Frayda thought it was a very strange way of determining chances. She paused a moment and then said, hesitantly, "I suppose it would be better for him to marry within the South."

Amarídi of Marazinople, one of Frayda's new least favorite people in the world, gave Frayda a patronizing smirk. "Are you not from the North?"

"...Yes."

Amarídi raised her perfectly sculpted eyebrows mockingly, in demand for an explanation. "Then you would abase your own country?"

"No. I don't think so. I mean, I didn't mean countries farther away from of Rumandy are less deserving. I was just suggesting maybe the world would—I don't know—be more peaceful if you kept things simple that way."

"Simple? I suppose that is quite like the North."

"What do you mean?"

"Oh, you know, everything is so simple when you live in an area devoid of refined culture and intelligence."

"Frayda," Priscilla tried to intercede, "I was just thinking about getting a glass of punch, are you thirsty?"

Frayda wanted nothing more than to punch Amarídi's painted face and watch her topple to the floor in fabric. But instead, she bit her lip and turned back to Priscilla. "Yes. Thank you."

Her mouth had been getting a bit dry, though she felt so uncomfortable in general she hadn't really noticed. As they turned to go, however, to Frayda's great shock and discomfort, a hand swung around from behind her head and covered both her eyes.

"Guess who?"

Frayda made no response.

"Oh, Bromley, you tease!" laughed Priscilla.

"Hey!" the prince's cousin objected, waving his finger at Priscilla. "You spoiled it, my lady—you're so terrible! I say you must now make amends by allowing me to kiss your fair face..."

"Absolutely Not!"

"Just on the cheek?"

Priscilla extended her hand with a proud, self-indulgent grin. "You may kiss my hand!" she said, and Bromley immediately did so, pecking a pattern of kisses to her elbow.

"Why, I declare!" Priscilla giggled, smacking the boy's cheek lightly. "That's quite far enough!"

Bromley took a sip of wine from a cup he carried. "Well, you know, it might be my last chance, my lady! In fact, I think it's a good idea I should do the same to all of the prettiest girls here tonight, since there's no telling who the prince will pick. And then she'll be off-limits for the rest of my life! Amarídi, you're looking marvelous..." he kissed her hand in the same way, and began to make his way through the circle of girls "Brigitte, yes, and Jaquetta. Simona, Dolce, nice pearls, both of you..."

"Tell us, Bromley," Amarídi inserted, playing coquettishly with the feathers of her fan. "You must know who the prince has chosen."

"Ha! Percy wouldn't be very shrewd to entrust such a secret to his treacherous, scoundrel of a cousin. Come now, I'm positively dreadful at keeping secrets!"

"But you must have an idea!" said Brigitte.

Bromley took another quaff of his wine, hiding a bit of a smile with the cup. "Well, maybe I know some things..."

The girls all squealed with excitement and drew the circle in closer. They pulled Bromley towards one of the open doorways leading to the palace piazza and begged him continue. The chilly night air was a welcome change from the stuffiness of the room. "I know several ladies he was considering," Bromley continued, "some of which are in this present circle." The girls drew in their breath and chittered and clapped. "But alas, my ladies, I have no knowledge of his final choice."

There was a simultaneous sigh of disappointment.

"Well," began Amarídi, "what eye color does he prefer in women?"

"Oh, blue! Definitely blue," Bromley replied without hesitation. "It's like looking in a mirror for him."

Priscilla nearly shrieked, "Oh, but *I* have blue eyes!"

"What about hair color?"

"Oh, it must be gold!" answered Bromley. "Nothing but finest gold for Prince Percival!"

"Like mine?" asked Dolce, turning herself round about in a circle to display her stunningly set head of golden hair.

"No, styupid!" said her sister Simona, "Mine is more gold zhan yours."

"Is not!"

"Both heads are absolutely lovely, ladies!" inserted Bromley, putting an arm around each of the twins, "And I don't think the prince can even tell you two apart, anyway."

"Oh, Bromley," said Priscilla, "You *must* surely know who it is! You *must* tell us!"

"I'm afraid not!" Bromley insisted again, "I only wish I did know! If I did, I'd kiss her at least seven times before Percy gets the chance. That would make my day."

"Oh, Bromley..." said Amarídi, "Give us your opinion at least. Tell us: if you were the prince, whom would you choose?"

Bromley paused a moment. Another smile slinked across his face. He folded his arms loosely across his chest and cocked his head. Then, without a moment of consideration it seemed, he stated, "That is easy, my ladies. Dear little Frayda of Lordale."

"Ah-ha!" Amarídi blurted out. She then silenced herself as quickly as if a ball of snow had been flung into her mouth. In fact, all of the girls withheld their usual outpour of excitement at Bromley's answer to the question. Frayda herself reddened slightly. She laughed a little and shook her head. "You jest, my lord. I'm afraid I am a poor receptacle for such humor."

"*Jest* she says? *Humor* she speaks of? My lady! You misjudge my advances entirely!"

Frayda's eyes began to widen with bewilderment, but she could not help but give into an embarrassed grin. "I do not judge you at all, my lord. But I'm afraid I cannot tell when you are speaking seriously and when you are acting like a buffoon."

Bromley smiled, and he did so as Frayda had never quite seen him smile before. It seemed almost pleasant and serious and not half as ridiculous. "I act like a buffoon whether I'm serious or not! But besides that..." He turned to the other girls, "Frayda of Lordale has something quite different about her, doesn't she, my ladies?" The princesses shrugged silently and fiddled with their hair and fans to avoid looking at the northerner. "She sort of sticks out in a crowd. Remarkably unique and yet not entirely obtrusive. Like a rare wild flower which has sneaked its way into a palace garden." He then turned towards her, leaning at ease against the column of the open doorway. "Don't you think you and I would go well together, my lady?" he said.

"Well...well, I..." Frayda contorted her eyebrows slightly. "Well...maybe?"

"Excellent!" Bromley cried, slapping his hands together loudly. "I think we should go tell Percy."

"Tell Percy what?"

"I mean, just talk to him. You know, to ask him how he is and tell him how we are. Make friendly conversation. Talk about horses and things..."

Bromley would have probably taken Frayda's hand and waltzed away at that moment had he not been rammed suddenly from behind. "Hey! Ahoy, there!" he said as a figure crashed into his back and the rest of his drink spilled to the floor.

"Cloeneth!" Priscilla exclaimed, "Whatever have you been

doing? I hope you haven't been walking about outside. It's nearly black as night out there now and it's starting to get cold!"

"It is night, ninny," Brigitte inserted.

Cloeneth looked first at Bromley, apologetically for the collision, and then her gaze wandered silently from face to face in the little crowd. Her own face was drawn and pale.

Frayda's brow wrinkled with concern, "Cloeneth, is something the matter?"

"Cloe, whatever is the matter?" Priscilla added. "You look as though you've seen a ghost."

The princess of Fairbourne turned her head abruptly back to the darkness out the doorway, and it was not till then that Frayda noticed her trembling hands.

"Something's wrong," Cloeneth whispered. "I can feel it. Something's not right. The night is so cold."

"Pardon?" asked Priscilla, continuing to flap her fan casually.

"I want to go home," Cloeneth said. Suddenly her legs seemed to collapse beneath her, and her brow, pale and dank as if from fever, bowed against the column.

"Woah, woah, there," said Bromley, catching her up and pulling her arm across his shoulders. Frayda moved forward as well and assisted him. "I don't think this one is feeling too well, my ladies," Bromley continued. "Probably just a bad oyster or something from lunch."

"No. Something's not right," Cloeneth whispered faintly. Her eyes were still drawn towards the night, northeast, towards her home country.

"Oh, do something, Bromley!" Priscilla exclaimed. "She's going to faint!"

"Maybe her corset is too tight," suggested Brigitte.

"Well, I'm not doing *that*..." said Bromley. "Here, let's get you something to drink, love, and maybe a biscuit or something...There's no point in starving yourself to impress Percy."

"I want to go home," Cloeneth whispered again. "Something isn't right."

After a moment, Bromley sighed through his nose, as if to give up a fight with himself and concede to a destined defeat. "Well...alright," he mumbled. "I'll take her upstairs."

"Oh, Bromley, you truly are a gentleman," said Priscilla.

"I know. It's a terrible condition. I'm going to die of it, someday...I beg your pardon, ladies, for I must cheat you of my presence and leave you to idle gossip for a moment."

"I'll help you with her," Frayda offered.

"Oh, no thank you, my lady," he insisted with a chuckle, "It will only take a moment and it'd be easier for only two to press through a richly clad and inconsiderate crowd than it would for three."

"No. I want to help."

"It's alright, my lady. You're a guest and a guest should enjoy the party."

"Well, I'm not enjoying the party, to be honest, and I'm more concerned with Cloeneth."

Bromley laughed and shook his head a little. "Oh, you are

wickedly wonderful, Frayda. I don't think there's anyone more lovely in the room. But I'm afraid if I let you come with me out of this room right now, I just may be tempted to take you away and never bring you back in."

And with that, Bromley winked mischievously and stepped away, walking with Cloeneth's head against his shoulder and her arm around his neck. They kept to the edges of the room until exiting the banquet hall.

"Well, are you happy, Frayda?" Amarídi asked, her backbone tensing as she straightened intimidatingly.

"With what?"

"Your success in making yourself a perfectly sore thumb in society."

Frayda bit her lip. "What do you mean? I didn't do..."

"You didn't do anything, of course you didn't. My mistake. It's just what you are, I'm afraid."

"That's quite enough, Amarídi," said Priscilla.

"Yes, it is. I've seen quite enough of Frayda waltzing around, cajoling her way up to advance her position in society."

"Excuse me," Frayda exclaimed, "I really have no idea what we're talking about."

"Games. Playing games. That's it with you—but for southern girls, for cultured girls—this entire matter is very important. So I suggest you step aside for ladies who understand the gravity of the situation."

"...It's a ball."

Amarídi let out a chesty burst of laughter. "You know, Frayda, you can put a wild pig into a corset and string pearls around its neck. But when it speaks, it grunts and snorts, and then there's no denying it's a pig."

"...I don't even know what that is suppose to mean."

"In other words your place is in the North."

"I know! For goodness sakes, I already know. I hate it here and I'm never coming back. I don't want to marry the prince. I don't want to be queen and I don't want to live anywhere near the South ever."

"...Oh. Good," said Amarídi. There was an odd shift from aggression to relief in her voice.

"Good."

"Yes, good."

"Alright then..."

"Alright."

And the conversation stopped at that.

At length, the guests were seated once again round the tables, and a feast more grand than any yet seen in Rumandy was set before them. Frayda was once again seated by the Borinoccian twins, who chattered incessantly in their now more recognizable but no less annoying accent.

After the dinner was over and everyone had their fill of food and prattle, the king and queen gave a few words. Or rather, the king gave a few words, and the queen gave a few thousand. Frayda had been giving about a fourth of her attention to the ceremony, and the rest of her thoughts strayed between the journey home in the morning and wondering about Cloeneth and her sudden bout of weakness.

"Well, now," the queen announced after a grand introduction Frayda didn't quite take in, "I'm sure you are all in such a hurry to get the ceremony going. I remember at your age I would simply boil up with excitement waiting for my name to be called in such affairs as these. Oh, what marvelous days those were! I was considered quite a beauty then. They called me—oh, what was it now, Lionel? Oh! *The Swan of Sophistication*! My, my! I'm always so embarrassed by that nickname..."

Frayda yawned through her nostrils. She tried to remember if she had already packed her cloak or if she had left it hanging in the wardrobe in the guestroom.

"Pst! Hey!"A close whisper and a hand on her shoulder startled her suddenly. It was Bromley, crouched and kneeling beside her chair with his back against the wall. "Sorry to scare you."

"How is Cloeneth?" she asked in a hushed voice.

Bromley shrugged. "I don't know. Seemed sort of weak and out of sorts. She said she probably won't come down again tonight."

"What wonderful days those were when I was young ..." continued the queen, "Well, anyway, with no further ado...Oh! This is just like a dream come true. I can hardly wait, myself! Look at my hands! Look how jittery! Oh, my! Girls, may I present to you once again," and she teared up a little at this point, "my son, Prince Percival Cornelius Vladimir Oswalden Edwalter Ambrogio Reginald Isidore Barnaby!" There was deafening applause as the prince stood up and minced to the center. Frayda pivoted around in her seat to add a few obligatory claps and then turned back to Bromley.

"She's a strange girl, that one" the boy said, "She did say she was worried she wouldn't get a chance to see you again before you left. Oh! Here, she gave me a…well, here, this is for you." He handed Frayda a little folded piece of parchment.

"For me? What is it?" Frayda asked.

"I don't know. What do you think, I read private notes between princesses?"

"I wouldn't be surprised."

"Well, I didn't understand it one bit, anyway." Bromley laughed and winked. He raised himself up halfway and began to crouch along the wall to his seat. Frayda laughed quietly as she returned her attention to the ceremony.

"Might I first present you all with my undying gratitude," began the prince. "For truly am I humbled by your adamant enthusiasm. Now is the time for which you have all been waiting, but, verily, it is a shame on my account, that I am limited to only one from among all the beauties the world offers me…"

Frayda tried to pay attention out of courtesy, but her fingers had already begun to unfold the note. Cloeneth's writing was small and delicate, yet the message itself was merely one line with no heading or signing. Frayda glanced up once more to pretend she had been listening, then quickly turned back to the letter.

On the left side of the fireplace. Two knives in an X.

Frayda raised an eyebrow. It certainly wasn't much of a

farewell note. She folded it, then reopened it to read it again—but something rather odd happened at that moment which prevented her. She thought for a moment someone had spoken her name, and suddenly the entire room was in upheaval with shouts and chattering and gasps and a sparse amount of applause. A hand grabbed her forcefully and pulled her to her feet. She turned to see that it was Priscilla, whose face was nearly drenched with tears and blackened from the paint around her eyes. She was grinning wide and embracing her, nearly to suffocation, and sobbing miserably at the same time. Brigitte also stood up and started to squeeze her, then suddenly the queen herself stepped into her face and started babbling about something inaudibly. It was only then that she realized the entire room was fixated on her. All her memory was choked suddenly from the shock, and she forgot entirely where she was and what she was doing. All she knew was that now she was being led to the center of the hall like a cow to the slaughterhouse.

The prince took her hand and held it chin level with his. "May I present to you," he said, "my choice as the future queen of Rumandy!" A torrent of blood rushed to Frayda's face and the rest of her body felt numb. Except her hand of course. She could not with any amount of effort or imagination ignore the fact that His Royal Highness Percival the Turkey of Rumandy was touching her hand. The feeling was repulsive, but not nearly as awful as the sound of the words he spoke. This clearly was a dream. A bad dream. A horrible nightmare. She gently felt her stomach with her other hand and tried to recall what she had eaten the night before.

"My decision may seem a shock to you," the prince said. "Allow me then to explain my thinking. I believe it quite proper that the South and the North should unite, and Rumandy should finally cultivate that end of the world which is so lacking in civility. From this alliance, I believe the world will profit greatly..."

But what if this was not a dream? Frayda blanched.

"And I also believe," the prince continued, "this union will not damper my own happiness, for the princess of Lordale I find to be splendidly adequate, if not a bit in need of polishing. But that does not worry me, as Rumandy is home to the finest stylist and hair-dressers in the world."

Frayda could feel her heart racing and her head throbbing, as if an iron bludgeon had smashed her skull.

"Your...Your Highness," she whispered. But the trumpets already started blaring suddenly in celebration. The crowd's commotion could not be spoken over.

"Your Highness? I..." He was still facing the crowd and apparently could not hear a word beside him. "Prince Percival!" She jerked his hand forcefully, and he cocked his head a little in her direction. He did not bother turning his full face away from the crowd, and gave her at best half his attention.

"My lord, forgive me. I fear you are making a mistake. I...I'm afraid I am an unsuitable choice to be—"

"Not to fear!" he said jauntily, then turned to the crowd again, hushing the musicians with a wave of his hand. "My lady feels she will be inadequate as Rumandy's queen. I can only say to her to put aside trifle worries. I am aware none can be entirely worthy for such a role, therefore my choice of her is quite as good as any that I could have made, despite her need for some grooming in refinement, which will be readily given."

Frayda cleared her throat of vexation, and continued trying to keep her voice down. "Your Highness, I fear you misunderstand me."

But the prince paid little heed. "In celebration of this engagement," he said, "you are all invited to remain as guests in the castle for as long as you wish. Feel free to visit any of my prized galleries or stables or whatever you will. And please remember to pay your congratulations to the newly selected future Queen of Rumandy, the fortunate princess to win a permanent position at my side every day for the rest of our happy lives!"

Frayda's eyes bulged. Suddenly, a single word tore out of her mouth before she could stop herself. "WAIT!"

The music stopped, trumpets and strings dying off with weak and flabby notes. The entire room became astringently silent, eyes intent on her.

"I'm sorry." She turned directly to the prince, trying with little success to ignore the penetrating glare of the crowd. "I'm sorry, but I...I must decline your offer."

The Prince's turgid smile remained, but his brow twisted in confusion. There was a long pause. No one knew exactly what to do at this moment. Not the crowd, nor the queen, nor the musicians, nor Frayda, nor even the prince himself. Madness!

That's what it was, or at least what they would call it. To Frayda, it was the first breath of sanity uttered in the entire room.

Suddenly a voice pierced the stagnant air. "I'll marry you!" It was Priscilla of Wilporsprings, now apparently fully recovered from her crying, smiling with her wide, painted lips and heavily powdered cheeks which still were streaked with tears and black paint from her eyes.

"How dare you!" came Amarídi, "If anyone has a right to interrupt, it would be—"

"Noh, noh! Zhe prince likes me zhe best!" came Dolce.

"*You*! *I* saw him first, you pudgy-cheeked, ugly little t'ing!" said her twin.

Another girl advanced in the attack, then another, and another. Simona smacked her sister's shoulder with her folded fan, and Dolce smacked back with her own. Suddenly the entire room was in chaos! No one was left in their seats, every girl flocking to the prince with outstretched arms, excluding Simona and Dolce who were still busy smacking each other with their fans. Promptly, the conductor of the band started the music again, possibly aiming to quell the bedlam. It was ineffective. Frayda was pushed aside somehow and found herself running wildly against the throng, faces flying by like a flock of mad pigeons. She slipped out the doorway, galloped across the vestibule, and escaped out the castle doors as fast as her feet could carry her, the echoes of pompous music and chaos ringing in her ears.

Chapter 10

Improper Conversations

Stormy nights are some of the most beautiful nights, I think. Precisely because of the secrets they try to keep, and yet cannot.

-The Journals of Bengolian

The night wind whistled through the bushes as Frayda tore across the grass of the courtyard. Only the torches on the piazza and the yellow glow from the palace windows broke the darkness. She fled even this, as if even the light from the South was laughing at her. She fumbled towards the old gardener's pathway and followed it blindly till she reached the open field behind the castle.

"Wonderfully done, Frayda," she said to herself. She thrust her fists against the palace wall and hid her face against the stone for a moment, as if it would conceal her from her own thoughts.

She turned herself around so her back was flat against the wall, then slid downward till her head found a place to hide between her knees. It seemed a very long time before she could bring herself to lift her face. Not that time would do anything to remedy the situation anyway. Hours could have passed and it wouldn't have changed the fact that Frayda had made herself the most obtrusive spectacle of unwomanliness in civilization.

At length, she heard a sudden creaking from the gate. A single light, like that of a large candle or a lantern, slipped through the crack of the doorway, and then another followed. Frayda started and pressed herself harder against the stone, but knew it would do no better to conceal her.

"Hullo?" came a surprisingly spirited greeting.

"...Bromley?"

As the boy came closer, the lights from his lanterns, one in each hand, lit up his half-smirking face.

"I brought you a lantern!" He plopped himself down next to Frayda and put the lanterns in between them.

"Thank you," Frayda muttered after some hesitation.

They were both awkwardly silent for a moment. Bromley crossed his legs and patted his hands rhythmically on his knees. "So..." he began, "That was, um...a nice party, wasn't it?"

Frayda was unamused and made no sort of rejoinder. "How did you find me here?" she said at length.

"Lucky guess," the boy replied spryly. "I mean, Percy and I did see you out here that first night, so I just sort of figured it would be a good hiding place. I mean, hey, I don't blame you."

Frayda drew in a breath and tried to exhale her misery. "It was the stupidest thing I could have ever done today. I don't know what I was thinking," she found herself thinking out-loud.

Bromley shrugged. "Well, if it's any comfort to you, I for one am not going to complain. Fact is, if you had said yes, I'd owe Percy a horse right now."

"...I'm sorry?"

Bromley laughed and rested his head back against the stone wall. "Kind of a long story," he said. "See, we made this wager earlier this week, Percy and I. I bet him I could win over a girl before he got his."

Frayda knit her eyebrows.

"Yeah, I guess it was sort of odd," Bromley acknowledged with a chuckle. "I have to admit, I was only playing the game on and off. I never actually thought I would have a chance to win it until recently."

Frayda sighed. "Well, he'll probably choose another princess tomorrow, and you'll be out of luck. As it seems I may be the only girl here who won't flail herself at his feet to..." her words trailed off as her thoughts shifted. Her eyes widened in the lantern light as she turned towards the boy beside her. "Wait a minute..."

"What?"

She paused and suspiciously searched Bromley's tensing face. "Were you...were you trying to make advances on me all along? And just because of your silly wager?"

Bromley dropped his jaw in poorly staged innocence. "What? No..." he said, unconvincingly.

"You little...tramp!"

"No, no...It's not what you think." He sat artlessly.. "I mean, that is..."

She began immediately to rise to her feet, "You're a...you're a wheedling, scheming . . ."

"Yeah, I know,"

"Immature, selfish . . ."

"I know."

"What do you mean, you *know*?"

"Yes, I know; I'm a bloody muttonhead. Now, would you sit down for just a minute? Just let me explain, and no, I'm not here because I still want to win...Not really. That is, I'd love to win, but I'm done playing if it hurts people. Now, to tell the truth, I did play around with the idea of you and me. I mean, why not? If there was one girl here who would have won the wager for me it would have been you. Am I wrong?"

Frayda settled herself back down upon the grass with a renewed sense of misery and embarrassment. "But it doesn't make any sense. You shouldn't have done such a thing. And I haven't the slightest notion where the prince would have come up with the idea of choosing me, anyway."

Bromley grinned. He shrugged and rolled his eyes away. "Well, I do," he said, as if confessing to some crime for which he was more proud than sorry.

Frayda's brow wrinkled in skepticism.

"I do! Really, now! You girls...you think you know the opposite sex so well when you haven't the slightest concept. See, what you need to realize, my lady, is that every specimen of the male half of humanity likes a good challenge. He might never admit it in his lifetime, but he just isn't satisfied with the easy reaches. That's why you stuck out, and that's why the prince picked you."

"Well, did he think I would change my mind about him?" Frayda disputed, "He must have known I can't stand so much as the scent of him!"

Bromley chuckled quietly. "You could fill a book with things Percy should know but doesn't."

The boy broke the banter a moment and looked out into the dense blackness. The sky, starless and carrying hardly a glow of moonlight, hinted at a night rain. The air felt heavy as well, and a chill ran through Frayda's already trembling bones.

"You know? I ought to thank you." Bromley laughed after his own proposition, so that Frayda once again was not altogether sure of his sincerity.

"For what?" she asked.

"For what? For putting a hammerhead to Percy's rear, that's what!"

"...Pardon?"

"I mean, I've personally been waiting for that for a long while," he laughed lightly, then paused. "Something I couldn't do for years. You know? I wouldn't doubt it if that was the first time anyone has ever said no to him in his entire life. First time I've seen it, anyway. Oh, and, let me tell you, it was a much needed breath of fresh air."

"I can't believe you're saying that."

"Why?"

"I would think you'd use more discretion when you talk about your cousin that way."

"Discretion?" Bromley laughed and slapped his knees. "I'm sick of being discreet. Discretion is like a toxic bile building up in my liver, waiting to make my entire body blow up into a billion little bits. And besides, I am being discrete! Look at us, we're outside where nobody can hear us, aren't we? See! This conversation is atrociously discrete! What more does discretion ask from me?"

"I don't know..." Frayda groaned quietly. "Maybe you should just keep things to yourself. Maybe I should keep things to myself. Maybe nobody should ever talk about anything."

"Well, that sounds like it could be either a very secretive and mysterious society or a very dull one. Plus, I'm terrible at keeping secrets. I never keep them."

"You've never kept a secret in your life?"

The boy laughed again, but hesitantly and quieter this time. He scratched a tuft of hair at the side of his head and raised his knees. "Well," he said, "I suppose everyone keeps at least one secret."

There was a stretch of silence, as if neither of them could find words nor cared to continue in the conversation. A drop of rain fell on Frayda's nose, followed by a light patter which quickly grew to a downpour. Bromley began to fiddle with the handle to one of the lanterns. "Well. A pleasure talking to you," he said.

"And you," Frayda replied, more courteously than sincerely. She took the lantern Bromley offered her and rose to her feet. "Aren't you coming as well?"

Bromley smirked. "I'll be a minute. Wouldn't want anyone to

catch us coming in from the night together. That would be treacherously scandalous."

Frayda rolled her eyes and turned away. "Goodnight then."

"Goodnight, my lady."

Frayda made her way to the gateway and her lantern's light vanished into the blackness. Bromley sat alone. Without a warning, the sky lit up with pale, crackling fingers of lightning, reaching across the blackened dome. A low grumble of thunder followed, like a hungry giant's stomach. At length, Bromley rose unhurriedly and shook his dripping hair to rid himself of the beads of rain which had been accumulating. He took the lantern and walked in the direction opposite of the gateway Frayda had gone to.

There was a small, opened window at the base of the palace's wall, from which came an orangey light. When Bromley reached it, he bent to the ground and peeped in. An old maid stood by a counter, scrubbing a pot half the size of Bromley. There was a heap of other pans and pots and cooking-ware, the meat-picked bones of a pig and fowls, a few piles of plucked feathers lying on the floor, and various jugs, barrels, and baskets lying disorderly about the little room.

"Hullo, there!" Bromley called in suddenly from the window.

The old maid started and dropped her scrub brush into the pot. "Bromley! Well, scare me to death, will ye boy?"

Bromley laughed mischievously.

"What are ye doing out there in the rain at this time of night? I won't have you catching cold!"

"Well, I can't very well come in unless the door is open. Let me in, woman, before I get struck by lightning!"

"Hold on, ye little rogue," the maid said, drying her pruned hands on her apron and walking around to the corner of the little scullery. A small, stone stairwell led her up to a barred door. Bromley rushed into the room the moment it was opened to him, immediately setting his lantern on the counter and shaking himself off vigorously. "Where are all those pretty little kitchen maids who are always scurrying about in here?" he asked.

"I sent them to bed early. Poor dears worked all day for the banquet, and...Aye! Mind where yer splashing that rain, boy! Ye're messier than a street dog!"

"Sorry, Mourha," he pecked a kiss on her cheek and began to rummage through the room's clutter. Finding a wine casket, he gave a short yelp of pleasure and began immediately to fill himself a cup.

"Aye-aye-aye!" Mourha admonished, tearing the drink away from him. "Not at this hour, ye don't!" She poured him a mug of milk from a little canister and forced it into his hand instead. "There. And I don't like the way ye've been taking to the drink. The prince and ye, both. The stuff spins too many man's heads for ye to be so taken with it," she muttered and shook her head disapprovingly. "And at so young an age."

"Ugh," Bromley grumbled, sniffing his milk. "Mourha, you're such an old lady, sometimes."

"Aye, that I am, sir," she said, proudly. She rolled up her sleeves, baring her thin but sinewy arms, and returned to her scrubbing.

"Who do you think is really older, Mourha?" Bromley asked. He hopped onto the counter and swung his dangling ankles below him. "Me or the prince?"

"Yer birthday isn't till December, isn't it?"

"Well, that's when they say it is. December 5th. At least, that's the lucky date that got stamped on me when they brought me in."

"December 5th is as good a date as any, I'd say."

Bromley shrugged. He began to whistle a tune as he continued to swing his feet like a little boy. Setting his cup down on the counter-top, he leaned back and propped himself up comfortably with his elbows. "My mum never really did bother to tell me when I was born," he said after a pause. "So, really, my birthday could have been in the spring. Or the summer. What if I am older than the prince? I'm taller than him, anyway."

"Congratulations."

"At least two inches taller!"

"Well, those two inches must make ye very proud, indeed."

Bromley laughed and picked up his cup again, swirling the milk around with a shake of wrist. "It's the only thing they can't control about me, really. I'm not allowed to best the dandified little jackass in any other area."

Mourha turned towards him reproachfully, "Hush yer mouth, boy!" she said. "Ye'd do better to sew those lips of yers together once and awhile. Or do ye want to be thrown out back where ye came from?"

"Pff," Bromley scoffed. "If the king and queen have gone this far in the game without the prince figuring out the little secret, it shouldn't worry me." He took a final sip of his drink, then looked down into the center of his mug, tilting it this way and that to watch the last milky droplets slide across the bottom. His smile shifted to an indignant smirk. At length, he laughed softly through his nose. "I wonder what mum would say if she saw me now. The distinguished cousin to His Highness Prince Percival of Rumandy!"

Mourha paused. "You told me you don't like to talk about your mother."

"Oh, on the contrary, Mourha darling. I only dislike it when you try and convince me she had anything of worth to talk about," he smirked.

"That I know."

"I only like to speak the truth about people; that's nothing to be reprimanded for, is it?"

"No."

"Truth is, she just doesn't have anything good about her to talk about. The shitty whore set me in a closet for most of my upbringing—am I suppose to talk about her now as though she were a candidate for sainthood?"

Mourha glanced over the half-cleaned pot hopelessly, then set the scrub brush down on the counter. She turned towards Bromley, leaning her back against the edge of the counter-top, and crossed her arms. "Ten years ago, when they told me to find the prince a wee playfellow, they said to bring back the cleanest, healthiest, and most mannerly boy I could find in the city. Yet, the one I found was lying cold, hungry, and barely dressed in the gutter of the street. More dead than alive. Why do ye think I picked that boy, Bromley?"

Bromley shrugged. "Probably because you felt sorry for the little bastard."

She turned back to her scrubbing. "Truth is, I didn't see any probability of worth in him. I saw only a probability of a corpse. And that's why yer here."

A bitter, halfhearted laugh escaped Bromley's mouth. "Oh, but everybody is a corpse waiting to happen. The only difference we have among ourselves is some of us know it and some of us don't."

"Ye don't really believe that."

"Right now, I don't really believe anything, Mourha. Except, maybe, that good old Percy is going to be incredibly put out tomorrow morning, and I just may get what I wagered for." He dropped his empty mug into a soapy pail of water and pecked another kiss on Mourha's cheek, but the maid's look turned uneasy.

"If these last ten years have given me the good sense to smell half of the trouble brewing in that mind of yers..."

Bromley only laughed. "Oh, Mourha, Mourha! You really are such an old lady sometimes!" he said.

Chapter 11

Sopping Clothes and Sopping Spirits

*Good people who are somewhere in between poor and
rich will often find it in their hearts to pity the poor. I,
however, pity the rich.*

-The Journals of Bengolian

The prince was in a terrible fit the morning following his
birthday. All the maids and pages in his service were dreadfully
worried of losing their positions and prepared themselves for
dodging any objects within the prince's grasp. He paced furiously
back and forth from one corner of the room to the next, spitting
out orders to the chamber maids, cursing and caterwauling and
pouting, hurling dishes and pillows and assorted flavors of
pastries to the walls.

"If there has ever been a more thickheaded, witless, feeble-
minded, piggish female, with a lesser sense of gentility and a
greater flair for savage manners—I am entirely disgusted at that
low-bred, tactless, entirely uncivil, woodenly clumsy, filthy...filth!
I've never in all my days come into contact with a more brutish
wench! How *dare* she!" A platter of apple cobblers suddenly

spattered onto the prince's wall-map, a direct hit from the prince to a certain northern country. "And *we*, so cordial as to invite even those on the outskirts of society... Why, we could have very well withheld the invitation; we should have withheld the invitation! But we chose to be civil! *Civil!* Unlike that contemptible, paltry, worthless tangle of trees and dirt and barnyards and pig scum they call *Lordale*, that shoddy landfill festering with barbarianism!" There was a faint knock at the door, immediately followed by a bowl of buttery crumpets clanging to its boards. "Come in!" the prince shouted. A cowering head peeped in just above the door handle.

"Um... Your Royal Highness?" said a messenger.

"What, imbecile?"

"H—her Majesty the Queen wishes to see you..."

"Well! What are you waiting for, fool? Send her in!" The messenger drew the door ajar and ran frantically away as the queen bustled in, sobbing and dabbing a handkerchief to her eyes. She extended her wiry arms, "My poor dumpling!"

"Mother..." His steaming expression sank to a pathetic, milksopping pout as she squeezed his head in her arms.

"Oh, why don't we get you a nice treat; how would you like a new hat?"

"Mother, I want to make war on Lordale."

"Oh, I do too, dearest!" she pursed her lips. "What a contemptible country. Oh, but your father would probably refuse... how about a new pair of shoes, darling?"

Percival grumbled and sank down on one of the cushioned

seats lining the windows, his eyes narrowing in on the part of his map where Lordale lay, now bejeweled in bits of apple cobbler.

"When I become king the first thing I shall do is build a barrier between Lordale and Ridgehaven so that the uncultured ways of the North don't defile the rest of the Free Kingdoms."

"Oh, of course, dear! What a wonderful idea!"

"Obviously I'll have to take control of Ridgehaven first in order to build on that land, but that shouldn't be too difficult."

"Oh, pudding-cake, you're so ingenious!"

"Yes," he agreed, smiling half to himself. His pouting was beginning to subside a little now that he was strategizing revenge. "Mother, has that little wench left the castle yet?"

"I haven't heard, darling. Oh, but let us forget about that disgraceful little girl. There is a world of better ones out there. Why don't you freshen up and come down for luncheon, and tonight we'll just have the entire party over again and you can pick a more suitable princess. We can forget last night ever happened!"

"I'm not in the mood for another party."

The queen gagged suddenly with her eyes turning as round as dinner plates, "Oh, but-but darling..."

He clasped his hands leisurely behind his head and set his feet crossed on top of a heap of pillows on the other end. "I'm tired of all those wretched people. Send them all away."

"...But."

"I fear all the excitement might worsen my health. I'd much prefer to rest today."

The queen's composure collapsed suddenly. "Oh, my

dearest," she fretted, "Are you ill? Call the prince's physician!" she yelled to a maid, "Quickly, before my darling faints. . ."

"It's nothing mother," mumbled the prince. "Just a little headache and a touch of dizziness and my stomach is a bit upset. . .and my smallest toe hurts a little. I think someone stepped on it yesterday."

"Oh, my darling!" The queen fell dramatically to her knees and assaulted Percival's head with kisses.

"For heaven's sake, mother, I'm not going to die," Percival declared, repelling his mother's pecks and then rubbing his eyelids mopishly with his fingers.

The queen frowned, "Oh, alright dearest...would you like me to send in Bromley for some company?"

Percival looked up. "Bromley?" He stiffened a little and sank deeper into the pillows on the seat "No." he said.

"What? But, sugar-dumpling..."

He put his fingers to his lips and forged a yawn, "No. . .no, I'm much too tired to talk to anybody right now, mother."

"Oh, well, if that's what you really wish, my darling," she gave her son a syrupy grin and pooched her lips for one final kiss on his forehead. "Now don't think too hard about anything, it will weary your mind!" She rose and bustled to the door, blew him one final kiss, and exited.

The prince lay silent for only a moment before looking to the servants, "Dismissed," he ordered sharply. They scurried out, bowing deep but hurriedly.

And where had Bromley run off to last night? Percival

wondered. Bromley had seemed to vanish in the confusion and never had reappeared. After the princess of Lordale scrambled off...

A thought occurred to the prince suddenly. *Impossible!* He sat up, startled.

"It's impossible...isn't it?" he blurted out-loud arrogantly, as if demanding an answer from an invisible servant. Could they have been conspiring against him? "Those cunning, little, treacherous tramps!"

They had always seemed to be sneaking around together. Like two renegades, two blackguards, two deceitful and scurvy mongrels! It was just like Bromley, too, to take things far beyond their measure. And that little shrew, Frayda of Lordale...

The prince paused. Whatever had prompted him to choose Frayda of Lordale in the first place? It seemed pure witchery. She surely wasn't the most attractive girl there. Or at least, there were girls who were much more resplendent in appearance.

Even as the prince grumbled and thoughts churned about in his mind, an unexpected spectacle out the window jolted him. He ducked his head beneath the sill and peeped downward towards the castle's central courtyard. It seemed the barbarian princess was taking her leave at last.

She was loading the horses herself, side by side to the servants, and looking dreadfully undignified. Her hair was being tussled about by the unusually windy day, and she looked entirely unrefined. Yet, when it came to her mounting the saddle, Percival was not so eager to see her go as he would have thought. The sight was not as satisfying as he hoped it would be. He was surprised then, when she dismounted, speaking a word to an escort, then scurried back through the palace doors.

The prince stuck his nose in the air and turned away from the window. After dallying in his chamber for another moment, he heaved himself back to the window as if against his will and waited for her to appear once more.

Frayda of Lordale, meanwhile, was entering the vestibule of the palace once more. She had just remembered she had left one dress, which, she would have been embarrassed to admit, was set outside her guestroom window in the sill's flower basket to dry from the night before. She told her servants only that she had overlooked one item, and had better go in herself to retrieve it. She forced herself back through the hallways, hoping desperately not to be seen by anyone who would recognize her. She had already made herself ready to leave, and retracing her steps through the palace felt entirely awkward. But she certainly did not want to stir up excess rumors by leaving behind her clothing on the roof of Rumandy's castle.

Fleeting thoughts ran through her mind as she hurriedly made her way through the lofty, empty halls. Why had the prince chosen her above all the others? Just to spite her, she was sure. He couldn't possibly be in love with anyone but himself, so what did it matter whom he chose? Every minuscule, trivial detail about him made her nauseous. His golden locks bounced their way frivolously into her head, curling out from underneath one of his ridiculous hats. That conceited, self-indulgent, condescending face of his, even if it were the most handsome face on earth, plagued her memory like a pestering wasp; she whacked and smacked with other thoughts but it kept buzzing in her ear.

When she entered the guestroom, she came to the window and saw that the dress was still quite wet, but had blown from the heavy morning winds a little ways away from the flower basket. She unhinged the window, swinging it as wide as it would go. The palace stood on all sides around her, towers and turrets projecting out. Frayda hoped no one witnessed as she carefully climbed a little ways upon the roof to reach the dress. Its burgundy color, and the green she was wearing now, clashed with the dull, blue-gray shingles of the roof, and it would have been a marvel if no one noticed. She rolled the garment into a compact bundle and inched her way back through the window.

As she was about to leave the room, however, she halted abruptly before the fireplace. Suddenly, she recalled the note Cloeneth of Fairbourne had given her the night before. *On the left side of the fireplace. Two knives in an X.* Frayda hadn't the slightest idea what the note was referring to, but she inspected the fireplace anyway. There were, however, no knives to be seen. Frayda had not seen Cloeneth that morning, but she had heard from a maid, to her surprise, that the princess of Fairbourne had already left Rumandy. Frayda scanned the whole room once more, pondering the note and subconsciously looking for a trace of *two knives in an X.* On finding nothing of the sort, however, she left the room.

Her servants were awaiting her in the courtyard, and she

quickly made excuses, put away the bundle of a dress, and mounted her horse. From behind the glass of one of the ornately framed oriel windows of the palace, a face caught her eye. It was not readily distinguished, but she guessed well enough by the raised chin and haughty stance that it was the prince. He cocked his head in his usual manner and abruptly strutted away from the window pane. Frayda formed a bubble of air in her mouth and blew it out, in disgust. She turned and did not look back again until she and her entourage were outside the palace's exterior walls.

That afternoon, the guests were cordially informed that their welcome was worn out, the prince being in ill spirits to receive them any further. This caused an uproar of disappointment. If Princess Frayda was ever unpopular while she was in attendance, now that she was gone she was subject to twice the infamy.

The prince sulked in his chamber till the evening as the guests made preparations for departures. He complained with inexpressible groanings he was too inconsolable to eat, and too ill to leave his bed. Of course, once the servants and physicians left him in solitude he immediately resumed his pacing around the room, helping himself to the feasts his servants left him.

He decided Frayda of Lordale was either as featherbrained as a hen or as villainous and sly as a scorpion. With all probability, both conditions were accurate. She clearly must have been some sort of unholy breed of hen and scorpion. And Bromley, of course, must have had some hand in the whole matter of the night's chaos because Bromley was obviously also part chicken and part scorpion.

What a queer girl that northerner was, indeed. Or apparently, it was not an unusual action in the North for princesses to climb out of windows and crawl along the shingles of palaces before taking their departure. Percival had witnessed this intriguing incident from the corner of his window. Whatever she was doing with a wet dress, he had seen the entire scene. He recognized the garment as the one she wore last night at the ball. Apparently she had decided to go waltzing in the rain after the delightful scene of pandemonium she created in the banquet hall. *Just like her to go running off outside somewhere*, Percival thought. He sat down and leaned against the back of his chair with his ankles crossed on the table, and he poured himself a second glass of wine

And where was Bromley today? In the stables no doubt. Dilly-dallying his day away, not caring at all what condition the prince was in. *Probably riding my horse, too,* Percival thought.

There was a rapping at the door. He quickly set his cup down and leapt back into bed.

"Come in," he said, coughing pathetically. It was Mourha carrying an empty tray.

"Pardon, Yer Highness," she said, nonchalantly as usual, "May I take yer dishes?"

"You may," he groaned and felt his forehead for his temperature. "Alas, I've scarcely been able to touch my supper."

Mourha began to collect his things without another word. He was a little annoyed she showed so little concern for his welfare.

"Where is Bromley this evening? Why hasn't he called upon

me?"

"Yer Highness said ye were too ill to receive company today."

"Oh yes, so I did," he coughed again. "Did you see him at all last night after all the mayhem?"

"I haven't been spying on the poor lad or nothing, Yer Highness."

"Did you see him?" the prince repeated, insistently.

"Well...yes. Actually, I did."

"Do you think he might have gone outside at all?"

"He was returning from outside, matter of fact. Is something wrong, Yer Highness?"

"No, no...Nothing's wrong at all," the prince smirked. "Was it raining when he was outside?"

"I think it was...I didn't quite get to asking him what he was doing out there, but he was wet to the bone, poor thing."

Percival sat up and leaned his head against the bed post. "Wet to the bone, was he?" A flash of fiery suspicion flickered in his eyes. "Where is he now?"

"His quarters, Yer Highness."

"Tell him to meet me in my fencing court."

"Fencing court, Yer Highness?"

"I'm feeling much better now, some exercise would do me good before I retire to bed, I think. You know...just a quick game of swordplay perhaps."

Chapter 12

A Quick Game of Swordplay

I once observed two very handsome white-tailed bucks
engaging in a smashing duel over a beautiful young
doe. Finally, at the break of day, they had both expired,
and the doe, having lost interest hours ago, was nearly
five miles away and very content to shun the company
of males.

-The Journals of Bengolian

The sound of Bromley whistling a tune preceded him into the prince's fencing court. On the walls of the room was displayed Percival's entire collection of weapons, and the prince stood inspecting the blades with his back to the doorway.

"You called, Your Most Re-cooperated One?" said Bromley as he entered. "I'd love to have the ability to heal from sickness as fast as you do, you know. It's extraordinary!"

The prince looked back across his shoulder laxly and took a rapier from the rack. "Thank you, Bromley. I take great pride in it."

"As well you should."

"You know, I just adore these blades. Aren't they exquisite? And they don't get used often enough, do they?"

Bromley leaned against one of the pillars outlining the fencing arena. He crossed his arms and chuckled patronizingly, his eyes twinkling as if shards of something playfully wicked had planted themselves there. "You know, Your Highness, I agree with you entirely."

Percival tossed the weapon he had been holding into the air, and Bromley caught its handle.

"Nice toss, Your Highness."

"Nice catch, Bromley."

"Oh, thank you, Your Highness."

"No, no...thank you, Bromley."

Bromley twirled his blade as Percival took another from the rack.

"So, Bromley, I'm just curious," Percival glanced over his chosen weapon, put it back, and picked another for inspection. "What do you really think about her?"

"About who?"

"You know who."

"...Dolce of Borinoccio? Sensationally good-looking; utter pinhead. It's a shame, really, but I'm glad you decided to go against her in the end. Besides, her accent would have gotten frightfully obnoxious after a while here, and I don't think I could have handled it...Or were you referring to someone else?...Simona?"

"If you were to think arduously on the topic, Bromley, I'm

sure you can figure out whom I'm speaking of."

"...Well," Bromley laughed and began to walk to the middle of the arena. "You really couldn't mean that straggly little northerner, could you?"

Percival seemed satisfied enough with his next choice of weapon. He advanced to the center of the arena and took stance. Bromley followed.

"Alright. I'll tell you what I thought of her," Bromley began after the first uneventful clash of swords. "Rather pretty. Sharp-witted. Pricelessly entertaining. And irresistibly charming for finding you to be the most detestable creature on earth."

"You met with her outside last night?"

Bromley paused a moment, then a wily grin spoiled his face. "*Touché*, good man!"

"Do you actually expect me to give you my horse for this?"

"Well, that was the bargain."

"She's not even here anymore!"

"I never said I'd *keep* the girl around, did I? Just that I would win her over before you did!"

Percival thought back to the exact words of the wager and dropped his shoulders slightly. "Well, what did she say to you last night?"

"Oh, Percy! Percy!" Bromley frowned, "A pox on you for asking so intimate a question! Why, I wouldn't give those tender words of affection away for the world!"

"You're bluffing...and you're not getting my horse."

There was an uncomfortable silence, broken at length by

metal clashes. The fight carried to the room's hearth, from which dwindled a fire, and silver flashes of the blades spiraled in the reddish glow. Suddenly the blade from Percival's hand was knocked to the floor, clanging noisily upon the stone.

"Oh dear. It looks as if I win," Bromley said emotionlessly, smiling only behind his eyes.

"Best out of three," the prince commanded.

"Fair enough."

The prince picked up his weapon and moved to the center of the room.

"Well, I already won two, if we're counting Frayda," said Bromley.

"Well, we're not."

Bromley laughed and followed Percival to the center, taking up his position once again and waiting for the prince to advance. The blades clashed with a bit more aggression than the previous round, but it seemed both of the swordsman were rather patiently holding back the rest of their energy. After a spell of clangs and clashes in which neither opponent was able to best the other, the two stepped back from each other and wordlessly agreed on a respite. Bromley loosened his muscles with a shake of his shoulders and Percival swabbed his brow with his sleeve.

"You know what I find amusing, Bromley?" the prince asked.

"Well, I can think of a few things *I* find amusing, Your Highness, but I doubt they're the ones you're thinking of."

"I find it exceedingly droll that you have no purpose in your life but to follow me around Rumandy and pretend you enjoy it."

"...That is rather droll, isn't it?"

"You know what I think, Bromley? I think your sad little relatives in Brushpool must have sent you here in attempt to pilfer popularity from me."

Bromley raised his eyebrows and twirled his weapon with his wrist. "Well, it's a good theory, anyway. But your lovely parents are much too smart for any kind of duplicity to go on behind their backs, don't you think? As to my purpose in life, I'm afraid you're entirely right, Your Highness. I have no purpose but to wait on you and keep you company. In fact, that's what most people in the world are for, isn't it? To indulge Percival of Rumandy in everything."

Percival suddenly advanced and knocked the sword from Bromley's unsuspecting hand. "Ha!" the prince exclaimed, pompously. "One to one. Final round."

A sour smile appeared on Bromley's face, but his eyes were cold as he looked from Percival to the blade upon the floor, the echoes of its clatter still reverberating in the room. "You know, it's a shame you can't understand my meaning in its entirety, but I think you just might be even more of a bastard than I am."

"Excuse me?"

"I don't think it's wise we should proceed with round three, Your Highness, because with our current tempers, I foresee there to be only two possible outcomes. Either, you will end up running me through, in which case I would be severely injured and possibly dead, or I will end up running *you* through, in which case I would most assuredly be dead. Both ends prove to be against my favor, and I do not wish to over-rely on the good fortune I've been receiving lately. I think I'd rather not face you in opposition again, Your Highness."

"I command you to pick up your weapon."

"What if I say no?"

Percival drew open his lips slightly and lifted his eyebrows in shock. He could hardly believe Bromley would seriously defy him, for such a thing had never been done before. Or rather, it had been done only once before, and the result was a ballroom full of pandemonium and love-crazed princesses. Now, however, there would be no one to gasp and swoon and sigh in shock. Percival, so shaken by the traumatic idea of people having wills not in accordance with his own, could find nothing innovative to say, and therefore had to repeat the command: "Pick up your weapon!" he yelled.

The foolish smile which had often sat on Bromley's face, that same smirk which could conceal a thousand different meanings, displayed itself now with perfect contentment before the perturbed prince. Bromley had clearly already thought his answer through, and seemed to savor it in his chest awhile before giving it up from his mouth. "...No."

That was all that was needed to be said. Percival threw his blade to the ground and charged forward, swinging a punch for Bromley's head. Bromley ducked and skirted it, then caught Percival's arm and brought him into a lock. Next, Percival stomped on Bromley's foot, causing the poor boy to let out a rather dumbfounded complaint. Bromley then took revenge with the rather primitive approach of ramming his head into his opponent's stomach. The artlessness of this maneuver probably did not win Percival's approval, but at the present, it served Bromley's purposes exceedingly well. The prince was plummeted to the floor with Bromley holding him down, and before Bromley could tell himself to do otherwise, he swung his fist once, twice, three times and then four into Percival's face until a bright red stream of blood appeared.

Percival's head hit the floor and he grimaced painfully, coughing and gagging. Bromley froze as he realized exactly what he had just been doing. He released his hold on the collar of Percival's shirt and rose staggering to his feet. This was the first time he had ever struck the prince. It was the first time anyone had struck the prince. Percival rolled over, smeared the blood dripping from his nose, and stood up disoriented.

There was a moment of arid silence before the prince screamed, "Guards!" and Bromley began to run. "Guards!" Percival shouted again. "Seize him!" He took hold of Bromley himself and tackled him to the floor to prevent him from running.

The nearest sentinels were a lengthy hallway away, but on hearing the cries they rushed towards the fencing court. When they entered, Bromley kicked the prince and broke free from his hold. The guards, however, did not move upon Bromley instantly. Either they had just been so thunderstruck at the sight of the prince being kicked in the gut, or they had always secretly wanted to kick him themselves, and were curious to see how it would actually look. In the next moment, however, they had no choice but to charge forward and lay hands on Bromley. They drove him down so his cheek slammed against the icy marble floor and they forced his hands behind his back. Meanwhile, Percival was bellowing out orders and charging Bromley of atrociously exaggerated offenses.

The smirk remained on Bromley's face as the guards brought him up and took him from the room. Percival smeared the blood from his noise again, with a great amount of self-pity, and followed them.

Chapter 13

A Boy Called Bromley

As previously stated, I emphatically pity the rich.

-The Journals of Bengolian

The king and queen of Rumandy were sitting in one of the palace parlors. In fact, they were sitting in one of the most ornate, comfortable, and superfluous parlors ever designed on the face of the earth. Light poured in through the grand paneled windows which extended up nearly to the lofty ceiling. The coral walls with white and gold floral designs gave the room a bright, posh, and wonderfully coquettish atmosphere. Above the fireplace hung a large painting of the queen sitting on a lovely swing with vines of roses growing up its ropes.

The queen was sobbing heartily on her cushioned settee, and the king was stroking his chin. The latter nodded after every few minutes of his wife's incomprehensible woes, adding a few sighs, yawns, and words of agreement where he saw fit.

"Oh! My poor little darling! My dumpling boy! My pudding-love-cake! Oh, Lionel, this is beyond words! It's *beyond words*, Lionel! And that wicked little boy who would dare to do such an abomination to our son! Oh, what a wretch! And on the day after our little darling's birthday! There are no words, Lionel!"

"No words," the king echoed. "Of course, my dear."

"Our dear boy has been mistreated and humiliated twice within twenty-four hours! What has our poor son ever done to deserve such a miserable treatment?"

"Absolutely nothing, my dear."

"*Nothing*, Lionel!"

"Nothing, my dear...No words. Just as you put it."

It should be marked that the king's birth name was, of course, Percival Cornelius Vladimir Oswalden Edwalter Ambrogio Reginald Isidore Barnaby the Third, but because of his lion-like temperament (that is, he yawned often and took long naps after his meals) he was known by this endearing nickname.

A knock on the door was just loud enough to be heard over the queen's sobs, and the king, perhaps a little eager to be relieved for a moment, readily bid the door to be opened. A page entered and announced, "To His Majesty and Her Majesty, enter the Lord Chancellor Magister William Pombraidy."

"Oh, send him in at once," said the queen, "And let us proceed with all haste in this traumatic ordeal!"

"Yes, bring him in," the king repeated.

Promptly, a prudish, judicial frown entered the room by means of a toadish sort of man named Pombraidy. He was dressed in expensively uncomfortable attire and had a stuffy, white powdered wig which went well with his nasally voice. "Your Majesties," he said, bowing. Behind him came a small servant carrying a stack of manuscripts which probably outweighed him. On top of the stack was balanced a quill pen in a small jar of ink.

Pombraidy seated himself at a desk in the room and ordered the servant to set the manuscripts there. Once everything was arranged to his liking, he set a pair of spectacles on the tip of his nose and dipped his pen into the jar of ink. "In the month of August," he narrated in monotone as he wrote, "the nineteenth day. Year nine-hundred and fourteen by the reckoning of the Free Kingdoms' Alliance." He looked over the rim of his glasses, "The accused?"

"Bromley Duccorio of Brushpool." said the queen.

"Bromley Duccorio of Brushpool," Pombraidy wrote.

"...Are we suppose to call him that in court?" the king pondered out-loud.

Pombraidy looked confused, a small wrinkle of questioning showing on his parchment-like brow. "Does the accused have another name by which he might be titled?"

"Well, Magister, you see, this is exactly why we called you in before the boy's trial," the queen explained. She sat up and dabbed the tears out of her eyes with a handkerchief. "The whole ordeal is, I am afraid, much more complicated than it would seem, Magister. I did say the accused is Bromley Duccorio of Brushpool, but you see, the boy who struck the prince isn't exactly Bromley Duccorio of Brushpool. In fact, there really is no Bromley Duccorio of Brushpool."

"There's a Findley Duccorio of Brushpool, I believe," the king put in. "And a Ferguson Duccorio. Then there was my cousin

Beaufort Duccorio—do you remember him, dear? Poor chap died of some sort of nasty urinary infection seven years ago. Good fellow. Excellent battledore and shuttlecock player."

Pombraidy remained looking terribly confused.

"You see, Magister," continued the queen, "we only wanted a playfellow for our son, but none of the servants had boys of his age. Lionel did have a few nephews, but for some reason or another they just could not get along with dear Percival."

"Couldn't get along?" The king grimaced sourly and shook his head. "That's an understatement to say the least—ha! Do you remember little Francesco Velinicci? When Percival put the snake in his pantaloons? I've never heard a higher pitched screech in all my life!"

"At any rate, Magister," the queen continued, "the relatives were indeed no help at all. And poor Percival demanded a playfellow, so we arranged for a common boy to be brought in. And, well, one thing led to another, and soon the little brat had practically slithered his way beside the thrown. Look how unruly he has become; he has dared to strike the prince!"

"I see," said Pombraidy. He puckered his bottom lip and looked at his notes. "The boy has no papers? No formalization of his identity?"

"None, Magister," said the queen. "No papers."

"Well, except for the ones we forged," added the king.

"Parents?"

"None that I know of," said the queen. "Though we might ask the servant who brought him in. Mourha, my son's old nursemaid." The queen turned promptly to one of her servants and ordered him to send for the maid.

When Mourha entered the room at length, she bowed, then stood neutrally with her arms at her side. Her face seemed a little grayer than usual, though she bore a rigid smile which might have hidden her thoughts.

"Mourha," the queen began, "this is the Lord Chancellor Magister William Pombraidy here to interview you about your involvement with the boy called Bromley who has been acting as playfellow and cousin to my son these past ten years."

"Yes, Yer Majesty" Mourha replied, politely, then added quietly, "I know of the boy."

"Ma'am," Pombraidy began, "Am I correct in believing it was you who first brought this boy into the palace?"

"Yes, sir, that is correct."

Pombraidy scratched something down on his paper. "Please continue to explain the circumstances of how you found him, ma'am."

Mourha paused as her gaze settled for a moment on the floor then returned to the magister. "He was in the street, sir, and I thought he looked like he had some good qualities to him. He seemed very polite. So, being commissioned as I was to find a boy, I chose him and had him washed and dressed and all."

"Did the boy have any parents?"

"Yes, Lord Chancellor. He had a mother."

"Name?"

"Rosalina O'Caelan, as I recall. I have only spoken to her that once."

Pombraidy took the name down on his paper. "Father is deceased?"

"The...father was unknown."

"Unknown?"

"Yes, sir. His mother didn't know who the father was."

"What? Indeed! What kind of loose harlot doesn't know who her own child's father was?" the queen remarked.

"Well, I'm sorry to say, Yer Majesty, but I'm afraid that's just what the woman was."

The queen gasped. "Do you mean to tell me that for ten year we have been harboring the bastard son of some salacious street prostitute in the palace walls?"

"Oh...no, I don't think so, Yer Majesty" Mourha answered. "Well. She...she worked at a brothel. That's not the streets, at least."

"Lionel, I want this boy removed from the palace immediately!"

"Of course, my dear...I agree entirely."

"How foolish we've been to treat such a filth as one of our own kind. Now, ten years later, we finally see him for what he is! How disgusting. And he struck our poor Percival! He struck him, Lionel! Oh, it sickens my stomach. Someone fetch me that plate of ginger tarts on the table in the corner there before I faint. I'm going to faint, I know it."

"My own thoughts on this matter can be simply put," said Pombraidy. He removed his spectacles and placed the quill into the jar of ink, then he laced his fingers prudishly upon the manuscript and frowned a little deeper. "Though he is young, the boy is of great danger. His disreputable character and unpredictable behavior renders him ineligible to receiving amnesty from the trial."

"You're absolutely right, Magister!" the queen applauded as one of the servants handed her the plate of tarts.

"However, to disclose in court what the boy truly is and where his upbringing is would be a disfavor to the Crown."

"Oh?" the king put in with sudden interest as he leaned over to snatch a ginger tart. "How so?"

Pombraidy made a croaking noise of consideration and lowered his frown yet another inch. "Your Majesty would think it unseemly for another country, let us say Felsacci or Borinoccio, to harbor an illegitimate miscreant in the palace for such a time. People would get suspicious. Rumors would spread."

"That's true..." the king considered, stroking his chin and blinking. "If that old sack-bag Ruggiero did anything of the sort over in Felsacci, I must admit I'd find it a most delectable story. I'd talk about it for weeks."

"Exactly, Your Majesty. One thing is certain, and that is, being that this ordeal is occurring at a time when nearly every country has a representative, in the form of a loud-mouthed young lady, still lingering around the palace, whatever decisions made in court shall be swiftly circulated to every corner of civilization."

"True..." remarked the king, contemplatively. "We must be very careful with how we handle this."

"Therefore," Pombraidy continued, "I will propose three stipulations. Firstly, no efforts will be made to squelch the guests' interest. Make the trial immediately. Make it public. Otherwise, it would be sure you are hiding something."

"Alright. Well, go on, Pombraidy,"

"Secondly, I am to be paid triple my usual salary for the trial. It must seem an extremely important case."

"That makes sense."

"Thirdly, the boy is to be tried for two offenses. That of striking the royal heir to the throne, and that of impersonating a nobleman."

Mourha, all the while standing silently, her presence nearly forgotten by the others in the room, shifted her weight uneasily.

"Impersonating a nobleman?" the queen repeated.

"Yes. Well. We'll just leave your part of the story out of it, and say that this boy deceived you for all this time, fashioning himself as your son's cousin."

"But what if the records don't agree with that?" the king asked, munching on a ginger tart.

"I write the records," Pombraidy grinned like a frog.

"Well...I think that's as good a solution as any," said the queen. "Don't you, Lionel?"

"Sounds wonderful! You're a genius, Pombraidy!"

"I do my part, Your Majesty. You need not fear, I will see to all of the minutia to ensure this trial goes smoothly and according to plan."

"I don't think that's very fair, sir," Mourha inserted, rather boldly. Each person in the room suddenly turned their attention to the maid. "Forgive me, but...ye're charging the poor lad for something ye did yerselves."

"We surely are going to get rid of the nuisance either way," the Queen replied, looking daggers at the maid, "All this plan does is ensure that the reputation of the Crown isn't tarnished."

"But...forgive me, Yer Majesty, but what exactly do ye mean by *yer going to get rid of Bromley?*"

"Exile. Execution. One or the other," Pombraidy said, plainly.

"Execution? He's just a boy, sir!"

"Mourha, you are very dear to the prince," said the queen, "and because of this, I will not consider dismissing you from your position here, but I warn you, you have no right to speak to us this way. These matters are above you. Dismissed."

Mourha pressed her lips together. She bowed and turned towards the door, and the other servants saw her out.

Bromley, in the meantime, had never been more content than when he was under arrest. He was being held in his quarters, two rooms joined together by a curtained portal and each area decorated almost as finely as the prince's own collection of rooms, though, of course, there were significantly fewer mirrors. Bromley had three splendid full meals sent directly to him that day, and he didn't need to go anywhere or do anything to get them. And the best part of it was that the entire day had not a single moment of Percival in it. The only downside to being under arrest, of course, was being locked inside his room, but most of the time he forgot about that.

Bromley had all day to be punished with doing absolutely nothing. Therefore, he amused himself by throwing blueberries at the chandelier, standing on his head, and singing songs he invented spontaneously.

He was never one for long periods of silence, particularly those forced upon him. Therefore, he did his best to make constant noise when alone, lest he come perilously close to contemplative thought. Take, for instance, thoughts about being in love.

Oh, of course, Bromley was not in love, Bromley had never been in love, and if luck would allow him, this status would never be modified.

Funny little Frayda of Lordale, though...Bromley chuckled to himself suddenly. He hadn't really realized he had been thinking about her until he said the name out-loud. What a fantastic partnership the two of them would have made! How deliciously wicked! He took a banana from the fruit platter brought in at dinner and started to peel it. He could just see Percy stomping and pouting and thundering out monstrous objections to their marriage. He laughed aloud at the thought of it.

And then, naturally, he and Frayda would ride Alcides into the western skyline—Percival moping behind them, shuffling little pebbles around the road with his feet. The mental picture was just too ingenious not to savor for awhile. Bromley had just stuffed the rest of the banana into his mouth and began chewing it to mush when a knock came at the door.

"Do come in!" he hollered almost incomprehensibly. His cheeks were puffed out like a hamster storing food, and his words were muffled by banana mush. "I just adore visitors in my sad state of imprisonment and desolation!"

A familiar old maid entered, carrying a tray with a milk pitcher and a large clay drinking mug.

"Mourha!" Bromley called. "Mourha, my love beyond reasoning! How are you?"

"Wipe that stupid look off yer face, boy!"

Bromley frowned traumatically. "Oh, how tortured is the unrequited lover!"

The maid slammed the tray onto the table, took the pitcher and mug and slammed them onto the table, and then proceeded to slam all of Bromley's dishes and leftovers onto the tray. "One day ye might learn the consequences of yer actions, though it would be wishful thinking to believe this is putting an ounce of wisdom into yer senseless head now!"

Bromley grinned with easy and unabashed wickedness and shrugged. "He deserved it."

"I don't deal out what the prince deserves and ye shouldn't neither!"

"But you do agree with me, though...You can't say Percy didn't deserve it."

"Are ye done with the fruit?"

"Mm, yeah, but leave the muffins." Bromley put his feet up on the table, and Mourha immediately pushed them to the floor.

"What goes through yer head sometimes, boy? I'll never

know!"

"Well, don't let it bother you. Half of the time, I don't know what's going through my head until it spills out all over the floor...And even then, I still can't make it out entirely. My head has a mind of its own, you know."

"And do ye always think someone else is going to clean up the messes ye make?"

Bromley folded his arms and laughed a little. "Come now, Mourha. When have I really ever gotten in trouble before? I mean real trouble? That was the very first time I've ever hit the prince in all these years!"

Mourha stopped her work and stared rigidly at the boy's face, but her eyes seemed agitated. "Don't you understand, Bromley? Yer not needed anymore here. The prince is growing up; he doesn't need a playfellow anymore. Soon enough, ye'll be nothing but a barnacle on the palace. A barnacle the king and queen will be most happy to be rid of! This isn't a good time to try yer luck!"

"Well, I'm not worried about it, Mourha, so you shouldn't worry your old head about it either. All it will do is give you a few more wrinkles and a few more grays. Now listen here, the worst case scenario for all of this is they chop this handsome head from its shoulders and the world is deprived of a rare breed of redhead."

"You're a fool."

"Then again, if they were resourceful, they could use my locks to decorate Percival's newest hat. Therefore, nothing would be lost in the matter!"

Suddenly, and as resolute and firm as a death sentence, Mourha's palm slapped across Bromley's cheek. Bromley was quite surprised by this. For a moment, he lost the confident sarcasm to his look, and could only feel over the sore spot with his hand.

"Don't ye dare speak another word of nonsense in front of me, boy!"

Bromley was truly lost for words from the shock, but had he thought of some artful pun, Mourha's tone would have silenced him anyway.

"How many pins can the jester throw into the air before they collapse down on him?" said the maid.

"What are you talking about, Mourha? You're the one who's not making a lick of sense now!"

"Here's what I want you to do, Bromley," Mourha continued to slam the rest of Bromley's leftovers onto the tray. "I want you to drink your confounded milk, I want you to think—if that's even possible for you—for a few minutes about the trouble you have gotten yourself into, and then..." As she turned away from the table suddenly, Bromley thought he noticed a glassy tear streaming from her eye. She seemed to forget the rest of her sentence.

"What's the matter with you, Mourha?"

Blinking, shaking her head, and pulling back a few loose strands of hair, she continued. "Then you can decide what to do." She picked up the tray, then slowly set it down again. She bent and quietly kissed Bromley's brow, then, taking up the tray once again, she left the room.

The door closed and Bromley could hear the maid's footsteps as they faded out into silence. He wasn't yet to the point of thinking of anything specifically, but he did feel rather unwell and uncomfortable. He was not sure whether this was because of the slap or the kiss. He came to only one conclusion: women were strange creatures, regardless of age. One minute they slap you, the other they kiss you, and if they can't decide what to do next, they leave the room in a frightful huff without explaining themselves.

Bromley sighed. He stood up and shook his head. There was only one sensible way of life he could foresee to yield a harvest of perfect bliss, and that was to scorn the company of women all together. "That's it," he said out-loud, "I've decided. I'm going to build myself a hut at the edge of the sea and be a celibate hermit until I'm too old to remember what *female* is."

He sniffed the milk from the pitcher Mourha had left on the table, turned up his nose, and set it back down. He jumped on his bed and lay with his ankles crossed and his hands behind his head, content to fall asleep inside his clothes and outside his covers. Since all of the lamps in his room were still lit, however, the room was far too bright to sleep in. So, he sat up. He paced the room for a quarter of an hour creating a rhyming poem about cranberry sauce, ate a muffin, and then laid back down. When he realized the muffin had left his mouth rather dry, and he was not going to sleep anyway, he went to the table and began to pour the milk Mourha had left from the pitcher to the mug. As he was yawning and staring lazily out the window, he heard a quiet *plunk*. The milk in the mug was rippling when he looked down.

"Well. That's disgusting."

He stared frightfully for a moment, gauging his thirst against the possible things which could have *plunked* into the drink. Then, deciding his thirst outweighed any of the possibilities, he brought the cup to his lips. The milk had a slightly metallic taste to it. He thought this was a little odd, but it didn't bother him enough to stop drinking it. As he came to his last gulp, however, something cold and hard met with his lips. A milky spray shot forth from his mouth suddenly and he dropped the mug, breaking it into three or four pieces on the table. He watched as the white droplets trickled onto the floor. Something else had fallen onto the floor as well.

"Hullo!" Bromley coughed. "Slap me, kiss me, then choke me, will you, Mourha? Really now! What's this?" He kicked the object with his toe, then stooped to pick it up. It was a key.

He stared at it in his hand for a moment, then slowly sank onto one of the table's chairs. "What are you up to now, you old maid?" he said quietly after a pause. He looked to the door. All of the sudden, the room seemed uncomfortably quiet and much smaller than it had been before. Bromley shook a few drops of milk off of the key and pat it dry on the fabric of his shirt as he silently imagined himself fleeing the palace. He could already smell the sweet fragrance of freedom, devoid of the dandified perfumes of royalty. Within a minute of imagining, he could almost hear the bustling crowds of the marketplaces on a warm, sunny morning. Then, after another minute, he could feel the mud. Real mud. Real, warm, oozing, disgracefully wonderful mud between his toes. It had been ten years, but he could remember his life before he was Bromley Duccorio of Brushpool as if it were yesterday...or rather, he remembered it with some significant bias towards the more idealistic moments.

He rushed towards the doorway and stuck the key into the hole.

It didn't fit.

"Damn it!" he said, his imagination crushed. The key was stuck and made considerable noise as he tried to jiggle it loose. "One would think if the woman went to the trouble of sneaking a key into my room, she would at least make sure it was the right one." He pulled it out with a jerk and then exhaled noisily.

He looked it over again, disappointed. It was too small for a door-key; he should have noticed that, at least. Perhaps the size for a cabinet or a window...

His eyes shot to the windows at the other end of the room. They were all closed and locked; in fact, they were seldom ever opened except when servants came in to clean them. Bromley never really thought of opening them himself. He made his way across the room slowly and touched his forehead and palm to one of the panes of glass. Before he could even bring himself to trying the key, he scanned the palace rooftops and walls for a possible route to scale and descend. There were a few that looked plausible.

He still could not bring himself to trying the key, his hands shaky with an unaccustomed nervousness. He went back to the table and gathered up all the food he could fit into his pockets. After a few moments then, he returned to the end of the room and slid the key into a slot in the window's frames. It clicked and turned in its place, and with a sharp creak the window was ajar.

Suddenly, a bold gust of night wind, fragrant and fresh, chilled Bromley's face, distancing him from even the smallest thought of staying behind.

Chapter 14

The Bizarre New Trend of Walking on Rooftops

Every once in a while, we are called to a great
adventure. But more often than not, we are dragged
into one without our knowing.

                                   -The Journals of Bengolian

Whereas Bromley could not be discouraged by punishments, Percival could not be appeased by indulgences. Just about every princess still present (which was approximately all of them) sent him perfumed letters with red kiss-stains and chocolates and candies and quaint little ribbons and other superfluous trills Percival ignored. The prince also received twenty-nine new pairs of shoes, (making an escalated total of one-hundred and sixty-six), three exotic birds, a Capuchin monkey wearing a delightful costume, a pair of red foxes, a python, and a white lion cub, four complete suits of new clothes, six boxes of cologne, and...perhaps it would be better not to mention the number of hats as it might startle you.

The prince was lying on his bed as an ensemble of chamber musicians played something like a dirge to sympathize with his emotions. At last, the song ended when Percival threw a pillow at the mandolin player, began caterwauling and making verbose orders and insults, and nearly suffocated a flutist with one of his bed-curtains. When finally all of the servants were bustled out of the room and/or discharged of their positions, the prince stood up, leapt from his bed, put on one of the hats he had previously refused, and began to pace around the room. He took out the lion cub from its cage and began to stroke it sulkily in his arms.

While previously he had only been leeching the world of esteem and adoration, Percival was now leeching it of pity as well. Most likely, he was now planning to keep himself locked in his quarters until every living thing in the vicinity had drenched him in sweetness like syrup drenches a buttermilk pancake.

He walked to one corner of the room and ogled his reflection in one of the mirrors. There was a bandage around his head (which he didn't really need, but it served to make him look more pitiable), an unsightly swollenness to his left cheek, and a little bruise underneath one of his eyes. He pulled back one flap of his lip to view the empty space which had once held his favorite molar. Of course, it wasn't his favorite molar until Bromley had knocked it from his head, but absence makes the heart grow fonder, you know.

Percival opened up a box of candied fruit, tried a few, and gave one to the lion cub. He then laid himself down on the cushioned oriel seat, one foot on the sill of the window and the other on a pillow, to ruminate over the misery of his life and count the unassuageable woes which harried him. When he was done with that, he was quite exhausted, and immediately required pistachio date shortbread. This was one of his favorite comfort foods for such trying times as these.

He sat up immediately and reached for his bell to signal his chamber maids. However, after a few seconds of vigorous and unanswered clanging (which caused the lion cub to jumped back into his cage, the birds to start squawking, and the costumed primate to cover his ears with his shirt), Percival realized he had sacked all of his maids that morning and no one had yet arranged for replacements.

Now, there are certain times even a prince of Rumandy must make sacrifices for the greater good, and since Percival's stomach was the greatest good he could think of, he decided to do the inconceivable. Yes. He would descend from the comfort of his room and venture unswervingly to the lowness of the servants' quarter recesses. All for the sake of his poor stomach's sudden necessity to be filled with pistachios and dates.

He immediately proceeded in this plan and made his way from the room to the corridor leading to the stairwell. His walk was rather brisk until he passed one of the palace guards and remembered that he was sick. A slight limp appeared in his leg then, as well as an ache in his stomach. It lasted all the way to the end of the hall, and once the prince turned the corner where the guard was out of sight, he seemed to recover considerably well.

This was a particularly quaint hallway leading to a side stairwell which was the most direct route to the servants' rooms. There was a lovely little line of windows which looked out past palace roofs and turrets and parapets towards the stables and riding grounds, just barely visible by the moonlight. Percival would not have had much time to take in the view, as his mind was absorbed with shortbread. However, something outside the window suddenly caught his eye. Stopping in his tracks abruptly, he nearly tripped on a wrinkle in the carpet, and his attention was immediately preoccupied in a little speck of a figure clamoring around a rooftop.

"Bromley?" he thought-out-loud.

The sky outside was already quite dark, so knowing for sure that the figure was Bromley was rather difficult. Then again, Percival did not know anyone else (besides Frayda of Lordale) who was bizarre enough in nature to do something as odd as scaling a rooftop. A new fashion, perhaps, for treacherous villains and uncultured clods.

The figure leapt a short distance from one turret to another, and by the almost puckish and impulsive flair added to the jump, any doubts of this being Bromley fled Percival's mind entirely.

"The devilish traitor!" he muttered. For a moment, he forgot all about his need for dessert and began marching back to fetch the guard. Then, he halted suddenly and stood as if his shoes had stuck themselves to the rug.

It occurred to the prince that running to the guards to fetch Bromley back would not be as deliciously vindictive as he would like it to be. He wanted to taste that sweet revenge for himself. Despite the fact that he had been whining and pouting in his room all day, he still considered himself masculine enough to face his cousin man to man. Therefore, he swung himself back around and continued down the hallway.

Bromley would be going to the stables, most likely. That would be just like him. Percival scaled the stairs speedily but passed the servants' quarters without as much as a snivel for pistachio date shortbread. Instead, he proceeded to the kitchens. Having been there only a few times in his life (Bromley and he had gone there on occasion when there were no other girls to flirt with in the palace but the kitchen maids) he spent some time getting lost and found and lost again. Eventually, he found his way to the washroom, now empty of servants. He climbed the old stone steps in the corner, unhinged the door there, and proceeded into the outside air.

His feet met the ground with a slopping slush in the mud. It was chilly outside. Much more than he had expected it to be. He was quite uncomfortable already, and he would have turned back around immediately had he not reminded himself that his will was made of iron and his fortitude primed to outshine any other prince in the whole of civilization. Or something along those lines.

It took Percival a considerable amount of time to cross the field. When at last he reached the stables, he had to pause a moment to mourn the death of his shoes, for they were now very muddy, hardly recognizable, and, sadly, irredeemable. They had been brand new, given to him this very morning with love and affection by one of the princesses. He couldn't, however, remember which princess it was. But since his feet were already a little sore, he was just beginning to think perhaps, when it came to shoes, style really did not always compensate for a lack of practicality.

Percival weaved his way in the shadows of the night and crept low and close to the walls and fences as he made his way to the stables. He figured he must have looked exceptionally debonair while dashing about in this way, but of course, he was so skilled in his stealth that no one would have the pleasure of seeing him if they had tried. Once inside, he promptly concealed himself in one of the stalls with an old, sleeping horse. The prince squatted low, alert and ready, and pressed his face to the opening between the boards of the stall.

Five minutes passed. Nothing happened. Percival's legs were getting tired in his squatting position. He sank a little and scratched his ear. It was a most disappointing thought to imagine Bromley could have been planning to go somewhere besides the stables and Percival had come all the way out here for nothing.

Suddenly, there was a sound of a gate creaking open, and the prince resumed his predatory stance. An orange lantern glow appeared from the back entrance where the supply shed stood, and as it grew nearer, Bromley's form was apparent. The boy hung the lantern on a protruding nail on one of the wooden columns, and then went back to the shed. When he reappeared, he was carrying a horse blanket and whistling softly. Suddenly, one of the horses began to fuss.

"Oh, shush" Bromley chided in a whisper. He went to one of the other horses and positioned the blanket on its back.

The noisy horse protested once more and began to stomp its

hooves.

"I said shush, stupid ass! What's with you, anyway?" Bromley stepped out of the circle of light and then returned carrying a saddle. The boisterous horse began to rear in his pen.

Percival repositioned to get a better view, taking the liberty of movement during the noisy spell. It was then that he realized the horse making all the ruckus was Alcides.

Bromley seemed to ignore the animal's call for attention as he secured the saddle on the other horse. At last, the noise diminished to quiet whinnies. Bromley finished what he was doing as well and dusted off his hands in his hair. He turned and leaned in against the wooden wall separating the aisle from Alcides' pen. Then, laughing quietly and shaking his head, he reached over to scratch the horse's forelock. "Look, I can't take you, alright?" he said. "You're just a bit too conspicuous, I'm afraid. They'd catch me and tear my head from its shoulders in less than an hour. Now maybe if I was trying to get myself killed, that would be a different story." He ran his hand smoothly down the horse's head and caressed its muzzle. "I'll miss you, boy. You're a complete jackass, for sure, but I'll miss you anyway." He went to the prepared animal, mounted it, and proceeded to ride out into the main aisle of the stable. "You know, I'll tell you what," he whispered, looking back to Alcides once more, "If worse comes to worse and I decide on suicide, I'll come right back for you, alright?"

Percival's eyes followed Bromley until he was out of the stable. Then, the prince puffed out a ball of air, almost disbelieving the atrocity he had just witnessed. Horse-theft. From his own cousin. He almost had the thought of gallivanting back into the palace and calling the guards on Bromley, but then he thought of a much more manly and gratifying plan of action. He waited a little while, until he was sure Bromley was far enough away not to hear. Then, he rose and went to the saddlery room.

He had never actually positioned his own saddle on the back of a horse before, but he figured he knew enough by having seen his servants perform the routine hundreds of times. He found one of his finest saddles and carried it, a little awkwardly, to Alcides.

The horse looked blankly at him and huffed lethargically from the side of his mouth. Percival placed the saddle onto the horse. Backwards at first, and then he switched it. It wasn't until he had buckled the saddle strap that he realized he forgot about the saddle blanket. Pressed for time, however, he figured the issue was a small one and proceeded to mount the animal.

The horse and the prince made their way into the aisle and then into the night air beyond the stable's gate. The shape of Bromley and the stolen horse were far ahead, almost hidden by the shadow of the trees beyond the riding grounds. Percival rode slow and cautiously as not to be heard. Alcides, being a very intelligent animal, probably guessed exactly what his owner was up to. Therefore, he trod quietly with the grace of a deer and the cunning of a fox, until they reached the midpoint of the field. Alcides then sent out a loud neigh and began to stomp.

"Stop! Whoa! Desist...You idiot, Alcides! Go forward!"

Bromley, hearing this, turned back across his shoulder and

immediately spurred his horse to a run. Meanwhile, the prince made attempts to steer Alcides, but the horse only turned in circles and continued stomping.

Finally, Alcides began to race forward, first to the right, away from Bromley, and then, seeming to concede to the prince's orders, in the other direction. Soon enough, Percival was at Bromley's tail, for Alcides had too much of a reputation at stake to let himself be outraced. They rode like this for some time through the field, with the chilly night air whizzing by their faces and the sounds of stomping hooves and panting in their ears. At last the castle was entirely lost in the shadow of night, and the riders approached the forest. Suddenly, however, just as Percival and Bromley were nearly side-by-side and the prince was preparing to jump at Bromley, Alcides veered away to one side and began to buck and rear. The saddle, which ostensibly was not buckled right, came loose, and Percival rolled with it off the back of the horse and onto the ground. Then, the last thing the prince remembered was a splitting pain in his side, a recognition that his waistcoat was atrociously dirty, and a loud *thump* at the back of his head.

Chapter 15

Ben

If you were a wise person, you would do well not to relate to fools. However, since it is more likely you are a fool, it probably doesn't matter to whom you relate.
-The Journals of Bengolian

A weak, reddish light crept back into Percival's eyes slowly, as if he had awakened in the middle of the night when the fire in his hearth had dwindled to embers. His first thought was that he was intolerably famished and would call the servants in for an early breakfast, the second, which hadn't occurred to him till he tried to sit upright, was that his body throbbed with inestimable pain. Actually, two things struck him in that movement. One was the sensation that a jagged knife was being twisted into a knot in the left side of his stomach, and the other was the ceiling. His head thwacked against a ceiling board, and he made a pouting groan. A cascade of dust came pouring down onto his face. This made him sneeze, which made a light beside him flicker, which made him realize for the first time that he was not in his own chamber.

There was one candle burning by him, the wax driveling into

a tallow-colored, warty mound and down the edge of a crude wooden nightstand. When his focus began to clear, he saw he was in what looked like a tiny, groundhog sort of broom cabinet, and he was lying on a primitive bed. Actually, the bed itself was more of a wooden crate stacked with blankets and furs. He noticed his waistcoat and hat thrown beside the nightstand, then looking over himself, found he was reduced to his shirt and hose and breeches and was bandaged round his head, his waist, one knee and an elbow.

He flinched when he heard a sound like shuffling paper coming from somewhere outside the room. The noise seemed to be from beyond a crack of light, which was just coming into focus on one of the walls. Percival heaved his aching body to the floor and crept warily towards the crack of light.

It was not a door, as he had assumed, but rather some kind of curtain or hanging rug made from the skin of a large animal. The room outside was lit with candles and lanterns and a hanging fixture in the center, just enough light to reveal its horrendous clutter. It was lined with bookshelves filled with stacks of papers and scrolls and dusty manuscripts, and torrents of other papers spilled out into the space. A desk stood in one corner, piled with trinkets and glasses and more stacks of books and papers, and somewhere beneath the mountain of it all came a murmuring and crinkling sound. Then two hands emerged from behind the mess, clamped a stack of paper from the table and dropped it to the ground. A beggarly figure came into view, dimly in the light, who, without so much as looking up from his desk, said, "Finally decided to wake up, have we, lad?"

Percival, deeply offended, stepped out with an immediate reproach. "Excuse me, sir, I suggest in the future you refrain from speaking to me in such a vulgar tone! I won't waste words on such ill-bred scoundrels as you, but I assure you, no matter what you think you will gain from bringing me here, I can promise you, your only reward will be a most uncomfortably extended stay in the dungeons!"

"...What?" the man looked up for the first time, his expression boyishly curious. His face was lined and weather-worn, his skin leathery, but his eyes had a peculiarly youthful glitter.

"For kidnapping me!" exclaimed the prince.

"Kidnapping? Is that what they're calling rescuing these days? Hm. It's very odd how the meanings of words change over time." The man paused, as if for comic timing, then suddenly burst out laughing, wagging his head from side to side and slapping the desk, very amused at himself.

Percival raised an eyebrow.

"Oh, no...never mind, lad. I do apologize. Haha! The littlest things can make me so entertained sometimes...Where were you?"

"Where was I what?" asked the prince.

"What were you saying?"

"I...I was..."

"Who are you?"

"I'm...do you not know who I am?"

"Of course I do! Haha! I was testing you! You're Prince

Percival Cornelius Vladimir Oswalden Edwalter Ambrogio Reginald Isidore Barnaby the Fourth of Rumandy."

"So...you recognize me, then?"

"No. It was stitched into the inside of your waistcoat. Is your name written on the inside of all of your clothes?"

"Most of them."

"Glory! Are you serious, lad? The entire thing?...Oh!" Suddenly the man's head jerked to one side. He shouted "Oh!" again and slapped his forehead. "Wait. Oh! That's it!" he shouted, wildly.

"What?"

"That's it! I've got it!"

Percival stood silently for a very confused moment.

"Oh..." Then the man's elated expression sank, "No. No, never mind...I lost it." His words trailed off underneath his breath as he squished his wrinkled face into his hand. After another moment, he snapped out of this dolefully befuddled look. "What were you saying?"

"...You're insane," Percival said, matter-of-factly.

"Maybe. But they call me Ben, usually."

"How long was I asleep?" the prince demanded.

"Good question...Well, let's see, you began to recover quite nicely after the first night...I figure your added beauty sleep was another twenty-four hours. But I don't know, I'm not very good at remembering things."

"And how is it you remembered my entire name from looking at my waistcoat if you have such a poor memory?"

"I never said it was poor. It's just selective." The man dipped a quill pen into a jar of ink and began scratching onto a corner of one of the pieces of parchment in front of him.

Percival, taking a moment to examine his bandages and sores, suddenly noticed an absent possession. "Where's my ring?"

"Your what?"

"The royal ring!"

"Royally gone, it looks like. Haha!"

"It's been stolen! *You* took it!"

"Oh, no-no-no. You were already robbed and knocked out cold when I got to you. Not a thing of value on you. Except your hat, interestingly enough. The thieves probably thought it stunk of cologne too much. You should know better than to go out walking at night so close to the forest, lad."

"Would you…stop calling me *lad*!" shouted Percival.

"My apologies, is there a preferential title which I may use to get your attention?"

"Your Highness Prince Percival."

"Your Highness Prince Percival! It is a delight to make your acquaintance!"

"Yes, well, whatever it was—Ben, was it? It's been an ineffable pleasure to make *your* acquaintance, but as I have more important things to do than speak to an old idiot, I'm afraid I must be on my…way." Percival's slight pause in his sentence revealed a hint of anxiety as he made a startling observation after turning to march out the door…There was no door.

Bookshelves lined every inch of the walls, leaving no way to escape from the rather asylum-like study.

"Where's the door?" the prince asked in a demanding voice, suppressing a slightly fearful quaver.

"What door?"

"The...exit door."

"Hm?"

"...Where are we?" the prince asked, helplessly.

The man stacked up another heap of papers and rose from the table. He was taller than he had seemed when he was crouched in his seat. Determining his age was rather difficult. He seemed to have the energy of a child; and perhaps the intelligence of a child. His face and greyish hair, however, gave evidence he could not be under sixty years. He stepped into the light, "Oh! You mean the door to the pantry! I never think of it as an exit or an entrance. Just a portal from one place to another."

"...Right. I suppose," the prince shrugged. If his only choice of a doorway was to a pantry, he would take that.

"Now, I have to find it...hold on, Percival..." He stretched his back and arms then began to scan the shelves lining the walls.

"What do you mean *hold on*? What do you mean *you have to find it*?"

"It's around here somewhere...will you be a lad and help me look for it?"

Percival, being quite eager to get out of the room, found himself rummaging around, searching intently for something without the slightest idea of what he was looking for.

"What did you say your name was, again?" the prince asked,

continuing to look around and finding nothing but paper and dust.

"What name?"

"Your...name."

"Which one?"

"The...name they call you?"

"Oh! That would be Ben!"

"Do you have other names?"

"Dozens! I forget them sometimes. But that's quite alright. I remember them when people call me by them. Any luck finding that door yet?"

Percival slid a stack of books across a shelf, "I haven't the slightest idea what I'm looking for."

"Most people don't, until they find it. AH!" Ben suddenly clapped; one loud clap of excitement which made Percival jump a little. "Here! Here it is!"

Ben waved Percival over from across the room. "Here, lad. Right here! Do you see it?"

"See what?"

Percival looked at an empty shelf.

"No dust," said Ben with a slight laugh. He ran his crinkled hand, gloved to the knuckles with black knitted wool, across the grains of the wood. "Yes, this is the place I always go to open the door. Now, if I can just remember how it works...There!" He pushed downward on the board, which shifted and made a clicking sound as though a lever had been pulled. Then, Ben effortlessly swung the entire shelf away. Seemingly it was built hinged into the wall; a perfectly invisible doorway. Ben took a candle from his desk.

"Come on now, follow me!" he said, stepping forward briskly. Percival followed with a bit of hesitation.

A thick smell of cheeses flooded forth, mixed in with the light and airy vapor of herbs and spices. It was a dark little room. Dark, but small enough that almost everything could be seen by the candlelight Ben brought with him. In the pantry, there were a few large clay jugs and hogsheads of ale, bread baskets with wrapped loaves, and bunches of herbs hanging from the ceiling. What was visible of the floor surprised Percival, for it seemed to be made of dirt. As his eyes began to re-adjust to the darkness, he realized the pantry was actually a domed cave with roots protruding from the floor, walls, and ceiling.

Ben set the candle in a fixture of tangled roots projecting from one of the walls. He went to the other side of the pantry and swung open another door. This time, light streamed in, along with the merry sounds of a summer morning in the forest. The old man sighed contently and drew in a breath of air as he stepped out.

"Glorious day!" he proclaimed.

With significantly less enthusiasm, Percival lugged himself out after him. The sun prickled his eyes in garish contrast to the dimness of the hut, or cave, or whatever it was. He turned around to get a look at the place which they had come from. The door itself was set in the side of a grassy mound. A tree grew beside it and its knotting roots billowed above and below the earth, entwining all around what would have been a front yard. Moss coated everything, including the door, making it easy to overlook the place.

On one side of the mound, between tangles of roots, there was a very old, doddering gray donkey, possibly the ugliest living creature Percival had ever seen. It was not tied to anything, and looked quite too pathetic to realize it could run off anyway.

"Your animal?" the prince asked.

"Aye, you could call him that, I suppose; Padgett I call him now and then. We've been through quite a lot together, him and I."

"Looks like it."

The animal brayed gracelessly. "Oh, don't take it personally, Padgett," Ben called to the donkey. "The lad is a little ornery after getting robbed and all. You'll have to excuse his rudeness."

Percival surveyed the rest of the area suspiciously, "This place is within the Barrier Forest, is it not?" he asked, sharply.

"The what?"

"That accursed forest on the edge of civilization," he sneered at the bracken and looked contemptuously at every tree. "I can understand now why they say this place is haunted, with lunatics like you inhabiting its marshes."

"Marshes? Are you insulting my landscape? First you insult my donkey then you insult my front yard! I'll have you know, this happens to be one of the most pleasant areas in the wood, thank you very much."

"Whatever you prefer to call this worthless place, I demand to be removed from it immediately. How far is it to the clearing? You will lead me back there, without any of your absurd gibberish—"

"Shh!" Ben put a finger to his lips and scanned the rustling leaves above. "Shh!" he repeated in a softer tone.

Suddenly, a twinkling of music resonated in the wind, and turning, Percival saw that the notes came from several sets of wooden and silver chimes strung upon the boughs of the tree which sheltered Ben's hovel. The morning sun in its golden luster sent fiery rays between the branches, and it broke into myriads of colors through glass prisms strung with the chimes. The wind blew northward, rustling the green foliage.

"What?" the prince demanded.

Ben listened, his gaze was distant and yet his eyes seemed to be lit with a vivid but calm light. Then a childish smirk reappeared over his furrowed features.

"It is beginning," he said. Then chuckled.

"...What?"

"I must be going, now. The wind has started up." Ben knelt down, crawling around the turf and examining it, as if searching for a mislaid object. Percival stared disdainfully with his upper lip curled up.

"Look here, your affairs excite not a fragment of my interest, sir, but I assure you, you will not be hampered from them, once you have escorted me back to the palace."

"Sorry," Ben said, and not exactly in the most apologetic of tones. "My way leads North," he picked up a straight, sturdy stick, suitable for a walking staff, and let out a sigh of satisfaction,

"Yes…this is the one," he mumbled, "Get ready, Padgett!"

"Wait one moment, sir. Do you expect me to simply find my own way in this abominable labyrinth of woods?"

"Well now, that is a problem, I suppose…" Ben tested the durability of his staff with a few taps against the trunk of a tree. "I don't suggest you wander about in the forest by yourself, it could be dangerous."

"Oh, really? There wouldn't happen to be any more halfwits and senile donkeys lurking about, would there?"

"Not that I've seen recently, but don't be too ready to dismiss the rumors of this wood."

"What rumors?"

"Oh, you know. That they're haunted."

"Oh, I'm shaking in fear," Percival said. "So what do you suggest? I stay here waiting until you get back?"

Ben scratched his stubbled chin and pondered the situation, his jaunty grin creeping back into his face, "I don't think that's a good idea. I might be gone for quite a while, judging by the wind. You're quite welcome to come along with me."

"Come along with…" Percival gawked, unable to repeat the sentence in its entirety due to the ludicrousness of the suggestion. "What sort of imbecile do you take me for? I will most certainly not come with you! That's the most ridiculous thing I've ever heard proposed in my life."

"You don't feel the slightest inkling for an adventure? That just may be what it's coming to!"

"…No. Of course not. You're insane."

"Could be, lad. I've been in that hut for a few days now at least. Insanity is a definite possibility. Oh! Excuse me, Percival. I've been calling you *lad* again and I remember you don't like that...that reminds me, I'd better pack!"

Ben quickly began to scurry back and forth from his hut and the donkey, piling the pitiful creature with various provisions of blankets, food, canteens, a heap of animal furs which sagged the pathetic beast downward considerably, and an assortment of manuscripts bound up in leather strings. These trips back and forth seemed never-ending, and every time he set one thing on the donkey, he would gasp and say "Oh, yes, and one more thing..." and scuttle back through the door. It surprised Percival then, when Ben abruptly stopped the pattern and simply starting leading the animal away, without so much as a curt farewell.

"Hey, w—wait a minute!" the prince said from a lofty throne he had established on an old log.

Ben looked back nonchalantly.

"You're...you're not just going to leave me here...Without even..."

"Was there something I forgot?"

"No, just..."

"Oh! Yes, I'm sorry, la—uh—Percival," he pointed to his right. "That way should take you to the road where I found you. The paths in the forest are old, but if you're careful, you shouldn't have too much trouble finding your way."

Percival stood. He took three steps, much more hesitant steps than he thought they would be, in the direction Ben had indicated. Ben continued walking his own way, humming softly as he led the donkey with an old rope. Percival felt that his feet had suddenly grown very heavy. "Where are you going, anyway?" he called out suddenly over his shoulder.

"I don't know yet," Ben called back over his shoulder. "But when I get there, I'll know!"

Percival bit his lower lip, and something inside him flared. He knew the words were coming, and he knew he would regret them after they were spoken. "Wait. I'll come."

"What was that, lad?"

"I said I'll...I'll go that way with you for a little while."

What a stupidly brash and irrational thing to say.

Ben looked back across his shoulder. He might have been pleased, but it was difficult to tell whether or not he was surprised, "Well, hurry up then, lad."

Percival hurriedly fetched his waistcoat and his hat from inside the hut. He was dazed at the sequence of words which had issued forth from his mouth. What was he doing? What a brainless thing to do! He pulled his waistcoat awkwardly over his bandages as he ran back into the open air. He hobbled after Ben, who was already yards away, apparently wasting no time waiting for the prince. Percival had not even bothering to tuck his shirt into his breeches or situate the hat correctly on his head. A princely wreck, and quite the sight for royal eyes to have seen, had anyone of importance been there.

JOSEPHINE ELI

Chapter 16

An Invitation to Tea

Friends can be found in the most unusual circumstances. Unfortunately, so can very bizarre people who you'd rather never have met. It's best to stay inside.

-The Journals of Bengolian

Within an hour after Percival had decided to walk with Ben, feelings of discontent and regret had already begun to seep through his clothing with his perspiration. Ben seemed to be growing more insane by the minute. He hadn't the slightest notion of where they were going. At moments he stopped to do something in the way of tracking, but instead of scouring the ground for markings or signs, he appeared to be listening to inaudible voices in the air. The most galling part of it all was his incessantly buoyant disposition, for Percival was not feeling at all in good humor, and to someone in such a cantankerous condition, a cheerful person can be as irritating as an unsmackable mosquito in the sweltering summer heat.

It would have probably been just after his usual breakfast time when they started off. Percival was very aware that he had not been given breakfast. After what seemed like an entire day's worth of trudging along aimlessly, the pestering sun had hardly seemed to change its position. Ben kept on, merrily as a drunken sailor at sea, while Percival lagged behind, grumbling over his injuries and moaning about how famished he felt and how rough and savage the terrain was.

It must have been around noon then, though it felt much later to the prince's stomach, when Ben finally yielded to sit down and rest for a moment. Percival crumpled, flopping himself onto the trunk of a fallen tree. The moss was sure to stain the backside of his attire, but he was at that moment too exhausted to be concerned.

"Exactly how long do you plan to keep to this absurd wandering?" he asked as Ben tossed him a canteen of water.

"Haha! I don't know!"

Percival took a drink and then stuck his tongue out in disgust at the bitter taste of the lukewarm water. "I should have guessed you'd say that," he added to his disapproval.

"Could be two days or six months! That's what makes it so exciting!" Ben handed Percival a chunk of crusty bread, a slab of cheese, and an apple. Though the prince was famished, he couldn't eat without a moment of hesitation.

"I'm not sure I should trust a stranger who offers me food. How do I know it's not poisoned, anyway?"

Ben tore off a a bit of bread from another loaf, "Well, that would be silly, since I packed it for my dinner. And anyway, if I were to poison you I would have done it with the water, that's much easier to arrange. I could carry my own separately, marking the canteens so as to differentiate between them. And of course, I would have purposefully withheld it from you till around the noon hour, knowing with the amount of walking you would be doing, your throat would be very dry, and you would hardly have time to consider whether or not it was safe to drink before you took a swallow. In which case, you would start to feel its effects right about..." he paused and raised his finger, "...now!"

Nothing happened.

"Your humor is revolting," said the prince, at length.

"I wasn't trying to be funny, lad. That's what would happen!"

Ben's expression was incomprehensibly glib, and Percival could only narrow his eyes and bite into his apple, spitefully. "How much food did you pack?"

Ben did not answer. Suddenly he sprang to his feet as if he had sat on burning coals. "Did you hear that?" he yelled.

"No," Percival took another bite of his bread, disinterested.

There was a peculiar silence as Ben picked up his walking stick and strode a few yards away, searching or sensing or doing whatever it was he did. He knelt and set his palm flat on the mossy turf, as if feeling its heat for a fever, then he looked up beyond the branches of the trees.

"Someone is coming," he said, his voice hushed and wary.

"I don't see anyone."

He made no reply except to rush back to Padgett to fetch his cap.

"Where are you going now?" asked the prince.

"Stay here, you should be safe in this area. If you wander far you may run into trouble. Goodbye, Padgett. I'll return within the hour."

"Within the hour? What am I to do sitting around for an hour?"

"Watch the jackass for me, will you?" Ben called over his shoulder, and without another word, he tramped off until his figure was lost within the tangle of leafy trees. Percival slumped back onto the tree trunk with an agitated grumble. Of all the incoherent, imbalanced, lightheaded, hallucinatory old loons in the world, Ben must surely have been the worst of them. And the prince wondered how he had somehow managed to become tousled in his affairs.

The minutes passed idly with nothing to see, nothing to do, and no one to blame it on but an ignorant donkey incessantly staring him in the face.

From the trees behind him, he heard a sudden rustle which made his heart skip a beat. About ten minutes passed. Fifteen. The donkey brayed. Percival swatted at a bug that was buzzing around his apple. Twenty minutes. He threw the apple core into the bushes. Twenty-five minutes. "Alright, I've had quite enough of this," he said out-loud. He was not sure whether or not he was talking to himself or the donkey. "I am finished with all of this idiocy. I'm going home, right now. It can't possibly be that difficult to find my way out of the forest."

After a few minutes of walking in a direction the prince

assumed was West, he heard a donkey bray directly beside him. His shoulders dropped in disappointment. He wondered if the dumb animal was following him, or if he had just been going in circles. Unfortunately, you see, every tree in the woods looks the same to a prince of Rumandy. Padgett lowered his head lazily and started to nibble on a tuft of grass. "Well, you can stay there!" Percival commanded as he continued onward...or backwards. Whichever way it was.

Walking seemed to become more unbearable as the day wore on, either because Percival was getting tired, or because the pine needles began regularly sticking to the bottom of his shoes, or because, as it seemed, the terrain was getting more and more savage. He collided into a bur bush and came out scratching and picking burs off of himself for the next quarter of an hour. The monotonous racket of breaking twigs and crunching leaves under his own feet began to irritate him tremendously as well. Suddenly, the donkey brayed in his ear again. "Why are you still here?" Percival yelled angrily. He scanned the area. It was most definitely not the same place as before, but now he had absolutely no idea which direction to take.

He sank down on a large rock and removed his hat. With a sorrowful sigh, he tore off one shoe and plucked out seven pine needles which stuck to his fingers as he tried to throw them away.

"What are you gaping at?" he shouted at the donkey, who stared almost as if he was amused at the prince's frustration. "If this were a civilized region and you weren't any less than a jackass, you'd hang for that look!" A sudden sharp sting pierced the prince's neck and he quickly smacked to death a blood-indulged mosquito. "Impudent little varlet..."

Although Percival had never before spent a great deal of time in front of a donkey and was therefore unacquainted with the animal's normal behavior, he was almost sure the animal was laughing at him. "No wonder your owner is insane," Percival retorted, "spending all day with no one to talk to but a dolt like you." His expression sank suddenly. "Wait a minute...I'm talking to you. Why am I talking to you?" he scratched his head and the pine sap on his fingers stuck to his hair. "Am I going insane as well?...So soon?" The animal began to nod his head clownishly and stomp his hoof on the ground.

Suddenly, a strap broke on the mound of baggage Padgett was carrying. Three of the heavy leather manuscripts fell to the ground, and one split clear through the binding into two tattered pieces. It must have been ancient, for the parchment was yellowed and the edges were decayed. Percival looked around the area cautiously, placed his hat back on his head, then reached over to pick up half of the torn book. At first, he thought Ben just must have had appalling handwriting, for he could not read a word of what was written. Eventually, however, he began to see that the characters themselves were unfamiliar. The entire book was written in some very strange language Percival had never seen. As he continued to flip through the pages, he saw that most of them were half covered in words and the other half in sketches. There were studies of plants and animals, peasants plowing fields, maids milking cows, dirty little boys and girls playing in mud puddles. All commoners.

Percival flipped the page once more and came to a sheet with only a single sketch and no writing. There was something particularly fascinating about this drawing, and perhaps a little bit familiar. But the prince could not quite place it. It was only a simple portrait of a young man, fair of face and hair. He wore militant clothing it seemed, and had a sword at his side. His expression, so masterfully captured by the artist, was alert and at the ready; audacious, yet with just enough vanity to make him appear regal.

"Got him!" came a nasally voice behind Percival's neck.

The book flipped out of the prince's hands. Two arms grabbed him from behind and heaved him up so that his toes dangled a foot above the ground.

"Oooh! What a pretty prize I found!"

"I founded him first, you lunkhead!"

"Did not!"

Whoever it was who had grabbed him turned him around and revealed themselves. Percival's face went pallid at the sight.

If these were indeed people, they were the ugliest people the prince had ever seen. One of them was holding him captive at the waist, and two others were standing close by, eyeing him with animal-like fascination. They were the prince's height, or perhaps a bit taller. Their skin appeared thin and slippery, blueish and nearly transparent, with dark veins and sinewy muscles showing through. They had long, twisted ears which curled over on themselves, and their hair, reddish and thick, was pushed up in streaks down the centers of their heads like the bristles of a horse-brush. They were dressed in patches and scraps of leathery gear and bits of fur, and metal rings and chains were strung from their ears, noses, lips, and eyebrows.

"Gentlemen!" came a fourth, suddenly appearing from behind. This one had a blue handkerchief tied around his forehead and tattoos carved into his arms and chest. "Gentlemen! What is the meaning of this lunacy? Now what have we here? Who in tarnation is this?"

"I found him first, captain!"

"You did not! I did!"

"He's so soft and scrunchable!" said the one who was holding the prince, giving him a tight squeeze.

Percival, panicking and not knowing what else to do with himself, suddenly yelled, "I'm going insane!"

"Huh?"

"It's really happening! I'm going insane!" he shouted again.

"Oh dear, Scrimp..." the first small creature whispered to the other, "This fellow is going insane..."

"Uh-oh. That's very unfortunate, Scallywag."

"I hope he doesn't die in front of us."

The other creature gasped suddenly and covered his mouth with both his hands, "Do you think it could be catching?" he squeaked, fearfully.

"Now, now! There's nothing to worry about," stated the one they called the captain. He spoke with an authoritative air which seemed to immediately alleviate the other creatures' concerns. "I went insane once and it's definitely not fatal."

"Oh good, that's a relief..."

"Now, gentlemen, hasn't the goodness of your krattkin mothers' hearts ever taught you manners?" the captain continued, "That's no way to behave to a perfectly innocent stranger!"

"Krattkin?" Percival squirmed in his captor's arms, "What do you mean *krattkin*? What the devil is a krattkin?!"

The expression on the smallest creature's face went flat. "He's never heard of us, captain."

"I don't believe it," said one of the others.

"So ignorant of the world..."

"We should kill him."

"No!!" Percival cried. "You're a krattkin. You're all krattkins. I understand. I'm sorry, I must have misheard you the first time—"

"*Krattkin* not *krattkins*! The plural form goes without an S."

"I'm sorry! Of course!"

"He doesn't know anything!"

"I bet he's one of those self-righteous prudes who thinks he knows everything there is to know. But then actually doesn't."

"All the curses in the world be upon him!"

"Now, now, now," the captain interrupted the others, "That's being a bit melodramatic, gentlemen."

He faced the prince, baring a line of rotting, pointed teeth. His breath was something like a mixture of decomposing fish and musty ale. "He's going to be a splendid guest today, I can already tell!" His lips curled up into a grin somewhere in between charm and utter grotesqueness. "Now, tell us all about yourself. We must know everything! Where you from? What's you name? Do you taste better with oregano or rosemary?"

The three other krattkin burst into laughter, ostensibly finding much more amusement in the question than Percival did.

"*Oregano or rosemary!*" one of them repeated, "How did you ever get to be so clever, captain?"

"I wish I was as clever as you," said one of the others.

"Oh, well..." the captain, rather pleased with himself, seemed to blush beneath his blue skin. He dusted off his shoulder proudly. "I do try. I do indeed try..."

"This is absurd!" Percival shouted suddenly above their laughter. All four creatures turned silent and looked him over oddly. "You're all not real. You can't be real. I'm hallucinating, that's it! Ben must have drugged me! Ben!" he called upwards, "Ben, wake me up right now!"

"What's...'allucinating?" said one of the smaller krattkin.

"It's...it's when you see things that aren't real," the prince answered.

"Really? That's very unusual, isn't it? Hey, Scrimp! Maybe we're 'allucinating!"

"Do you think we could be, Scallywag?"

"I'll slap your face and you can tell me if it hurts...if it does, I'll bet this is real."

"Alright...Wait. What if we're both real, but this fellow we found here ain't?"

"...Me?" said the prince.

"Yeah, you!"

"Well, of course I'm real!"

"I don't know if we should trust him..." the smallest krattkin pulled out a dagger and poked the prince's stomach. "He looks suspicious."

"There's only one way to know for sure," snickered the creature who held the prince. With a knavish tone of voice, he added, "I think you all know what I'm talking about!"

The captain clapped his hands together gleefully. "The taste test! Good thinking, Quagmire!"

"The what?" the prince asked, his skin suddenly losing its color.

"Oh, we haven't done that in ages!"

"I...I guarantee you, I'm—I'm not tasty at all, really," the prince insisted. "And look, I'd be a meager dish anyway; hardly any meat on me, see? Skin and bones!"

"I like bones!" said one of the smaller ones. "You can gnaw at them all day long and they keep your teeth nice and sharpened!"

"Alright, alright. Now, now, now, settle down, gentlemen! Settle down," said the captain. "We're forgetting our manners! This fellow needs a proper introduction! Now, sir," he addressed the prince, "I'm Captain Lickspigot, at your service, that krattkin who's got you around the waist there is Quagmire, and these two young gentlemen here are Scrimp and Scallywag."

Scrimp and Scallywag saluted. Quagmire snatched the prince's hat and placed it on his own head. "Oooh! I like this! Can I wear it for a bit?"

"No! Give that back immediately!"

The krattkin ignored Percival's request.

"And we," the captain continued, "are all formidable members, myself the esteemed leader, in fact, of the Barrel-Cat Brigade!"

"The Barrel-Cat Brigade!" the other krattkin announced triumphantly in unison.

"Now," the captain said to the prince, "we here, as you can see, pride ourselves on being real gentlemen. And what do real gentlemen do?" He asked the other krattkin in a quizzing tone.

"Real gentlemen always invite guests to tea!" the other krattkin answered enthusiastically.

"...Tea?" the prince repeated.

"Can we have biscuits too, captain?" Scrimp asked. "The ones we've been saving in the back of the lavatory?"

"Scrimp, you always have the best ideas!" the captain replied. "I think this occasion does indeed call for such a delightful treat! Now, onward, gentlemen!"

Chapter 17

The Taste Test

*The other day, I found the most delicious recipe for a
raspberry strudel. It was the perfect formula in every
detail. Unfortunately, the place I found the recipe was
in between a thought and a daydream...and forgot to
write it down.*

-The Journals of Bengolian

As much as Percival would have liked to have thought
otherwise, he was becoming more and more convinced the
krattkin were in fact, not a hallucination.

"Um, excuse me," he tried with little success to interrupt
them as they pulled him along. They were all singing some sort of
nonsensical song as they paraded through the woods up a
winding path which grew increasingly rocky and difficult to
manage.

"Excuse me?" Percival said again, "Uh, thank you very much
for the invitation, to uh...tea, or whatever it was, but I'm afraid I
have to...be somewhere else."

"Sing with us!"

"...Alright then!" Percival was easily and instantly cajoled into joining them as Quagmire pressed a rusty blade to his stomach. The prince followed the krattkin lyrics on a slight delay for about a quarter of an hour until he began to memorize a refrain they repeatedly returned to. He had utterly no idea what he was saying, of course, but tried his best to sing along for fear of otherwise getting stabbed.

The band of krattkin lugged their hostage forward and up the steadily sloping terrain, until they came to a rocky place at a clearing in the woods. Large boulders with patches of moss and strange symbols carved into them decorated the area. They led him through a crevice of rocks which sank deeper into the earth until it became a covered tunnel. The darkness blinded Percival, but the krattkin made their way as easily as if it had been broad daylight. Their cackling and joking and singing echoed in the tunnel along with the noises made from the dozens of squealing rats that scurried past them. Percival thought he heard more krattkin voices ahead. And, to his great disappointment, he was correct.

They turned a corner and entered a large space with ceiling barnacled with stalactites and dozens of krattkin brawling on the floors and climbing up the walls. At the center of the room, a fire crackled and a few of the creatures wrestled, laughing chaotically as they nearly threw each other into the flames. Others were playing what looked like king of the mountain on a pile of sacks, barrels, and wooden crates. Dishes and chairs and all sorts of other objects were being thrown about the space in every direction. Suddenly a jug came hurling towards the prince and crashed into pieces against the wall next to him.

"Gentlemen! If I could kindly have your attention!" said the captain. His voice was suppressed by the havoc, so he tried again by whistling piercingly and yelling as loud as his voice would go: "Aye! Aye! SHUT UP, you idiots!"

"Hey! The captain's back!" said one of the creatures, excitedly.

"Hello, captain!"

"Afternoon, captain!"

They all began a rather awkward process of straightening themselves out and attempting to look civilized.

"Look at this place, it's an absolute atrocity!" the captain chided. "What an embarrassment you are; you should be ashamed. Now clean up right this minute! We have company."

"Company?"

"I love company!"

"Who is it this time, captain?"

"Bring him forth, Quagmire!" the captain commanded.

"May I introduce, today's distinguished dinner guest..." Quagmire chomped his teeth together and shot his face back to the prince. "What'd you say your name was, anyway?"

"I'm...uhm."

"Cat got your tongue?" said a krattkin in the corner.

"A cat got my tongue once, it bled for two days straight," said another.

"I bet we can guess his name, captain!"

"I think he looks like a William."

"What about Charlie?"

"Horace!"

"Rickrock!"

"Wolfslayer!"

"Wolfslayer?" another krattkin repeated. "Now that's a good name!"

"That sounds majestic!"

"Let's call him Wolfslayer!"

"Have you ever killed a real wolf?" one suddenly inquired of the prince.

Percival, finding himself in a rather speechless state, froze a moment before he could answer at all. "I...well...no."

The gang let out a lugubrious sigh of disappointment.

"Hypocrite!"

"Now, now, gentlemen!" the captain said, raising his hands to quell the uproar of dashed hopes. "Let's not get carried away with details. We have far more important matters to attend to. Now would one of you idiots please get out the silverware?"

"The...silverware?" said Scallywag, widening his eyes in awe.

"What's the occasion, captain?"

"We haven't used silverware in ages!'

The captain slapped Percival on the shoulder then gave him a squeeze. "Well, gentlemen...We are having ourselves a taste test!"

Percival was not exactly sure what that meant. But he was significantly less enthusiastic about it than the krattkin gang appeared to be. Every one of them jumped up and cheered and squealed and slammed themselves into each other chaotically. Apparently, that was one of their ways of expressing excitement.

Suddenly, four or five gritty hands grabbed Percival and began to pull him towards the fire-pit at the center of the room. He could only think of a few possibilities of what would be happening next, and none of them seemed overly appealing. He tried with little success to break himself free. "Excuse me, I'm terribly sorry," he cried out, ineffectively, "I'm sorry but unfortunately I really do have to be somewhere else today. This is all very kind of you to include me, but it's all happening too fast..."

"Include you?" said Quagmire, "Why, you're the most essential part of the taste test!"

"The honorary guest!"

"My good sir," the captain added, "the likes of you as company is a delightful treat we seldom have the opportunity to experience. It is, in fact, our deepest pleasure and not a trouble at all. Could somebody get out the hand-ties and the blindfold, please?" he asked suddenly with disturbing politeness.

Two krattkin were just setting down a large, rickety chair with old upholstery tearing at the seams. Percival was pulled down and immediately bound with chords of rope to the arms and legs of the crude throne.

"I really don't think this is a good idea!" he shouted, but was entirely ignored amid all the excitement.

A squat, potbellied krattkin carried out a tray of dishes—a teapot and a set of matching cups which looked strangely out of place in the trashed room. "Tea is ready!" he shouted.

Another krattkin took out a tablecloth and spread it over a large crate next to the chair, creating a make-shift dinner table which was quickly decorated with empty candle-holders and dead flowers.

Another krattkin entered with a tray of bowls stacked chaotically on top of each other. Different colors of goop spilled out from each bowl onto the tray. That was the last thing Percival saw before they blindfolded him.

"There we go!" the captain proclaimed. "All is prepared! Now are you gentlemen ready for the taste test?"

A louder cheer rose up. Many things flashed through Percival's mind at that moment. His inheritance. His perfect reflection in the mirror. A beatific vision of his funeral. A coffin, bedecked in jewels, containing only fragments of bone, picked clean of meat from the krattkin. Such perfect and beautiful white bones wearing his finest suit of clothing.

The vision was spoiled suddenly when Percival felt something shoved into his mouth. He gagged for a moment. It was lukewarm and gloppy.

"Now..." the captain's voice said into the prince's ear. "What's it taste like?"

"I...it..."

"Come on! You can do it!" Scrimp's voice cheered.

"Think green!"

"Think of splitting somebody's skull in half!"

Percival swished the mush around in his mouth for a moment. It didn't taste all bad. And surprisingly did not seem too foreign of a dish. "...Split-pea soup?"

"Correct!"

A roaring applause flooded the room.

"He's good at this!" said Scrimp's voice

"That was an easy one! And you gave him hints!" Scallywag's voice argued.

Another ladle-full of slop was forced into Percival's mouth.

"Now, for round two!" came the captain's voice.

Percival was just at the point of thinking he was going to vomit when the scene was interrupted by the sound of another voice. It was farther away, perhaps near the doorway to the room.

"Pardon me, but what exactly is going on here?" the voice said.

It was not angry, but it did not sound pleased. It was not a krattkin voice, but it was familiar. Full of energy and yet not a young voice. Percival only needed a moment to place it. Earlier that morning, he never imagined he would be so thrilled to hear that voice.

"Ben!" he screamed. "Ben! Is that you? Get me out of this chair!"

"Just what exactly do you think you're doing with my house-guest?" Ben asked the krattkin platoon. "And what the devil are you doing strapped to that chair, lad?"

"We was just having ourselves a taste test," said the captain, politely.

"Just some honest fun!" Quagmire added.

"We wasn't going to eat him afterwards or nothing."

"Raw meat upsets my stomach anyway."

"Of course you weren't going to eat him," said Ben. "Now somebody get those bindings off him and give him back here!"

Another bout of disappointment filled the room.

"But he didn't even get to try the cat-brain pudding yet!" said Scallywag.

"Nobody ever guesses that one right," said Scrimp.

Percival immediately spit out whatever was in his mouth as one of the krattkin, with great reluctance, removed his blindfold. Another two krattkin followed by beginning to untie the ropes at his ankles.

"Wait a minute, wait a minute!" the captain interrupted, sourly. "Now, Ben, we found this guest fair and square and not on your property, neither. What gives you the right to just take him away from us, just like that?"

"He's our honorary guest!" Quagmire said in defense.

Ben's attention, however, seemed to have drifted to something else. He took a step closer to the scene, his eyes fixed on the table by the fire. "Where did you get that?" he said.

"Get what?" said the captain.

"That banner."

"What banner?"

"The tablecloth."

"Oh! That."

"How did you find it? And where?"

The krattkin captain crossed his arms across his chest. "Well, that there is our specialest tablecloth we have. It's been in the brigade for years and years."

"I'll buy it from you."

"We couldn't possibly sell that! No! It's too precious."

"What's your price?" Ben continued.

The captain hesitated. He turned to chat with a couple of the other krattkin then quickly looked back to Ben. "A firestone—no—three firestones. One blue, one red, one green."

Ben chuckled. "Oh come now, an old tablecloth for three firestones? I'll give you one firestone for the cloth and the boy."

"Three or there's no deal!"

"Two."

"Fine. One green and one blue."

"Fair enough." From somewhere in Ben's folds of fabric, he took out a little leather sack which jingled as if it was filled with marbles. He put his hand into it and took out two round, smooth stones about the size of large walnuts. He examined them, replaced one of them with another from the bag, and rubbed them between his palms. He stepped towards the fire, and as he approached, the krattkin seemed to all simultaneously move back in awe, with all eyes fixed on the old man.

Ben put his hand a few inches above the flickering flames, and with a strangely elegant gesture, he seemed to snatch up some of the fire's glow. He brought it to his other hand which held the stones. Then, slowly and gently, he raised them to his mouth and blew upon them. Immediately, the stones ignited in glowing flame—one blue and one green—and the krattkin gasped and shouted in amazement. Percival gasped and shouted as well, though his reaction was significantly leaning more towards fright than amazement.

"They are not hot to the touch, as you will find," said Ben, "and the fire will last a number of weeks."

"What sort of sorcery is this?" said the prince. He was entirely ignored.

"Alright, alright! Give them here!" said the captain, excitedly.

"Not until you hand over the boy and the banner."

The other krattkin, now eagerly, untied the rest of Percival's bindings. With much excitement, they knocked the candle-holders and the dead flowers off the table, bundled up the tablecloth, and handed it with every attempt at politeness to Ben.

Carefully, as if transferring a newborn baby from one person's arms to another, Ben handed the burning stones to the captain, who received them, fearful but mesmerized. Every krattkin eye was fixated on the stones.

Percival, who was now entirely forgotten by the krattkin, stood up from his chair and began to sneak as far away from them as he could get.

"Let me hold one of them!" Quagmire insisted, grabbing at the stones.

"No you don't!" said the captain.

"I'm second lieutenant! I should get a chance to hold one!"

"You will after I'm done looking at them, Quagmire!"

"Now, now, let's not argue about the petty things..." Ben interrupted.

Suddenly Quagmire pulled out a knife. "Just the blue one!

That's all I want!"

"You're a crummy krattkin, you know that?" said the captain, pulling out his own knife. "Isn't he, gents?"

"Don't listen to him!" said Quagmire, "He's gonna keep them all to himself as he always does with nice things!"

"Look, I'm the captain and I say these stones are off limits for the next three hours."

"And what about after that?"

"Then I'll decide how long they're off limits after that."

"He's just tricking us!" said Quagmire. "WAR!"

"What? This is mutiny!" said the captain.

"It's not mutiny, it's rebellion against tyranny!"

"That sounds smart, whatever it means!" said Scallywag, and a ruckus of arguments ensued.

And whatever in fact it did mean, Percival had a very bad feeling about it. He got Ben's attention and they mutually signaled an attempt at escape. Ben somehow managed to move towards the entrance with relative ease, but Percival found himself trapped. All of the krattkin began to take out their knives. Apparently, they all had them hidden somewhere on their persons. More arguments broke out until each krattkin was fighting with another and objects were being thrown about the room. Breakable objects, sharp objects, heavy objects, edible objects, flammable objects. Percival ducked and dodged and tried to run towards Ben.

"Come on, lad!" Ben called out.

The prince was almost to the entrance, and just sensing a

rush of relief running through him, when he realized it might have been too soon to celebrate his escape. Something hit him. At the back of his head. He had no idea what it was, and only about two seconds to guess before he blacked out. He saw the cave spinning for a moment, and then his face hitting the hard ground. And that was the end of the tea party.

Chapter 18

Ben and Company

Whenever I meet a person for the first time, two things immediately enter my brain: curiosity as to what this person's story may be, and utter dread that perhaps I have actually met this person before and I've entirely forgotten them.

-The Journals of Bengolian

The first thing to come into Percival's consciousness was the sound of a mosquito buzzing by his face. He opened one eyelid and then the other to a view of two rather oddly shaped faces peering down at him, silhouetted by the colorless evening sky. As his eyes focused, he saw that one of the faces was Ben and the other was the donkey.

"Hold on, lad!" Ben said. He reached out suddenly and slapped the mosquito, smashing it onto the prince's face. Percival jerked up to a sitting position. "Ouch!"

"Got it! Good morning, lad! Of course, it's almost night now, but it always seems more appropriate to say *good morning* to someone waking up, regardless of the time of day, doesn't it?

Would you like something to drink?"

Percival made a groaning noise and shook his head, repulsed as he wiped off the mosquito smear from his face.

"You must have been out cold for a good three hours at least. You do love to sleep, don't you, lad?" Ben quaffed down the rest of his drink and sighed contently. "But it's a good thing nothing happened to you while you were lying here."

The prince glared at him blankly. "Nothing happened to me?" he said with a croaky, dry throat.

"Besides mosquito bites, I'm sure. I am sorry to have left you alone for so long, lad."

Percival brushed off the dirt from his waistcoat and scanned the woods around him suspiciously.

"Is something the matter?" Ben asked.

The prince felt the back of his head. There was certainly a tender spot there, but it was difficult to know whether the soreness was from that day or from the previous. "I must have had...an exceedingly vivid dream."

"Really? About what?"

Percival furrowed his eyebrows as he recalled. "I was...taken by some sort of strange beasts and dragged into a cave where they tied me to a chair and fed me. And then you...came in with magic rocks or something like that. And traded the rocks for a banner they were using as a tablecloth."

Ben's face went expressionlessly flat. "What the devil have you been drinking?" After a moment of stillness, he burst out into the kind of laughter which is only enjoyable to the one laughing, and altogether galling to the person being laughed at. He stood up and stretched his arms, cracking his neck and back. "Well then! On our way!"

"Wait just a moment!" Percival insisted.

"For what?"

"I'm not entirely convinced."

"Convinced of what, lad?" Ben chuckled.

"That...well, I don't think I trust you."

"Well, surely you don't believe any of that nonsense of a dream was real, do you?"

Percival squinted his eyes and looked Ben over warily, trying with little success to read his expression. "You're not a normal person, are you?" the prince said.

"You know, I was actually just thinking the same thing about you, lad."

"What do you mean?"

"You're very strange. It's not normal. Did you ever realize that?" Ben loaded his sack of supplies back onto Padgett. "Quickly now! We must be off! You must meet my companions up ahead; they've already started a fire, I'm sure. We'll stay with them tonight!"

"Companions? What are you talking about? You never said anything about companions before."

"That's because I didn't know I was going to have companions! What a pleasant surprise! I met them along the path while you were having your lovely dream about being captured by krattkin. Haha!"

The prince paused, then stood up suddenly. "Wait just a minute! What did you just say?"

"What?"

"What did you just call them?"

"...Hm?"

"You called them krattkin."

"Called who krattkin?"

"I never mentioned what the creatures were called!"

"What?"

"It did happen! I knew it! I knew it, Ben!"

Ben let his emotionless face break into spastic laughter. "Well, of course it happened, lad! Don't you understand sarcasm?"

Percival's expression went askew. "...I don't think it's very funny."

"That's because you're pitifully desiccated of a sense of humor. Haha! Now come along!"

They walked a little ways without much conversation, with only Ben's incessant humming and murmuring to breech the silence. It must have been well past supper time, and the light was just becoming muted enough for glowing eyes and creeping shapes to haunt the woods.

"Come along now, lad," Ben called over his shoulder to the prince. "Keep those lily-petaled feet of yours in motion! Unless you feel no shame in being outdistanced by an old man and his donkey. He stopped suddenly and stared forward. "Ha! There they are! There's the glow of firelight ahead." "Hello there!" he called out, waving his arm as he continued to walk forward.

Though the daylight was almost entirely gone, Percival could make out the forms of three men and three horses around a fire. One of the men caught sight of Ben and stood, signaling back as he began to walk towards them.

"Pavlock!" Ben called out. "I've returned at last with this poor lost cause of a boy."

The man's steps came quietly, though his bearing was stoic and austerely resolute as he approached them. "We were beginning to fear something had happened," he said. His voice had a steady and sagacious quality to it, though his face could not have seen more than thirty years. He was tall in stature, lean but solidly built. Percival looked him over distrustfully. He was clad in what seemed strange clothing to the prince; rather archaic and rough. He wore a pale coat with a high collar, a leather belt and scabbard with a sheathed sword, and dark, worn boots which had seen much travel.

"You were worried something might have happened?" Ben repeated, laughing. "Something always happens. The question is, is the something going to be good or bad?"

A humble crease appeared on Pavlock's brow. "Of course. Forgive me, sir."

"Apology accepted! Now quickly, let's go back to the fire. The sun has set and with it the warmth of day—how strange a season it is, to be so warm in the day and so chilly after nightfall. My bones are so brittle, Pavlock, so easily affected by the elements! How does one live like this? It's a very strange feeling and I don't think I'll ever adapt to it. Oh! By the way, this is Percival. Funny little stripling; he'll grow on you though."

Pavlock acknowledged Percival with a shallow bow. His deeply set eyes were half concealed by the fading twilight, veiling any expression. The rest of his face was weathered and unshaven, and his flaxen hair hung loosely to his shoulders. He turned away abruptly and walked with Ben, the two of them muttering quietly. Percival dragged himself behind them by a few yard, feeling for perhaps the first time in his life, the entirely foreign sensation of insignificance.

Up ahead, the two men slouched against logs by the fire, laughing and chatting. They did not seem to be of the same stuff that Pavlock was made of, for their manners and expressions were quite different from the stolidity of the man to whom Percival had just been introduced. As they drew closer to the ring of firelight, the younger of the two men, enthralled in conversation with the other, said between laughter, "It's impossible! I mean, *you*? Five or six I could understand. Seven is just smashing, but, I swear, *seventeen*? How is that even mathematically possible?"

"You really don't believe me?" the other said.

"Oh, I believe you, but your wife must want you dead for it!"

"She probably does."

"Pavlock," the younger man called out, "Where does someone as ugly as Brunwick get the nerve to have *seventeen* children with one woman?"

"A little quieter, please, Orion," Pavlock upbraided.

The younger man laughed, pulling back the volume of his voice a little. He scruffed his coal black hair and rose from his seat.

He was probably not much older than Percival. Twenty or twenty-two at the most, the prince figured. His clothes were that of a peasant's; his sleeves rolled up informally to his elbow. He wore a coarse, dark green rag-cravat tied loosely around his neck, like a rustic who would have liked to think himself dignified.

"Seventeen..." he said, "That's inhuman, Brunwick. Hey, has anyone seen Phyllis anywhere?"

"No, thank the gods," the other man replied.

"Brunwick, you ornery bastard, you know I can't think straight unless I've got my fingers on that girl. What'd you do with her?"

"I didn't do a thing. It's around here somewhere."

When Ben reached the fire, he outstretched his fingers towards the crackling flames and sighed contently. "What a splendid fire! And is that a soup I see simmering in the kettle? Delightful!"

"It's almost good enough to eat," laughed the younger of the two companions, walking around the site with eyes tied to the ground as if looking for something.

"Percival, are you hungry?" Ben inquired without waiting for an answer. "Acquaint yourself with these two chaps and get yourself something to eat. Pavlock and I will be back in a moment." And with that, Ben and Pavlock walked out into the darkness and began speaking again in murmurs too low to hear.

The prince stepped up to the fire and looked into the kettle beside it skeptically. "What's in it?"

"You like venison?" the younger man asked. "Shot it this

afternoon. I shoot things, Brunwick cooks things."

"Fresh kill. Wanted to make a warm welcome for Ben and you," said the other man.

Percival sniffed it from a distance as if fearing too close an encounter would poison him. "I am accustomed to eating only food which had been properly prepared with the highest degree of attention," he said.

The two companions shot each other underhanded smirks, then let their amusement spill out into a torrent of laughter. "Alright then," said the younger, "Nothing wrong with high standards. Here now!" He rose to his feet and extending his arm, "I don't think we've been introduced by the book. Pleasure to meet you. That's Brunwick over there; I'm Orion."

Brunwick saluted with a hand to his brow as Orion gripped Percival's hand, giving him a single, astonishingly vigorous handshake.

"There's an extra bowl and spoon over there by the sacks," said Brunwick, leisurely propping his legs up on a log. "Help yourself, mate."

Percival hesitated. "I'm suppose to serve it to myself?"

"Well...that's the idea," said Brunwick.

Percival let out a peevish sigh and lugged himself to the sacks to fetch the bowl and utensil.

"I'm thinking our next meal should include seven courses, Orion," laughed Brunwick, removing his cap and scratching his short, dark ringlets of hair around the ear, which was pierced with a small, golden ring.

"Oh, Brunwick, please now!" Orion replied, lightheartedly. "He's going to be so much fun, I can already tell. It'll be like having the Prince of Rumandy come visit us in the flesh."

"Oh, please! No more talk about him!" said Brunwick.

Percival, returning with his eating ware, halted suddenly when he heard his title. "I take it Ben told you, then?"

"Told us what?"

"...Wait. What did you just say?"

"Oh, never mind," Orion laughed, "I didn't mean to offend you. It's a running joke. Here, let me dish some of that out for you, there's a certain trick to finding the best bits." He ladled a large scoop of soup into Percival's bowl.

"What do you mean it's a running joke?"

"Ever heard of the Prince of Rumandy?"

"...Yes."

"Well, you know how it is; everybody poking fun at him all the time."

"Excuse me?"

"Well, Brunwick never heard of him before so I had to give him the whole scoop. And so now every time someone has even the slightest attitude of superiority or superciliousness, I call him a prince of Rumandy. But don't worry, you can't possibly be as bad as him," he handed the bowl to Percival. "Careful, it's a little hot." The prince looked at Orion speechlessly, then dropped his face, quite disgruntled, down to his soup.

"Where is Phyllis?" Orion mumbled to himself, scanning the area again.

Percival sat down on one of the stump seats. "Wait a minute; how do you even know who the Prince of Rumandy is?" he asked after an awkward silence in which he could do nothing but smash bits of venison with the spoon.

"Is there anyone who doesn't? A fellow can't walk through the marketplace without hearing *the Prince of Rumandy is doing this* and *the Prince of Rumandy is wearing that*. Especially these days, with that big old birthday party or whatever it is he's having."

"He already had it," Percival corrected resentfully, tasting a nibble of the soup.

"Did he really?"

"It's over."

"Well, it's about time! Maybe the talk will all start to simmer down then. Everybody I know is terribly sick of hearing about him, anyway. I was starting to feel like vomiting. So, how's the soup?"

Percival took a discontented spoonful and did not answer.

The twilight was all but faded and night sweeping in steadily. Ben and Pavlock continued to murmur a little ways away from the fire, where the orange glow bordered with the blue shadows of night.

"I suppose I'd better see to the horses then," Brunwick said at length. "Since apparently I'm the only one who does anything useful around here."

"Well, you definitely are the most productive one around here, I'll give you that. Damn, seventeen children."

Brunwick chuckled and marched off to see to the animals.

"Apparently there are seventeen miniatures of Brunwick living rather fatherlessly up there in the High North," Orion said to Percival.

"The High North? Is that where he's from?"

"Indeed he is. Beyond the border. He and Pavlock both. Brunwick is Pavlock's right hand. They're always traveling, but they rarely journey this far to the South."

"And what is Pavlock's line of business?"

"Oh, he's some sort of knight of a kingdom up there. Goes around settling discord and rescuing women. Something like that."

Suddenly, Brunwick called back towards them. "Orion!" he said, thumbing through baggage sitting by the horses. "It's over here."

"What is—oh! Good, you found her." Orion rose eagerly and dusted off his hands on his breeches. "Thanks, Brunwick, can you give her here?"

Brunwick handed Orion a package bound up in cloth, which Orion readily accepted. He sat back down on the ground by the fire and laid the package on his lap. The firelight glowed on the object's lusty cherry-brown surface as Orion unveiled it.

He turned to Percival and his grin widened. "This is Phyllis," he introduced. "She's my darling."

"...It's a fiddle."

"Well of course she's a fiddle," he laughed. He locked the bow between his side and elbow and plucked the strings of the fiddle with his fingertip, turning the pegs till the notes pleased him.

"Plays the damn thing constantly," Brunwick complained, returning from his work with the horses.

"I'm pretty damn good at it, too," Orion held it into position, propping it between his chin and shoulder, and played a flight of notes.

Ben presently re-entered the circle of the fire's glow, still talking to Pavlock at a few steps behind him. "Well, that's the silliest thing I've ever heard you say, lad. You don't need to flatter me to convince me to go back! I think I already had a sneaking suspicion the road to the North would be my call—I'm hungry. Percival, have you eaten already? Good."

"Let me to get you a bowl, sir," Brunwick offered, formally.

"Ah, thank you, Brunwick," Ben said, sitting down next to Percival. "That's very kind of you."

Percival stared a moment at Brunwick as he prepared Ben the soup. "He made me go and fetch it myself," the prince pointed out, indignantly. "I'm the one who has been through the most today and I'm in the worst condition right now, and yet everyone is serving everyone else like kings."

"No," Brunwick correct. "Only one person is serving one other person like a king. Haha! Thank you, Brunwick!" Ben rubbed his hands together and gratefully accepted the bowl from Brunwick. "You three will have to excuse the lad's manners. He is the Prince of Rumandy, after all."

"Yes, I know!" Orion agreed. He played another flight of notes on his fiddle and laughed again. "That's exactly what I said!"

Chapter 19

The Prison of Fairbourne

*The human mind holds onto memories while they are
still needed. Or while one is trying to let them go.*
-The Journals of Bengolian

The golden rays of the setting sun and the white stone stairs
of Fairbourne's palace contrasted with the dark garments of the
man who walked upon them, increasing the austerity of his
appearance. He descended the steps swiftly but with such
formality and rigidness his form seemed to equal the hardness of
the stone. A carriage halted at the foot of the portico, and the man
dismissed the footmen as one with authority. He opened the door
of the carriage and gave his gloved hand to the girl seated within
it.

"My lady Cloeneth," he said, bowing his head as she stepped
to the ground.

"Lord De Mourté," she acknowledged. Removing her hand
from his.

The man sighed, drawing his lucid gray eyes upon the girl.
His face was handsome though sullen, his dark hair swept back

and his beard trimmed stoically along the sides of his jaw.

"Forgive my poor welcome, Your Highness," he said. "There have been most tragic happenings in the time of your absence. If I may, I will beg your audience in my study at once."

Cloeneth's gaze swayed to the palace doors and then back to Lord Ormont De Mourté.

"My parents," she said.

His eyes flashed with astonishment. "You have already been told?"

"No. What is it?"

The chancellor hesitated. "If you will follow me, my lady, I will explain everything inside."

"What has happened to my parents, Ormont?" Cloeneth demanded.

Ormont held his breath a moment before letting the words escape. "They were killed."

Though her eyes remaining fixed on Ormont De Mourté, Cloeneth's vision clouded.

"If you will follow me, my lady." De Mourté turned to ascend the stairway, and the princess followed him silently at a distance.

As she reached the vestibule, a crow landed on the marble railing of the stair. It crooked its neck and leered at Cloeneth, its right beady black eye glistening. Its other eye was torn and scarred. It cawed brashly, and Cloeneth's heart jumped at the sound. She turned away from the bird quickly and entered the palace. She had once seen it there before.

The study of Ormont De Mourté was a stark and ascetic place.

It was lined with shelves carrying the historical and political records of Fairbourne, and yet there was only one small window, allowing for a scant amount of reading light. There was a single desk which had nothing on it but a candle and small wooden box. In the corner of the room, an empty bird cage stood. There were two chairs, one behind the desk and the other in front of it. Ormont De Mourté and Cloeneth seated themselves accordingly.

"I scarcely know where to begin, Your Highness. No one your age should have to bury their parents."

"But many do." Cloeneth said, emotionless. She sat tall in her chair, her hands laid across her lap and her face like stone. She waited for Ormont to begin.

"We do not yet know all the details," he said. "Their lives were taken two nights ago. The night of the seventeenth. It would have been futile to send a message to you when you were so soon to travel back home."

There was a long silence as specks of dust drifted in the last sparse rays of the evening light.

"You seemed to have had some premonition of this, my lady. I do not wonder at it. It seems we feel it within us when those close to us...pass."

The air was heavy and stagnant.

"My lady," Ormont continued, seeing that Cloeneth would remain silent. "This is a pain to you I cannot begin to fathom. I am sorry. But you must know the hatred I feel towards those who would cause you so much pain, be it even those of my own blood." He paused a moment, seeing the change that came across

Cloeneth's face.

"What do you mean?"

"Your Highness...my brother has been imprisoned."

"Terence," Cloeneth whispered and shook her head. "I don't understand."

"I am quite sure you do, my lady."

"No. I don't. Terence wouldn't have—"

"Cloeneth." Ormont interrupted her softly. He breathed a heavily sigh, lowering his eyes to his desk. "We don't know his motives or what state of mind he was in, of course, but there is no question as to Terence's involvement."

Cloeneth's heart began to beat faster. Her eyes seemed torn between the figure before her and the shadows of her own thoughts. She set her gaze on the floor near her feet. "That's impossible."

"As much as I would hope for his innocence, the evidence is too strong to refute. My lady, you perceived what sort of life he led. Even in your youthful modesty and innocence, you must surely not have been blind to the diminishing of his virtue."

Cloeneth pressed her pallid lips together.

"Your Highness, did you not know his sporadic visits here, sometimes once a fortnight, sometimes twice a week, were strictly in the matter of begging me a replenishment of the money he squandered in taverns and brothels?"

"...Yes. I did know it."

"I had feared his life of debauchery and dissipation would lead him to his death, but I could never have foreseen such an end as this. I am sorry, Your Highness."

"He is not a murderer."

"Are you quite sure of that, Cloeneth? How well were you acquainted with him, after-all?"

Cloeneth clenched her fist around a handful of fabric in the lap her dress. She breathed in deeply but quietly as her eyes met Ormont's, and she stared at him without expression, her breaths coming shallowly from her chest.

"Terence was identified by a prostitute about a half mile down the river," Ormont continued. "He carried the crowns of your parents and was bathed in their blood."

"I will see him now," Cloeneth said suddenly.

A glimmer in Ormont's eyes flared. He shifted his weight uneasily in the chair. "Your Highness..."

"I will see him now, Ormont." Cloeneth repeated, a little more insistently.

"As your father's advisor and chancellor, I am by law your lord protector and counselor upon your parents' death. It would be wise not to relate to him until after a trial. I most ardently advise against your seeing him now."

Cloeneth rose from her seat, and the rich fabrics of her dress rustled as she went in haste to the doorway.

"Cloeneth!" Ormont called out brusquely. Just as she put her hand on the door's handle, he continued, "Do you recall this object, Your Highness?"

She turned across her shoulder to see Ormont holding out a small golden object. It was a chain bearing a pendant, an ornately engraved oval with a rose carved out of ivory. Cloeneth parted her lips as her eyes remained fixed on the necklace.

"Terence refuses to confirm or deny anything since his arrest the night of the seventeenth. However, this was found in one of his pockets. " Ormont rose and came towards Cloeneth. The sound of his footsteps fell morosely in the dark room till he stood close beside her. He presented the necklace to her gently, but his eyes were incomprehensibly cold. "Cloeneth, we are both grieving from the loss of those whom we love. You need not think of yourself as alone in this."

Cloeneth seized the necklace and locked it within her fist.

"You speak as though he was already dead."

Ormont set his hand on the girl's shoulder. "Cloeneth...you know I love my brother dearly. He led himself to this."

She turned away from him abruptly and left the room.

The sun was now beneath the horizon, and the cell of Terence De Mourté was dank. The prisoner sat in the corner, his back slouched against the wall. He picked up a piece of straw from the floor of the cell, ripped it in half and then into quarters, then into eighths and so forth until it was nothing but a collection of tiny yellow bits. He threw the little straw flecks up into the air and let them rain down on his shirt. Then, he picked up another straw and began the process over again.

A sound of rattling chains and the screeching of an old iron door echoed through the prison, but Terence, barely rolling his head in the direction of the noise, remained unmoved. A small-framed guard with mousy hair and a round face, stubbled with an attempted beard, came forward and stood at the bars of the cell.

"Good evening, Perkins," said the prisoner, with an inappropriately untroubled smile, "Where have you been? I've been so bored the last half hour without you staring at me. I'm supposed to be under constant watch, you know."

"Shut your mouth, rat."

Terence gasped. "Well, that was rude. What terrible service in these cells. And I'm starving, by the way."

"Dinner's in an hour."

"Can't you bump it up a little on the schedule? You should never eat after sunset, you know. Gives you cramps and terrible nightmares."

"Is that so?" the guard said.

"I get really frightening ones too. Mostly about your mother in her negligee. She really let herself go recently, didn't she?"

The guard's expression went indignantly flat.

"Must be getting close to three-hundred pounds, no? Shame. She used to be such a cougar in the sheets."

"I swear, you better watch yourself, De Mourté."

"Well, it's not my fault. Your mother's the one giving me nightmares. I can usually get through the night if someone reads me a bedtime story, though. Know any good ones? Bedtime stories?"

"No."

"Why did they even hire you, Perkins?"

The guard grinned disdainfully and folded his arms, "You know what? I do know one. Once upon a time there lived the most worthless scumbag in the world."

"Alright. Good start. Promising concept."

"Everybody hated him until one day, finally, he was executed. And then everyone else lived happily ever after."

Terence grimaced with disappointment. "The climax was too abrupt. And there weren't nearly enough twists in the story-line. Terribly predictable. I'm disappointed. You should think about getting a new career."

"You have a visitor."

"Oh, god. It better be either a whore or my fairy-godmother."

"Her Highness, the Lady Cloeneth."

The prisoner fell silent suddenly. Then, he laughed caustically and turned away so that his face was cast in shadow. "Well, that's not my fairy-godmother, anyway," he muttered as Perkins left the prison corridor. After a moment, he returned with Cloeneth close behind him. The torchlight glimmered upon the wavelets of her golden hair, which hung freely past her shoulders. The softness of her face matched her pale garments.

"You may leave," she said to Perkins.

"My lady," the guard started, "I was given orders not to leave you and—"

"I say you may leave, and you may."

A worry-wrinkle appeared on the guard's brow, but he bowed promptly and followed her orders. "Yes, Your Highness."

"Are you well?" Cloeneth asked the prisoner at length.

Terence was silent a moment before responding, his eyes remaining fixed on the stone of the floor. "I'm fine. Thanks."

"One of the guards told me you had a cough. I'll have a doctor sent to you."

The prisoner fidgeted and moved his head away with agitation, "Make sure I'm in perfect condition for my execution?" he said, trying his previous sarcasm, but it seemed to grow awry. "Rather counter-productive."

"Had you been drinking?"

"I'm always drinking."

"How did you do it?"

"Do what?"

"Kill my parents."

There was another long silence, and the crickets outside the prison walls were beginning to make their nighttime music. The crackling of torches was the only other sound.

"I really don't remember anything," Terence muttered.

Cloeneth extended her hand past the bars of the cell, and the red torchlight glistened on something gold within her hand. "Do you recognize this?" she asked. Terence reluctantly rolled his head towards her, studied the golden object for a moment, then turned his attention back to the shadows.

"It's a necklace you used to wear."

"It's a family heirloom. My father gave it to me. But I haven't been wearing it lately; do you know why?"

"If I'd have to guess, I'd say because you lost it."

"How?"

"Maybe I took it to pay off a whore."

"Then how did you get it back? It's been missing for years."

Terence exhaled and turned his eyes towards the girl. "You know, these are all lovely questions, but I think they're better saved for the trial, Cloe."

"I'm trying to help you, Terence. I don't believe you did it."

"Oh, you don't?"

"No."

"So much faith." Terence smirked and shook his head. "You know what's funny? I wouldn't think someone as immaculate as you could even stand to come and visit me down here. Not a very nice place for you. It really doesn't have the best smell, does it? Kind of a sweaty crotch smell. Add liquor and it'd be exactly like the whore-house on Leistriver Street."

"Stop it, Terence."

"Then there are the rats too. You afraid of rats? I'd be if I were wearing that. They could crawl up your skirt and get inside all kinds of places. That'd be awkward."

"I said stop it."

"Be kind of ticklish up there, I'd imagine."

"Stop."

"Stop what?"

"You're being crass."

"Well, I'm sorry; it's my nature. I'm a crass ass, Your Highness."

"I don't care how much of an ass you are, I am the heir to the throne of Fairbourne, and you are not permitted to talk to me like that."

Terence paused. "You just used the word *ass*."

"...I'm sorry."

"No, it was hilarious."

"I was—"

"I don't think I've ever heard you say the word *ass* in your entire life."

"Terence, I..."

"Your mother better wash your mouth out."

Cloeneth paused. Then swallowed.

He closed his mouth suddenly, as if regretting his last words. "Sorry," he said.

After a moment of silence, Cloeneth wiped away a sniffle from her nose. She smiled through misty eyes. "You know, I was just thinking about the—um—the rose garden. How it took you almost the whole afternoon to find me. You remember that?"

The prisoner made no reply.

"You didn't think I would actually be foolish enough to hide in the thorns. I came out all scraped and cut. My arms and cheeks, my dress, everything."

"Yeah. You were always pretty bad at hide and seek. No offense."

Cloeneth laughed, combatting her reddened cheeks and eyes. "Well, you had a definite advantage. I was only eight. You were sixteen."

"Oh come on, if anything that's a disadvantage. You were smaller, you could have hidden yourself just about anywhere. If you hadn't been afraid of the dark and closed in spaces and drowning and heights and insects—"

"I was never afraid of insects."

Terence laughed pleasantly for the first time that night, revealing a glimmer of boyhood. "Alright, fair enough," he said. "But you were afraid of every other goddamn thing in creation."

"It took me a few years before I figured out you always knew exactly where I was hiding the whole time. You'd just look everywhere else first to make me feel clever. Except when I hid in the rose garden. That was one time you really didn't know where I was. You were very angry with me for hurting myself just to win the game—do you remember that?"

Terence swallowed and made no response.

The prison was static except for the flickering of torches and the glimmering spangles cast by the firelight. At length, Cloeneth continued.

"Then you reached into the bushes and cut your own hands, pulled out a bunch of roses. And when you gave them to me you said, *See, Cloe? Now we're both bleeding, and two crying together is better than one crying alone.*"

Terence opened his mouth to say something, but instead turned away curtly. "Do yourself a favor, Cloeneth..." he started.

Cloeneth waited, but he did not continue. "...What?"

"Do us both a favor. Don't think about all that anymore. You can't save me."

"I'm not trying to, I'm just—"

"I don't want you here, Cloeneth. Is it that difficult to understand?"

"...You told me you loved me."

"I lied."

"I don't believe you."

"I was drunk and I wanted you and I lied."

"I don't believe—"

"Well, you better!"

Cloeneth swallowed with difficulty, as though a sickness were welling up within her and she fought to keep it down.

Terence shook his head with annoyance and turned away. "Get out."

After only a moment, in which Cloeneth's unrequited gaze fell upon Terence, she turned and left the prison. After a quarter hour, Perkins brought in a meal which stayed untouched till mice discovered it. And Terence remained the rest of the night lying on the cold floor of the cell.

JOSEPHINE ELI

Chapter 20

The Other Prince

Each person is an entire universe, and there is always
something in each one to surprise you.
                                    - The Journals of Bengolian

Percival had not recalled falling asleep, but he awoke in the same position he had been in, slouched against a stump by the fireside of the camp. He had been covered with a rather dirty and scratchy woolen blanket, and his back and neck were considerably sore. The sun was high and the forest all alive with its usual chatter.

"Breakfast?" came a voice above him. It took Percival a few minutes to place himself in his current situation and to remember the people who surrounded him. He reflected a moment. There was Orion, who was some sort of irritatingly energetic peasant a little older than Percival. Brunwick, who was a squire or something like that. Ben, who was...well, Ben. And then...Percival couldn't remember the other man's name; the knight or whatever he was.

Ben, sitting by the smoldering fire, threw the prince a slab of hard bread. It hit him square in the face and he groaned. "Good morning, lad!" Ben said. "You've had quite an exciting day yesterday, and I thought it was best to let you sleep it off. But I think I ought to give you a brief explanation of what's going on now that you're awake. After making such a fool out of yourself, you deserve it!"

Percival sat up sluggishly and rubbed the sleep out of his eyes as Ben continued, "You see, yesterday, when I departed to see who was approaching and you were getting yourself into a terrible fix, I ran into these three—Pavlock, Brunwick, and Orion—riding towards me along one of the paths. They seemed to have recognized me immediately, and they practically pounced on me with excitement to have come upon me there, though I admit I was entirely oblivious to their identities at first. My own fault entirely, I'm afraid. Of course I have met each one of them before. But it's this feeble mind of mine, you see; I barely remember my own name. Anyway, where was I? Oh. Well, when I first laid eyes on Pavlock I saw from his garb he was a man of Armidia, but it wasn't until he began to speak that I recognized him, though his voice makes considerably less of those awkward cracking noises now, haha!"

Percival yawned and scratched his thigh. "I didn't understand anything you just said."

"Oh, I'm sorry. Armidia, you see, is the kingdom in the High North," Ben continued. "Beyond the forests and the mountains. That is where our journey will take us."

Percival stared blankly, then sighed. "Right. Well, I'm tired and in exasperating bodily discomfort and quite prepared to accept any brash and ludicrous thing you have to say to me. So please continue."

"That was it."

"What?"

"Anyway, it's getting late; are you ready yet?"

"Ready for what?" the prince asked.

Ben did not answer. Instead, the entire group began scurrying around the campsite like worker-ants with various tasks to be done in preparation for a journey. Percival hadn't any idea what was going on, to tell the truth. But a thought struck him, suddenly. He was sure he had some vastly important destiny to fulfill. This destiny, whatever it was, would place him even higher above everybody else in civilization than he already was. And it would be foolhardy to reject the opportunity just because all other persons involved in the adventure were undistinguished idiots.

The party of travelers consisted of three horses, one rickety old donkey loaded down with half of Ben's hut, four men, and one prince of Rumandy. Therefore, they had a rather slow start that morning.

Percival shared a horse with Brunwick, Orion rode alone, and Ben and Pavlock walked on foot just behind them. Pavlock gently led his grey horse by the reigns as he and Ben conversed in low voices about matters probably pertaining to whatever it was the company was doing. Percival had very little idea what they might have been talking about, and he had no idea whatsoever what the company was doing, so he only bothered trying to listen in a few times before finding himself disinterested.

"So, Percival," said Orion, "Me and Brunwick are curious as to how you got those shiners."

"What?"

The prince had almost forgotten that in the past few days, he had been savagely beaten by his infernal cousin, tragically jolted onto the ground by his ass of a show-horse, left for dead on the road until Ben found him, hustled through a forest by insane, greasy creatures, and then knocked out by being hit in the head by some sort of object which will forever remain a mystery. All of these activities were drastically contrary to his usual routines of life, and his body did not agree with them. If he had been able to see himself in a mirror, he would have been aghast to discover all of the bruises and swelling parts which decorated him.

"I don't see you being the young, brawling drunkard type," Brunwick remarked. "Where are you from, anyway?"

Percival was not sure he should yet reveal his true identity to these travelers. "I'm from the southern countries," he said, "A little farming village called Brushpool outside of Rumandy. I'm certain you haven't heard of it." He took some pride in the lie, considering himself quite ingenious for cloaking his identity so smoothly.

"That so?" Orion said. "Funny. I didn't see you as a farm boy, either. Look at those rose-petaled hands of yours! You must be more of a dreamer than a plower. Hey, do you sing?"

"Why?"

"Because I feel like singing! What kind of adventure is this, anyway, if we're not making music?"

Brunwick groaned, "Can we please have one day without you singing, Orion?"

"You know, you people are cranks. Austere, unpleasant persons. I swear, before we get back to Lordale, I'll have the both of you singing all the songs every respectable adventurer in the world is required to know."

Percival's expression drooped.

"He's been singing and playing that damn fiddle all the way down," said Brunwick.

"And it's been so lonely singing alone! My poor poetic soul cries tears of heartbreak until you join me, Brunwick. You too, Percival! I don't want to hear any excuses!"

Percival's thoughts were still caught up in Orion's previous statement, which he was sure he must have misheard.

"I'm sorry," the prince said, looking a bit dazed. "Can you repeat that?"

"Repeat what? About the music?"

"No, no, no...where did you say we were going?"

"Lordale."

"Lordale?"

"Didn't Ben tell you that?"

"He somehow managed to leave that part out."

"Just stopping in, I think. Is that right, Brunwick?"

"Aye," Brunwick answered. "Before Pavlock and I head to the North with Ben. I suppose you'll be going with us then?" He said to Percival, "If you're Ben's companion."

"Ben's companion? What does—wait." Percival's level of discomfort was increasing at an exponential rate. "What's in Lordale? I mean, why are we stopping there?"

"Well, it's my home country, for one." Orion said.

"...You're from Lordale?"

"Indeed, I am! I'm looking forward to being home, too. My sister should be back by now; seems like I haven't seen her in forever. She went to that one Prince of Rotundity's ball."

"Rumandy," the prince corrected.

"Right," said Orion.

"Wait."

"What?"

Percival paused. He opened his mouth but his words seemed to stick to the back of his throat while a horrifying wave of revelation choked him.

"You alright?" Orion asked with a chuckle.

"Your sister is—I mean, so then you would be..."

"Prince of Lordale. Don't worry, you don't need to bow or anything. I'm not even the oldest."

"...So you're a prince. Of Lordale."

"It can be alright, but most of the time it's so relentlessly tedious. That's why I have to take occasional holidays from it."

Percival felt a sharp queasiness in his stomach all of the sudden and began to think he was going to regurgitate his last meal.

"And then what exactly are you doing with Pavlock and

Brunwick?"

"Oh, they were just stopping by Lordale on their way down. I volunteered to go. Ben knows my father. I've met him once as a child."

"...And so—what did you say your sister's name was?" he asked, trying to sound nonchalant and probably not succeeding.

"Which one?"

"The one who went to the ball."

"Why?"

"I...might have heard of her, I think."

"Frayda?"

Percival cringed. "No. Never mind. Never heard of her."

JOSEPHINE ELI

Chapter 21

Engagements Elsewhere

*I believe everything a woman says is entirely
incomprehensibly to a man. Either because her
thoughts are always so far above him, or because she is
speaking too fast.*

-*The Journals of Bengolian*

It had not yet been three weeks since the guests had left
Rumandy. They had been extricated rather suddenly after the
peculiar run of circumstances involving Frayda of Lordale. The
whole story caused quite a stir in the courts and countrysides
alike, and Lordale had never before received so much attention in
well-to-doers' conversations. As gossip runs its usual course of
progress, the story was inflated fifty times its actual size, and
lovely little heinous embellishments varied from place to place.
Most countries claimed their own princess was in fact Prince
Percival's original preference, and the young, ill-mannered vixen
from Lordale had something to do (her actions were usually
debated) with splitting the two asunder. Then, of course, when
Percival of Rumandy had gone missing...well, if you can imagine

a bolt of lightning strike a golden idol and burst it into bits when the entire civilized world had been dancing merrily around it in song, you have about pictured the idea. Surprisingly, however, one of the first to recover from the incident was Priscilla of Wilporsprings. That is, she had become engaged.

Priscilla was to marry a certain Prince Alfonso of Felsacci, and had quite suddenly gone from mourning her disappointment and destitution to basking in vanity. And for good reasons. Felsacci was second only to Rumandy in wealth and prestige, and Alfonso himself was nearly as toothsome as Prince Percival. And was almost as conceited.

Alfonso and Priscilla had met briefly at Percival's ball and had thought little of each other until the day of their departure. The story being circulated was that as Priscilla was on her way out of the palace of Rumandy, she tripped on her petticoat and collapsed down the stairwell leading into the vestibule. Alfonso happened to be swaggering by when he saw the damsel in distress toppled over in fabric, and he immediately came to her rescue with artful and debonair flare. Priscilla had sprained her ankle, and Alfonso heroically carried her all the way out the portico to her carriage. Then, he sent her an engagement ring straight away to solidify the connection.

"Look how it glistens in the sunlight, Gitty! It's wonderful, isn't it? It's perfect!" Priscilla waved her hand, flaunting her newly adorned finger to a circle of princesses gathered around her. "Sweetheart Alfonso of mine! He is a darling, isn't he?"

It was ideal weather for an engagement party, and almost all of the important, wealthy, beautiful people in the world were in attendance at the palace of Wilporsprings. They stood in groups conversing and enjoying the fresh air and edible refreshments.

"It's so beautiful, Priscilla!"

"Congratulations, Priscilla!"

"How I wish I had a ring like that!"

"How I wish I had any ring at all!"

"It looks a little tight to me," Brigitte mumbled, "You must have added a little fat to your fingers in the last day or two. Too many parties."

Priscilla withdrew her hand sharply from the attention of those surrounding her, inspecting it with sudden alarm. "What are you talking about, Brigitte? That's ridiculous!"

"Oh, she's just jealous, Priscilla," said Isolde of Hastineve.

"Jealous! I am not!" Brigitte retorted. "Why would I be jealous? I wouldn't want to marry Alfonso, anyway."

"You're always, jealous, Brigitte," said Priscilla.

"I am not!"

"If Percival of Rumandy had asked me to marry him," Priscilla toyed with her ring in adoration of its beauty, "I'm sure you would have been just as indignant. You would have said, *Oh, I didn't want to marry him, anyway*. That's just what you always do, Brigitte!"

"I do not!"

"You do! Just ask Cloe! Cloe?" Priscilla scanned the circle to discover Cloeneth was missing. A wrinkle of concern creased her brow. "She was just here a moment ago, wasn't she?"

"Oh, how should we know?" Princess Amarídi of Marazinople said, picking up a glass of punch from the table beside them. "She rarely talks when she's present anyway."

"She has been acting so odd lately," said Fiamette of Veracci.

"Probably off sulking somewhere again," said Jaquetta of Delamúre.

"Well, I wouldn't blame her, given her situation," Amarídi murmured in a tone which practically obliterated all reservations on gossip.

"What situation, Amarídi?" asked Fiamette.

"Well, surely you must have heard about the happenings in Fairbourne? Oh, it's a disastrous mess..."

"What do you mean?"

"Well, the king and queen were murdered, of course."

"No!"

"Yes!"

"Oh, how dreadful!"

"Will you believe, it was during Prince Percival's ball! In fact, the very night of his birthday."

"On zhe night he schose Frayda?" inquired Simona of Borinoccio.

"While we were all dancing and having such a grand time!"

"And now Cloeneth is an orphaned heir," said Amarídi. "And the Lord Ormont De Mourté is her lord protector now, until she reaches her eighteenth year."

"Zhe lord who?" asked Dolce.

"Ormont De Mourté. He is the chancellor to—well, I mean, he

was the chancellor to the king of Fairbourne. And what's more, Ormont and Cloeneth are engaged to be married!"

"No!" the crowd of girls gasped.

"Yes! Or at least, De Mourté has asked her. I didn't quite hear it out yet that Cloeneth has accepted him."

"Oh, but he must be nearly forty!" exclaimed Brigitte.

"True. But between you girls and me, Cloeneth may have hidden motives for the marriage," said Amarídi.

"What do you mean?"

Amarídi held the girls' unwavering attention as they drew their circle of conversation tighter together. "You see, the murderer—the person who did the deed—was none other than Terence De Mourté. The little brother of Lord Ormont De Mourté!"

The flock of princesses turned aflutter with feathered fans.

"No!"

"Yes!"

"And he did it when he was completely inebriated."

"No!"

"And he was identified that night by a prostitute with whom he had relations!"

"No!"

"And it has been said that—this isn't proven yet, of course, but it has been said—that Terence had an affair with Cloeneth. And killed her parents because they had discovered them." The girls gasped and lifted their fans to their mouths to curtain the scandal. "And that's why Cloeneth has agreed to marry Ormont.

Ormont could grant Terence freedom if he was convinced to do so."

"So, Cloeneth is marrying a man she hates in exchange for her lover's freedom?"

"That's so romantic!"

"I wish that would happen to me!"

"Now, that's absurd," Priscilla inserted. "I've known Cloeneth for a very long time. She's never said a thing about him."

"Of course she wouldn't. The man sleeps with everyone. She was ashamed."

"The man has affairs with all kinds of people."

"I heard he even had an affair with Frayda of Lordale."

"Oh, that vixen, I can't stand her."

"All she ever did was flirt with the prince."

"Not to mention his cousin."

"Eef it were noht for zhe princess of Lordale," Dolce started, "zhe prince would have..."

"Schosen us!" finished Simona. She locked arms with her sister and the two clasped hands to comfort each other. After the warfare in Rumandy was over, the twins had re-allied, and neither seemed to realize that *both* of them could not have married Percival.

"I had a dreadful premonition about her the moment I first laid eyes on her."

"What a minx!"

"Wait just a minute!" interrupted Priscilla, uneasy with the topic but lacking the audacity to refute the statements. "How did

Frayda get thrown into this all of the sudden?"

The girls paused for a moment to trace back along the path of conversation.

"Oh yes, she was having an affair with Terence De Mourté," said Amarídi. "Now, where was I..."

Amarídi had just closed her eyes to help her think when something rather odd and upsetting happened which prevented everyone from continuing the conversation. First, a voice called, "Watch out!" and immediately, a dish of banana bread pudding and a bowl of fruit custard found their way from the dessert table to Amarídi's dress. This is how it happened.

Directly after the warning and before anyone had time to process it, a boy rushed into the area and collided with the table standing beside them. It was overturned, and a good deal of its contents suddenly became edible embellishments for Amarídi's dress. The rest of it splat to the ground, and the boy tromped through the puddings and baked goods swiftly, escaping before anyone could even make out his face. Then, a little round man in a sizzling frenzy rushed by waving a rolling pin in the air, and another man followed with a carving knife. Amarídi screamed and flapped pathetically with her fan at her ruined dress as the rest of the girls gasped, wide-eyed in shock. Then, two more cooks and three palace guards followed. One of them crashed into another table, sending a bowl of delectable red punch onto Simona and Dolce of Borinoccio.

Finally, the last member of the chaotic parade, a very bombastic and corpulent man, calling out commands and curses while panting for air, slogged into the area. He was holding a large butcher knife, and his apron and chin were stained with meat juices.

"Rupert Trapani!" Priscilla exclaimed. He was the head-chef of the palace at Wilporsprings. "What is the meaning of this?"

The fat man heaved to catch his breath and felt his heart with his hand. "He take'a my pork chops," he began with a heavy accent, "heez'a head going to get'a chopped from heez scrawny neck! Dogs of zhat sort end'a up in my stew for less—"

"Trapani! Stop that gibberish, I cannot understand a word of it," said Priscilla, "Now, for goodness sake, there had better be an explanation for this most dreadful interruption of my party. Look here! How close I was to getting a stain on my dress!"

"Forgive'a me, your'a highness," said the chef. "Zhere eeza beggar boy sneaked into'a ze kitchens."

"A beggar in the kitchens? Is that all, Trapani? Why hasn't anyone shewed him away yet?"

Trapani glowered. "He'za very fast! And heez'a sneaky!"

"Well, when they find him," Amarídi said through tears, furiously wiping off some of the custard from her clothing, "I assure you, I will see to it he is hung from a gibbet before sunset!"

"Oh, Amarídi, dear," said Priscilla, "you're always over-reacting. And you're not the one in charge, anyway. Now go inside and freshen up; you're embarrassing me."

Amarídi trampled off sobbing towards the palace entrance. Trapani apologized and staggered black to the kitchen, and a dozen servants were sent out to clean up the mess. The rest of the group began to dissipate slowly, some to change their clothing and some to eat and some to spread gossip and engage in other idle prattle. Priscilla turned towards the end of the piazza and caught sight of Cloeneth, who leaned against a railing separating herself from another group of guests playing games on the grassy yard. She made a few steps towards her, paused timidly and turned back, then mustered the courage to advance towards her once more.

"Hello there, Cloe," she said, clearing her throat a little awkwardly.

"Hello."

"What are you up to, my dear?"

"Just watching."

"The games?"

There was a pause.

"I didn't know you enjoyed watching croquet," said Priscilla.

"I don't."

"Oh." Priscilla looked down at the croquet players, flirting among themselves more than actually playing the sport, as was typical. "Cloeneth, is it true what everyone is saying?"

"That depends on what they're saying."

"That you're going to marry Ormont De Mourté."

Cloeneth turned around, leaning her back against the railing. "No. It isn't true."

"Oh, good!" Priscilla exclaimed. "He's a fine gentleman, I'm sure, but Cloeneth, you can do far better than him! Have you ever met Otto of Capris? He's a good friend of Alfonso's—"

"I'm not going to get married."

"Oh, don't be silly, Cloeneth. Everyone gets married, you know."

"No they don't."

"Well, everyone besides ugly people. You're the only heir to your kingdom."

"I'm well aware of that, Priscilla. I do not have to get married if I do not wish to do so. I can easily name someone as my heir."

"I suppose so. There are so many parties to be lost in staying single, though."

Cloeneth lowered her chin as she stared listlessly back towards the croquet players. "That may not be an awful thing," she muttered.

The rest of the day was spent on food, dances, and further gossip concerning things which may or may not have been true. When the skies faded to night above the merry troupe of royals, the celebration concluded with a brilliant display of fireworks. But many of the princesses remarked that Cloeneth's apathy towards the party only increased as the night wore on. She retired early to her guestroom.

The room was ornately decorated but cold. It was lit only by a small oil-lamp, a candle sitting on a writing desk, and the moonlight. The smoky air still smelt of fireworks as it poured in through the open window. Cloeneth opened the window a little wider so she could take in the view above the courtyard. Most of it was masked by the branches of a large tree, but it was a beautiful view of the night nonetheless. A full moon climbed high above her, hanging like a silver fruit amid the leafy branches. She unpinned her hair and let it unravel around her shoulders, and the wind rushed into the room, making her shiver. Suddenly, she heard a faint sound like the snap of a branch coming from beneath her. She looked down out the window, but in the three stories between herself and the ground, she saw nothing more than lightly swaying branches.

Only mildly wary, she moved away from the window to the writing desk at the other end of the room. The tepid flame of the candle flickered in the soft draft of night air. On the table sat a little wooden jewelry box. Cloeneth opened it slowly and took out an oval pendant attached to a chain. In the thinning tones of bluish light, she studied the design engraved on the ornament, fingering the ivory rose set into the gold.

Cloeneth put the necklace into her pocket. She went to her nightstand, poured some water from a pitcher into a basin, and began to wash her hands and face. The room was very quiet, but she did not feel entirely alone. Suddenly, a branched snapped near her window. She turned around swiftly to see a hand reaching into the room, pulling up the rest of a body, visible only as a dark silhouette against the moonlight. Cloeneth immediately grabbed the pitcher, ran to the window, and smashed the intruder's head.

"*Ow*! Damn it! *Ah*!" The figure fell awkwardly through the window, groaning and clutching his head.

As the moonbeams touched the intruder's features, his fiery red hair glowed distinctly in the pale light. Cloeneth stood with gaping eyes, clutching the handle of the smashed pitcher, bits of porcelain garnishing the floor.

"Bromley Duccorio?"

He paused, looked up with sudden shock, and met her eyes.

"Oh. Hullo," he said, awkwardly. He stood to his feet hastily and brushed off a few pieces of pitcher from his shoulders. "Hullo. Hi. Your Highness."

"It's Cloeneth of Fairbourne," Cloeneth said after a moment, noticing Bromley's obvious want of words.

"Oh, yeah, no, I remembered it. I just...yeah," he said. "So...how are you?"

Cloeneth stood speechlessly. She crossed her arms and raised an eyebrow, then examined the window and the bits of broken pitcher. "What are you doing here?"

Suddenly, there was a noise from the ground below them, and Bromley, shushing Cloeneth's last words, crept back against the wall amid the shelter of the curtains.

"What's going on?" Cloeneth demanded in a whisper.

"The guards are looking for me."

"Why?"

"No reason."

"Somehow I find that difficult to believe."

"I just took some leftover scraps from the palace's kitchens for the sake of my sorrowful stomach, alright?"

They heard sounds like footsteps and the rustle of guards' gear, a few ill-humored voices, and then the courtyard returned to silence.

"Why were you stealing from the kitchens?" Cloeneth asked.

"Hasn't anyone ever told you that incessantly asking superfluous questions is extremely unmannerly?"

"So is sneaking into a lady's bedroom at night."

Bromley, unable to parry that offense, turned back towards the window. He tilted his head cautiously over the sill and scanned the courtyard. After a pause, Cloeneth set the handle of the pitcher down on the nightstand."What is going on?" she asked, folding her arms in front of her.

Bromley examined the boughs of the tree and the stones of the palace wall. "Well, after the prince's birthday, I decided to...take a holiday."

"By disrupting an engagement party? A rather unusual way of spending a holiday."

"What can I say, Your Highness? I'm an unusual boy."

"Is the prince with you?"

Bromley knit his eyebrows, "What are you talking about?"

"Prince Percival. He's gone missing."

"Missing?"

"You haven't heard, then?"

"Well, apparently I haven't."

"And you don't know where he is?"

"Why should I know?"

Cloeneth sighed exasperatedly, knelt to the floor, and began to pick up the bits of porcelain.

When Bromley solidified a proper escape route, he turned over his shoulder towards the princess. He felt a sudden ache in his side as he looked at her, though he wasn't quite able to put his finger on the reason for this uncomfortable sensation. "Hey, uh...Look, I'm sorry. I really am pretty much the worst person in the universe. That was rude and I...I hope I didn't frighten you."

"I'm fine."

"I was just climbing up, you know, trying to not be seen and..."

Cloeneth glared at him indignantly as she rose from the ground. She kicked away a few bits of the pitcher, then put the pieces she had gathered up on the bed. It was clear to Bromley that a prolonged apology would fall on deaf ears.

"Alright, well...sorry again. So, bye." He stuck one leg out the window, then the other, and climbed into the leafy branches.

"Wait," Cloeneth said, loudly enough to stop him, but rather timidly. She rushed to the window and leaned over its sill. "My father's adviser—my lord protector—has asked to marry me."

"Oh. Well...congratulations," Bromley said.

Cloeneth paused. Bromley continued his climb down the tree. "I'll be sure to send you a fruit basket or something, my lady."

"Wait! Please!" Cloeneth called again softly. But when Bromley looked back, she hesitated. "Take me with you," she said.

"...Excuse me?"

"Please."

"...Is that a joke?"

"I think I have to get away."

"Wait, what?"

"I have to get away."

Bromley laughed. "So, you want me to just. . .volunteer to be your escort or something?"

"No, I'll pay you."

"How much?"

"I don't know."

He smiled and squinted his eyes at the girl. She was quite pretty, but terrible at convincing people to do what she wanted. Presently, however, he was toying with the idea of bringing her along. He figured having a female accompanying him had its drawbacks, but to tell the truth, he was a little wanting of company. "Well, you're inheriting a kingdom, aren't you?"

Cloeneth's face hardened. "Yes."

"And you're pretty rich."

"I suppose so."

"Well, see, that's some leverage you can use on people whom you're trying to manipulate."

"I'm not trying to manipulate you. I just want you to take me with you."

"Well see, my lady, you can't just ask people to do what you want them to do. You have to be clever about it. Now, where do you want me to take you?"

"I don't know yet. For now, just away from here."

"Well, that's fair enough. That's a good move; you don't want to be too demanding when you first start the manipulation game."

"I'm not manipulating you."

"You're trying to make me take you along. That's

manipulation."

"Well, will you take me with you then?"

Bromley put on a half charming face laced with a smirk. "If I'm going to take you with me, I'll need some kind of deposit."

"But I don't have anything with me."

"That's fine. We can just seal the deal with a handshake or a kiss or something."

"A what?"

"You know; we could. It could be a thing. To seal the deal. People do that sometimes to seal deals."

"Kiss?"

"Maybe. Sometimes."

"I'd rather not."

"I'm just joking!" Bromley laughed. He had been partially joking, of course. But sometimes he had good luck with things he had been partially joking about, so he was still a little disappointed. He extended his arm. "Alright then. Handshake."

"Fine."

"Here do I swear to take care of you so long as you're under my custody, my lady."

"And I promise to repay you when I return to my country."

They shook on it, and Bromley gently pulled her forward. She climbed out onto the window's ledge, surprisingly less awkwardly than Bromley had imagined. In fact, he was almost a little intimidated to see how well she climbed down the tree with him. But to tell the truth, he was glad to have some company. Since he had left Rumandy, he had been enjoying his time of absolute independence and complete lack of responsibility. But one can only take so much of that kind of lifestyle before getting utterly bored to tears. So now, Bromley felt as if he had been given a new sense of purpose. It was a small, inconsequential purpose: see to it that this princess doesn't die. Nonetheless, it came with an energy and an excitement he had not felt in quite a while, and he was glad for that.

JOSEPHINE ELI

Chapter 22

Brunhilda Wimbleton

If a person gives a flower a name, does that change anything about its nature? It is what it is, whether or not it has a name.

-The Journals of Bengolian

One night, Orion awoke to a strange sound. That is, the sound itself was not entirely strange, but it was strange to hear at that hour when all the other men in the group were asleep. He was suppose to have been keeping watch, though since they had never come or been come upon by anything more dangerous than an opossum for the last three weeks, he had taken the liberty of closing his eyes for a bit longer than he would have admitted to.

The sound itself was a little like metal chimes, or the brassy bells which jingle on a carriage or sleigh. It came from the general location of the horses and baggage, though the fire, now hardly more than glowing embers and wafting cords of smoke, revealed little of that area. Again he heard the jingle, followed by some general shuffling noises, like a raccoon scouring for food.

Orion rose from his position and crept over the sleeping bodies strewn around the campsite. He found a log which looked just about the right length and thickness to be utilized as a cudgel. Just as he took it in his hands, however, he started to make out the figure standing by the horses more distinctly. He then decided a weapon was unnecessary.

It appeared to be a small person. Rather, it was either a small man or a well-proportioned woman. As he came closer, he saw that the latter was true. Her dark hair was all tousled around her shoulders, one of which was bare, for her white, oversized shirt hung loosely around her, tucking sloppily into her belted skirt. She continued to rummage through the bags until Orion was almost standing directly behind her.

"Looking for something?" he said over her.

She immediately turned to run, still holding one of the bags. There was another sound of the jingling as she started, but Orion grabbed one of her arms to stop her. She turned back and, with a solid fist, clouted Orion's chin. It was a surprisingly good clout, and Orion was a little stunned for a moment. She escaped his hold and ran, making the jingling sound with every step until Orion overcame her. She tried to swat him with the bag, but he fended off the blow and took hold of both of her wrists. He brought her down, pinning her between the ground and himself.

"Got you!" he smirked.

She spit in his face. "Get off me, you son of a-"

"Watch it! There could be ladies present."

"Get off right now."

"You let go of the bag and I'll let go of you."

She let go of the bag.

"...Ok. Maybe I lied."

"Jackass."

"Ouch. Speaking of pain, that's quite a cuff you got there. Where'd you learn to hit like that?"

The girl tried to struggle out of Orion's grasp, but failed and set her head back on the ground.

"So, going anywhere interesting tonight?" Orion continued.

"You expect me to talk to you in this position?"

"I expect you to run off the second I let you out of it."

"You're very intuitive."

"Thank you. I try."

"Do you try to be so repulsive too? Or does it just come naturally?"

"Hey, now! That's harsh. It's difficult to keep up on one's appearance when he's on the road, you know. You're doing very well with it, though. It's fairly rare to see such a beautiful girl wandering around in these woods."

"Thank you. I was thinking the same thing when I saw you."

"Touché."

The girl stared relentlessly at Orion, as though her eyes could burn a hole into his head.

"How about this?" Orion began, "I'm going to get up now, and you're going to sit up too, and we're going to have a nice little conversation and figure out what's going on. Alright?"

He started to sit up, still holding her wrists in check.

"I'm Orion, by the way."

The girl said nothing.

"Normally, this is where you would tell me your name."

"Don't have one."

"Wow. That's interesting…Must be hard to get your attention."

The girl said nothing again.

"So what are you doing out in the forest by yourself?"

"Just enjoying the night air."

Orion chuckled. "I like you; you're funny."

"I'm really not."

"I'm going to have to give you a name. A good solid name for a nice, strong girl like you…How about…Brunhilda Wimbleton?"

The girl stared at Orion blankly without any trace of amusement.

"Or, you know, maybe not. It was just a suggestion. I think it's kind of cute."

Orion adjusted his grip on her wrists, and in doing so, caused her to flinch as if she were trying to conceal pain. He felt a rawness to her skin, and looking down, saw that her wrists and hands were torn and bleeding. He moved his hands to avoid touching the marks, then met her eyes.

"Are you alright?"

Once again, she didn't answer.

"What happened here?"

"I'm fine."

"Oh, when girls say that they're always lying. Now, I can wake up the rest of my crew here and we can collectively decide what to do with you, or you can tell me what you're doing here and where you came from, and I can let you go."

She shifted her weight, and as she moved her leg, Orion noticed the jingling bell sound again. "I came from that way," she indicated northward with her head. "A town up there."

"Ok. And why do you jingle?"

"I'm sorry?"

"Every time you move you jingle."

She paused unresponsively, then brought out her foot to show a metal band linked with bells around her ankle. It was obviously not for ornamentation, but appeared to be some kind of social indicator.

"Oh. Interesting. Looks like something worn by a...you know."

"A what?"

"A...woman."

"A woman?"

"I mean, you know. A woman of the night."

"A whore?"

"I was trying to be polite. So, is that what you...?"

"You wish."

"Hey, just asking! I'm not judging you."

"Wouldn't have cared if you were."

"So alright now; let me sum up what I've learned about you thus far: your parents forgot to name you, you have brutal fists which have no forbearance towards men's faces, and you're not a prostitute."

"Pretty accurate."

"So, do you want to know some things about me now?"

"No."

Orion frowned. "How many times can a boy be slighted in one night? I should tell you some things anyway, otherwise it just wouldn't be fair. Let's see. I'm Orion, I have a dog named Oberon, I like parsnips but abhor brussels sprouts, and I am also not a prostitute...We have something in common!"

"How charming," the girl said with dry sarcasm.

"I'm already feeling a connection. We should do this again sometime."

"Are you going to let me go now?"

"What were you doing in our baggage?"

"I'm sorry. I was looking for something to eat. I haven't eaten in two days."

"Liar."

"What?"

Orion reached forward suddenly and wrapped his arm around her, pulling out a little sack tucked into her belt at her back. The girl tried to snatch it back, but Orion held it away. "That's interesting," he said, "You can't eat the contents of a money sack, can you?"

"Alright. I couldn't find any food so I was going to take a few coins to buy something with."

"You could have asked us for money once we were awake."

"I could have also killed you in your sleep, but I was trying to be polite."

"Good manners do get you far in life, I've been told."

For the first time that night, the girl started to display something like emotion on her face. Her eyes reddened and her cheeks seemed flushed. She opened her mouth to say something, but Orion cut her short:

"Not going to work, Brunhilda."

"What do you mean?" she said, blinking her eyes.

"You're trying to look cute so I'll let you go."

"What?"

"Don't bother."

The girl paused and her face returned to its callous state. She sighed heavily. "Well, I'm really very tired of this, so perhaps I should just ask nicely, after-all. Please let me go?"

Orion smiled and raised his eyebrows. "Now that was pretty polite, actually. Sounded nice." He held her in his eyes for a moment, but she turned her face away. Suddenly, she tore one of her hands from his and punched his jaw again. She immediately rose to her feet and began to run.

"Ouch!" Orion yelled. The girl was already a ways down the road when he got to his feet. "Now come on, that's not fair!" he called after her. "Don't I even get a name? It's going to drive me insane not having anything other than Brunhilda Wimbleton to think of you as."

"That's easy. Just don't think about me," she called back.

Orion grinned. "Nah, that'll be too hard to do," he said. The girl continued down the southern path till her figure was lost in the shadows. Orion crept back to the center of the camp, stepping over the sleeping bodies. He rekindled the fire until it blazed pleasantly, and then found where Percival was lying. "Pst! Hey! Your turn to keep watch," he said, shaking Percival's shoulder until the prince began to groan and make slurred refusals.

"Tell Brunwick to do it."

"Brunwick's been doing it for you for the past...every night. Besides, it's been quite exciting so far."

"Oh really?" the prince mumbled sarcastically. "Did you see any unusual kinds of moths?"

"Not quite that exciting, I'm afraid, but close. A girl."

"A what?"

"A girl. You know what that is?"

"Oh, shut up. What are you talking about?" Percival's voice was raspy and lethargic, his eyelids half-opened at best. He slumped himself to a sitting position and wrapped his blanket around his head and shoulders.

"She was over by the horses rummaging through the baggage."

"What? Well, where'd she go?"

"Back down the road."

Percival turned his head towards Orion sluggishly and narrowed his droopy eyes. "If you're making up this story just to get me to wake up and take over the watch for you I am most assuredly going to kill you in the morning."

"She had on some kind of anklet thing with bells on it."

"So."

"I just thought it was funny for a girl who's trying to sneak around a campsite to be wearing an anklet with bells on it."

"Hilarious. I cannot tell you how amused I am right now."

"It's a shame, I didn't get her name." Orion laid himself comfortably on the ground and linked his hands behind his head. He grinned and crossed his ankles. "You missed out, Percy. She was really pretty. She had this long, dark hair; kind of untidy. Gorgeous eyes."

"I am missing out right now on a good night's sleep."

Orion laughed. "Is that how you stay so beautiful, Percy?"

"Yes." Percival yawned and pulled the blanket tighter around himself. "So are you going to tell Ben and Pavlock about it?"

"About your beauty secret?"

"The girl."

Orion shrugged. "Don't think there's much need for it. She didn't take anything."

Percival yawned. "Well, if she did take something, it's coming out of your rations because you're the one who was supposed to be keeping watch."

Orion laughed lightly. "Well, in case she does come back, tell her I'm dreaming about her all night long. And don't let her hit you, it hurts."

Within the next five minutes, Orion was asleep, and Percival took an uneventful watch.

Chapter 23

Brother's Keeper

There are two offenses that are most detrimental to a person's long-term well-being. The first is presumption, when one admits to doing no wrong, and the second is despair, when he thinks nothing of himself but that he has done wrong.

-The Journals of Bengolian

"Perkins. Perkins...Pst! Perkins!" Terence De Mourté was slumped against the bars of the prison cell, redundantly tossing flakes of straw into the aisle-way. The guardsman sat at the other end of the jail, pretending with much effort and vexation not to hear him.

"Oh, Perkins..." Terence said again. He let out a heavy, theatrical groan. "I'm so lonely these days. Nobody cuddles with me...Say, how has Mrs. Perkins been treating you at home? What's her name again? Cassandra?"

The guard remained silent.

"...Oh, don't blame her for it, Perkins. If I were married to you, I wouldn't want to make love to you either." Terence allowed a moment of silence to fall in the room, until he was overcome with another bout of boredom and tried another subject. "How's your mum these days, Perkins? Has she lost any weight recently, or is she still as fat as a ham?"

Perkins breathed out in exasperation, rubbing his head as if to relieve a headache.

"Poor woman must be spending a fortune replacing the buttons that pop off her clothes after she eats," Terence continued. "I worry about her sometimes, you know. She was much thinner when I slept with her."

"My god, do you ever stop talking?"

"...I'm your god now? Well, I certainly feel unworthy, but I'd be honored to take up the part. When do you start worshiping me?"

"What do you want this time, De Mourté?" Perkins asked impatiently.

"Funny. It's always the mother insults that get to you," Terence grinned. "I wonder why that is."

"What do you want?"

"That's a first-rate son, right there. Always ready to defend your mum. You stay just like that. Loyal and true, Perkins. Loyal and true. Right up until the day your mother explodes after eating her last eight course meal."

Perkins crossed his arms. "Unlike that tart whose stomach you crawled out of," he said with a taunting chuckle. "What was it they said about how your mother died? She strung herself up, didn't she? Oh, yes! I remember it now. They say your father beat the old bawd till she went mad as a loon and hung herself from the rafters. That all true?"

Terence lowered his chin. His face hardened and his eyes flared, but a sardonic smile creased his lips. "From the stairwell, actually."

"You know what I find fascinating about you, De Mourté?" asked Perkins.

"My strikingly handsome features and alluring physique."

"I find it fascinating that of all the bastards I've had to watch down here, you're the first one who seems to know his life isn't worth keeping."

The prisoner shrugged, leaned back comfortably, and stretched out his shoulders. "Well, you must understand death is like a whore, Perkins. Most men who call themselves respectable avoid her dark enticements. They think so poorly of her. But I'm far less judgmental. Far be it from me to call death an evil. And why should I be afraid of her? There's no reason for that. On the contrary, I'm quite enamored by her. Death is gorgeous and sickening all at once; which is exactly my kind of woman." Terence returned to playing with the straw on the prison floor to entertain himself for another pointless stretch of time.

The midday sun contained no warmth, only a stony brightness. It shone through the bars of the jail windows, casting long shadows upon the cell and the prisoner. Terence sprawled himself out on the floor, put his hands behind his head, and began to whistle a flimsy melody. After some time, the door of the prison's hallway creaked open, and Perkins stood to his feet in respect to the austere, darkly clad figure who entered through the portal. "Sir," Perkins bowed.

Terence lifted his head from the ground to peek at the visitor. "Why, if it isn't the good son!" he laughed. "Perkins, bow down in worship! Shield your eyes lest you be struck down by the sheer wonder."

"You may go, Perkins," the man said.

"Yes, Lord De Mourté."

As soon as the guard had shut the door behind him, Ormont De Mourté set his eyes on his brother.

"You're looking well, Ormont," said Terence. "A cheerful disposition as always. Is that a new coat? Looks like a new shade of black. How marvelous for you to be able to afford such nice things."

"I hope you're well, brother. As well as can be, given the circumstances."

Terence propped himself up and crossed his ankles nonchalantly. "Oh, you know. The place could use some curtains and picture frames and things, but I'm making do."

Ormont paused and seemed to study his brother inch by inch. He smiled sparingly from one corner of his mouth. "Come, Terence. Let us be friends for as long as time allows us."

"You mean until they decide to publicly execute me?"

"Most likely."

"Oh, Ormont. What is there in you that's not to love? But, that's the difference between us in the end, isn't it? You're perfect, and I'm perfect shit."

Ormont shook his head and laughed cheerlessly under his breath.

"It is funny, isn't it?" Terence said with a salty smile.

"Am I to blame for your mistakes, brother?"

"Blame? You?" Terence rose to his feet, patting off his backside. "Oh, no! Good heavens, no! Who would ever blame you for anything?" He went to the corner of the cell where a small wooden table stood. "You're the good one." He picked up a clay mug of water from the table and put it to his lips, rinsed his mouth, then spat on the floor. "Saints and angels look down in envy upon you, don't they, Ormont?"

"You attempt to mock me."

"Well, what do you know? He's a man of brains as well."

"Do you think I took pleasure in watching my own brother sink into such a depraved state? It does not gladden me to see you as a reprobate who bears the hate of the entire kingdom."

"Oh, you do put it nicely, Ormont. From whom did you inherit your charm and eloquence? Certainly not father."

"Terence, I did come to see you today for a reason."

"And to think, here I am with nothing but good looks and bad manners. I drew the short stick, apparently."

"I have something to tell you."

"Well, it better be interesting."

"It is."

Terence clapped his hands together. "Well, praise whatever gods still listen. I'm tired of the excretion of words from the mouths of lesser humans. Perkins is a bore and never has anything interesting to say. I'm deprived. My mind is emaciated. Oh, do feed me, Ormont! Feed me the nectar of your expansive knowledge."

"Terence, I'm afraid Cloeneth is gone."

Terence's eyes darkened. He stood still for the first time in hours and stared intently at his brother. "What do you mean *gone?*"

"Missing."

"Missing? What the hell does that mean?"

"Her attendants reported her missing during her stay in Wilporsprings. She never returned."

Terence laughed a little from the corner of his mouth. "So...you lost her? I'm not sure this Lord Protector career is working for you, Ormont."

"Or perhaps fragile little dolls like Cloeneth get misplaced when they fall into the hands of unruly boys."

"Whatever the hell that means. I didn't touch her, if that's what you're insinuating. I'm in a goddamn prison cell."

"I don't mean now, I mean before."

"Before what?"

"Terence, have you or have you not had Cloeneth?"

Terence paced the floor of the cell. "I was unaware you were so interested in whom I've slept with."

"I'm asking as her guardian not yours."

Terence made no answer.

"It is of little consequence." Ormont took out a pair of gloves from his coat pocket and began to slip his hands into them.

"It is, isn't it?"

Ormont grinned tepidly. "I believe I understand you more than you will credit me for."

"Is that right?"

"You have, it seems, a hypnotic way of making insecure, stupid girls adore you. But the pity and affection they give you, you both crave and abhor. So much so that you always have to find a way to kill it, don't you? You always have to make them hate you. By one way or another."

Terence turned away from Ormont, setting his gaze towards the little window near the top of his cell. The sharp sunlight hit his face, and his eyes squinted as he stared upward.

"I'll find Cloeneth. And she will eventually forget you," Ormont continued. "She never loved you, she was too naïve."

"Don't say the *L* word in my presence please, brother. It gives me stomach cramps."

"Very well." Ormont paused. "It may take her a while to adjust to your death. I observed she was rather infatuated with you."

"Yeah, I'll bet you *observed* her."

"I beg your pardon?"

"Or didn't you know I noticed?"

"Noticed what?" Ormont asked sharply.

"How you'd watch her."

Terence felt his brother's stare on the nape of his neck. He felt the tightening of Ormont's fingers on the prison bars as though it was his own flesh. He turned back around to face him. "If you lay a finger on her, Ormont, I swear I'll kill you."

"That might be difficult once you're dead."

Terence paused. He smiled icily. "Oh no, brother. You can never get rid of me. I'll always be there."

"Is that so?"

"Yes. In the darkest hours of your nights, when you can't sleep because you feel cold fingers walking up your spine, I'll be there. I'll be at the bottom of every cup and in the face of every mirror, just waiting for you to notice me. And finally, when you die, Ormont, I'll be the devil sent to drag you to the deepest ring of hell."

Ormont lowered his eyes and smiled, shaking his head as if conceding to forfeit his efforts. "I had hoped we might be on better terms before the end, brother."

Terence smirked. He leaned against the prison bars and shrugged. "Well, you know, you could leave now, get yourself a lovely carriage and drive it westward until you fall off the edge of the world. Then we'll be on pretty good terms...brother."

"Goodbye, Terence." Ormont turned away from his brother emotionlessly. His steps echoed as he walked the length of the stone hallway then vanished through the portal. Terence remained leaning against the prison bars. Soon, Perkins re-entered the room. The guard stared a moment at the prisoner, shook his head with a sneer, and positioned himself in his usual seat at the far side of the prison.

"You two look alike," he remarked. "Your brother and you." Terence was silent.

"It's a shame you never did anything but whore around and

drink; you might have made something of yourself like him."

Terence stood against the bars for an hour, and then another. Perkins closed his eyes and began to snore when the afternoon was fading, and still Terence stood. The sun sank and night assumed its dominion, with it came the incessant droning of crickets. A single torch was lit in the hallway, and the rest of the prison was set in shadows. And Terence remained standing.

Chapter 24

Why Women Always Cause Problems

Quiet women, like flowers, are very good at telling lies.

-The Journals of Bengolian

Bromley had configured himself into a comfortable position, somewhere between sitting and laying, across the branches of what might have been the sturdiest apple tree he had ever found. He hummed softly in between munches of the tree's crisp fruit. The apple in his hand dripped with sweet, sticky juice down his chin and collected in the creases of his palm. Suddenly, he looked down with excitement at the golden-haired girl beneath him. She sat against the tree trunk brushing through blades of grass with her fingers. "Cloeneth, do you know what? This is probably the best day of my life."

The girl looked back up at the boy and answered only with a doubtful smile.

"I'm serious! It's sunny, I have zero things to worry about, and this apple is fantastic!"

"Good enough to make it the best day of your life?"

"Well...I'm only eighteen. I haven't had that many days to

compete with the present day. It may as well be the best day. Yes! I think it is!" He bit off another juicy wedge from the apple. "The only thing that could possibly make it any better is a basket of Rumandorian blueberry muffins. Did you ever try them, my lady?"

"I don't recall."

"Well, you must not have, because if you had tried them, you would have remembered. And that's terrible, by the way. There are only three reasons to come to Rumandy, my lady: the prince, the prince's horse, and the prince's muffins."

Cloeneth laughed quietly. She turned away and tore off a bit of grass.

"Ah," Bromley sighed in blissful remembrance, leaning his head back against a branch. "Blueberry muffins. If there is a heaven, I think I would like to spend all my eternity eating Rumandorian blueberry muffins."

A corner of Cloeneth's lips curved up in a grin, but her mind seemed elsewhere. Bromley could not say why, but her expression made him sorry for her, and he felt compelled to continue the conversation until she would change it.

"Do you ever think about heaven?" he asked, biting into his apple again.

Cloeneth shrugged. "Not really."

"Me neither. Of course, my mum used to tell me if I was bad the devil would drag me to hell when I died. I don't think she really believed in the devil. It kind of scared the shit out of me though."

"I don't like to think some people would end up in one place and others would end up in another."

Bromley dropped himself down from the tree's branches and sat with a thump beside Cloeneth. "Well, there's some people I'd rather not spend eternity with, wherever I go. So I think I'd be alright with having some options. I mean, you probably know at least one person you'd rather not be stuck with forever, don't you?"

Cloeneth hesitated. "I suppose so."

"All I can say is whether I end up in heaven, hell, or a hole in the ground...I hope there's blueberry muffins there."

This time, Cloeneth laughed more openly, as though for a moment whatever had been on her mind was forgotten. It was the change of expression Bromley had been hoping for. And at that moment there was something in her eyes which Bromley quite enjoyed looking at.

A little green caterpillar was inching its way towards the princess's feet, and she leaned over her lap to inspect it. She set her finger beside it, and it made its way onto her skin.

"You know...you're very pretty," said Bromley. He was rather surprised at himself for saying it out loud. Cloeneth looked up from her caterpillar.

"What?"

"I said...I said you're very pretty."

"Oh. Thank you."

"You're welcome." Bromley smirked. He leaned back against the tree and tested his arm strength by throwing the apple as far away as he could. Cloeneth aligned her hands and let the caterpillar crawl across them finger by finger. She pinched her face into an embarrassed grin, trying to avoid eye-contact.

"You know," Bromley continued, "Simona of Borinoccio was deathly afraid of every bug that innocently made its way across the earth. She was sitting by Percy once during the party, and a grasshopper hopped onto her lap, and do you know she started yelping and wailing and flapping that silly fan of hers all around like she was on fire!" He laughed, then paused for a moment. "Now that I think of it, it could have been Dolce. But there really wasn't much of a difference between the two. There wasn't much of a difference between any of them, I suppose. Or most of them, anyway."

Bromley crossed his ankles and laced his fingers behind his head. He was surprised he hadn't really noticed how beautiful Cloeneth was until after Rumandy. Most girls, he figured, would look less and less fetching while traveling like this. Once their hair was disheveled and their powder and paint worn from their faces, there was usually nothing very extraordinary about them. But Cloeneth seemed to be more pretty today then she had been at the ball. The sun hit her face in such an effortless way it would have shamed the princesses who try with such a fuss to imitate that radiance.

"You know?" Bromley continued once again, "There's something very secretive about you, my lady. I think you might be hiding something from me. Oh, don't worry, I won't pester you about it. But one of these days—I'll find out what it is."

"Why would I be hiding something from you?"

"Well, maybe you're not hiding it from me, specifically, but just from people in general. From everybody." Bromley began whistling a tune into the fragrant, apple-crisp air. At length, he asked the princess, "So, where are we going, by the way? I don't think we ever really decided yet."

"Is it up to me?"

"Well, you're the one who's paying me for escorting you, remember? I'll take you wherever you'd like to go. Within reason, of course." Bromley stood up and began to inspect the clusters of apples on the tree. Beside Cloeneth lay a little bag which he had acquired from a farmer a few towns back. Bromley picked it up and shook it a few times to remove the dirt, then began to pile in some of the apples.

"How far are we from Lordale?" Cloeneth asked.

"From where?"

"Lordale."

"...Lordale?"

"Yes, as in—"

"As in Frayda of Lordale?"

"Yes."

"Well, what a splendid idea! I don't rightly know. I should think it's a good week's hike at least."

"I think I'd like to go there."

"Really! Why is that?"

Cloeneth hesitated. "I don't have very many friends. I liked Frayda. I'd like to see her again."

Bromley chuckled. "Indeed. I liked her too." He knotted the

end of the bag of apples and slung it over his shoulder. "Well then! To Lordale the princess commands her knave!" He offered his hand to Cloeneth and helped her to her feet.

It was rather late into the evening once they finally arrived in the closest little town. They had spent the last hour of their journey on the back of a wagon, alongside several cartons of chickens who were especially garrulous to be receiving company along the way.

The town they entered was called Figstock. Ironically, there were no figs anywhere to be found. According to the wagoner with the chicken crates, it was called Figstock because nobody gave a fig about it.

It was a town of coming and going and very little staying, and it was not kept up very well. Paint was chipping off the old, rickety buildings, and the streets were dirt. There were crowds gathered here and there, many of them pouring out of taverns, laughter and cheap music emanated with an orangish glow of lantern lights. It was an hour of transition between a busy day and a busy night. A band of traveling gypsies was setting up a place in a street corner, tuning their stringed instruments and rolling out exotic rugs which clashed fantastically with the mundane environment around them. There were entertainers of all sorts; acrobats, jugglers, and magicians, all competing for attention on faces and money in pockets.

Suddenly, as they turned a corner, their walk was blocked by a dense crowd, a large canvas covered wagon, and two men quibbling beside it.

"I have reread the contract, Mr. Ratsuccio, and you have a two year warranty," said the shorter of the two men. "I am entitled to a full refund of my purchase and I demand you carry through with the policies you have stated."

"Ah, ah, ah! But the warranty does not cover *missing* girls. Only *dead* ones," the other man answered. He was a tall and thin man with an oily sort of appearance, despite his tailored vest and a pricey looking cravat. "The ones up for full sale are guaranteed to live for at least two years. And if they don't live two years out of no fault of your own, you can return the body for a full refund with proof of purchase. But, Mr. Frounche, I see no body and no proof of purchase."

Bromley took Cloeneth's arm gently as they tried to walk away from the scene. It was difficult to move as the chatty and quarrelsome crowd stood around them. The taller, oily man beside the wagon caught sight of them, and with a wily eye, looked Cloeneth over as if inspecting merchandise.

"I paid eleven hundred for a girl that ran off before I even got her home!" said the shorter man.

"Oh, that, sir, is a frightful shame. But nothing can be done on my part, I'm afraid. Should have just paid for a night or something. That way neither one of us would have lost something. Which one did you purchase, anyway? It escapes my memory."

"The slattern never said her name. She said she didn't have one."

"Oh. That one, haha!" the taller man threw his head back as

he laughed. "I know just the girl! Doesn't surprise me. I am very sorry about that, sir. I'll tell you what, come to another of Ratsuccio's Foreign Delight Nights, aye? You'll get your pick from another collection. All shapes, colors, and sizes. Half price on Thursdays. What a deal."

The shorter man continued gruffly, "Mr. Ratsuccio, I'll have your head for this! Your business is dishonest and unprofessional."

"Now, now, Mr. Frounche! My honesty and professionalism is, as you might say, on a different spectrum than that of other classes of businessmen. I'm very sorry you never got to reap the riches of your harlot, but there's really nothing I can do about it, see? Now, perhaps you can come to my next auction; it'll be a week from today, in Ackridge. I'll even give you a special deal, just because I like you. Have a good night, sir! Goodbye!"

The taller man shewed the shorter man away like a fly, who then trudged off, irate but too annoyed to continue the argument. The tall man noticed Cloeneth and Bromley again. "Excuse me, there!" he called out, his voice sickly sweet like the smell of rot. "Little blondie!"

Bromley put his hand a little tighter on Cloeneth's arm, drawing her away.

"Wait, wait, wait! I just thought I'd present the lady with my card!" the man put his hand in his vest pocket and procured a small, yellowed paper.

"No thank you," said Bromley.

"I was offering it to the lady, not to you, sir."

The man took a step towards Cloeneth and handed her the card. "Here you are, love. Mr. Andre Ratsuccio, at your service." He bowed.

Cloeneth eyed Ratsuccio warily, then took the card in her thin fingers. It read, in a gold script, *Andre Ratsuccio, Corporal Delights.*

"I run a reputable little business which relies on the talents of beauties like yourself. The lower scum and slaves get sold now and then of course, but with real classy young ladies like yourself we leave it at more of a nightly rental situation. And of course you'll receive a generous percentage of the profits."

Bromley's face lengthened. "I'm sorry, sir, she's not interested. Have a good night."

"Does the lady not speak for herself?" Ratsuccio chided Bromley. He then turned his attention back to Cloeneth. "What an unpleasant sort of boy you keep in your company, miss. Always leading you around like that. A girl like you can take care of herself, I'm sure. And you must be wanting of finer men's company."

Cloeneth gave the man a surprisingly world-wise smirk; an expression Bromley had never seen the girl wear before. "The lady does speak for herself, sir," she said. "Do you have any girls who look like me?"

Ratsuccio's eyes glimmered with snake-like charm. "Why, I've got many different sorts, but none quite as lovely as you."

"But do you have any others who look like me? With similar hair, maybe?"

"Oh, not at the moment, I'm afraid! It's a rarity to see that type of head around here. I'll tell you, men love it though."

Cloeneth sighed with disappointment. "What are the chances you'd find another girl who looked like me?"

Bromley, meanwhile, was listening to this conversation in utter bafflement and growing annoyance.

"Well, darling, if indeed I'd find another one like you, I'll tell you this much: you'd be a rich little lady working for me. Twins are gold in this business."

Cloeneth squinted her eyes at the man. She raised her chin and looked down at the man's card. "Thank you. I'll keep your card."

Ratsuccio showed his full line of rotten teeth with a greasy smile. "Excellent. I'll be in town here till tomorrow night, come find me out and we'll have ourselves a little chat."

"Thank you, sir." Cloeneth pocketed the card and quickly turned away. Bromley followed hesitantly.

"Cloeneth," he protested, once they were no longer in Ratsuccio's sight. "Cloeneth get rid of that man's card!"

"I'm keeping it."

"Do you have any idea what kind of business he runs?"

"Of course I do."

"That man was dangerous, Cloe! We can't afford to get mixed up with people like that. Give me the card!"

Cloeneth stopped in the roadway and looked intently at Bromley. Her face was entirely unreadable, as usual.

"What?" the boy said. "I'm being serious, Cloeneth! You can't play around with people like that on the street."

"You just called me *Cloe*."

"What?"

"You've never called me that before."

"So? What are you talking about? *I'm* talking about Mr. Ratsuckero and the fact that you just took his card for his prostitution business! Give it to me right now!"

"I'm not interested in working for him, Bromley."

"Well, I know that!" They continued walking in silence for about ten seconds before Bromley continued. "So why the hell did you take his card then?"

"That's my business, Bromley."

"No. It's *my* business because I'm your bloody escort."

"Why does that make it your business?"

"Because...because I'm not going to endanger my own life by putting up with your stupid life decisions! You're going to get us killed unless you realize we're no longer in a palace with two dozen armed guards protecting us!"

"It wasn't that bad, Bromley."

"Oh, yes it was!"

"You're exaggerating. And I have my reasons."

"You know what? Never mind. It doesn't matter. I don't even mind."

"Then why are you complaining?"

"I'm not complaining!"

"Then may we please stop arguing and find somewhere to spend the night?"

"I'm not arguing!"

"Really?"

"You know what, Cloeneth? Just...It's just...I care about you and I don't want you to get hurt."

"I know."

"What do you mean, you know?"

"I know you care about me."

"...I mean I don't care about you that much."

"Yes you do."

"...Well, alright, I do! I care about you a lot! Why, is that illegal?"

A smile slowly stretched across Cloeneth's face and culminated in laughter. It was the prettiest laugh Bromley thought he'd ever seen, though he now found himself exhaustively uncertain about Cloeneth. Then suddenly, without the faintest idea why, he found himself laughing as well.

Cloeneth set her hand gently on Bromley's forearm. She drew him in a little, her eyes magically luminous, and said, "I'll explain later, Bromley."

The boy could not argue with that. In fact, he didn't want to. To tell the absolute truth, his curiosity towards the princess had now tripled since the start of the day.

Bromley had a very good plan for a place to spend the night. Bakeries always had convenient storerooms above them, providing a perfectly free one-night lodging. As long as they were not caught. He spotted the town's bakery, and led Cloeneth there.

They found a side-stair which led up to a storeroom, just as

Bromley had expected they would. He picked the lock on the door with a scrap of metal he had pocketed earlier on their adventure. He was rather good at figuring out questionable procedures such as picking locks.

The storeroom proved to be a rather nice little place, if only a bit drafty. This night was chillier than the previous. There were large brown sacks of flour stacked in rows around the room, and the little crevices in between them were just the perfect size for a person to fit snugly lying down. Bromley tested one of these potential sleeping areas by squishing himself into a crevice. "Perfect," he said. "We couldn't get better beds if we had paid for rooms at an inn! And those are always filthy, anyway. Who knows what goes on in them."

Cloeneth went to one of the little windows of the room. It was just high enough for her to rest her chin on the sill, and she set her hand there to pull herself up and peer into the dimly lit town.

"Can you see anything out there?" Bromley said, coming forward to the window and standing beside Cloeneth.

Only certain areas of the town, places where lanterns hung or fires burned, could be seen in the now growing darkness. A gypsy girl was beginning to dance to a band of mandolin players in one of the street corners, and a few people were gathering around them to watch. Other crowds were singing tavern songs, and a few young urchins in the streets were engaged in something in between a game and a fight.

"There's so much going on," Cloeneth said.

"Yeah; I love it," Bromley mused. He crossed his arms and leaned forward on the windowsill. "I love every part of it."

Cloeneth bit her lip and smiled. She studied the village figures, more like living shadows now than people, but so full of life. "I've never seen anything quite like it," she said.

"Yeah, I can tell, the way you behave in front of common people is ridiculous."

"What are you talking about?"

"You act like nobody would ever have the guts to hurt you just because you've got royal blood in your veins."

Cloeneth met Bromley's eyes, but hers were curiously wintry. "Unfortunately, you misread me."

"Well, you know what, Cloeneth? I want to tell you something I usually don't tell anyone. I hate being royal. I absolutely hate it. All those stuffy clothes and stuffy people. Sometimes, I wish I could just be a hapless street urchin."

"Is that why you ran away from Rumandy?"

"Well...yes and no." Bromley continued to study Cloeneth's face as she turned her gaze back towards the scenes of villagers in the streets below them. "You know, Cloeneth? I think I do far too much talking."

"You're probably right."

"Well, hey now! Alright then, let's correct it. You talk; I know hardly anything about you."

"You know things about me."

"No, for instance, I have no idea why you'd take the card of a man running a prostitution wagon."

"You just will not let that be, will you?"

"I certainly won't!"

"I'll explain it to you later."

"Fine."

Cloeneth grinned, but her lips seemed to bear a touch of sadness which she seemed determined to conceal. It only increased Bromley's curiosity.

"Then tell me something else I don't know about you. You owe me a delicious secret."

Cloeneth rolled her eyes. "Alright. Well, I ran away from home when I was thirteen."

Bromley's jaw dropped. "You? Ran away? I don't believe it."

"I did."

"No."

"I was gone for three days."

"Where did you go?"

"Just to the forest outside my palace."

Bromley laughed and turned himself around, leaning his back against the windowsill. He crossed his arms in disbelief. "How does a princess like you run away without being caught?"

"Well, I just did it again, didn't I?"

"I suppose you did. With my help...What else am I going to learn about you, my lady? First you're a runaway, next I'll bet you're a criminal, and then a day later I fancy you'll prove to be some luminous goddess in human vesture."

"No," Cloeneth laughed quietly, "I'm not a criminal. And I'm certainly not a goddess, I'm sorry to say. I'm not one for disguises."

"Well, it's not much of a disguise."

Cloeneth paused, smiling shyly. She shivered a little as a draft entered the room from the window.

"You look cold."

"I am a little chilly."

"Here..." Bromley stepped closer and put his arm around her. Their eyes met for a moment, and they stared silently. Then Bromley wrapped his arm tighter around her, drawing her closer to himself. He leaned his face towards hers until their noses touched. Suddenly, Cloeneth flinched. She tore away from him and struck his cheek with her palm so hard there was a loud slapping sound followed by an immediate shriek from the boy.

"Sorry," she said.

"Ouch! What the hell was that for?"

"I said I'm sorry."

"You are not sorry! You don't slap somebody and then be sorry about it a half a second later! Regret doesn't even have time to register in the brain that quickly!"

"You tried to kiss me."

"I..."

"You shouldn't have tried to do that."

"Obviously! Damn it, ow! It was just a...friendly gesture!"

"Then I must ask you never to give me any sort of friendly gesture like that again."

Bromley rubbed his cheek pitifully with the back of his hand. "Fine. I won't." He turned away and threw himself back into his crevice between the flour sacks. "Why are women always slapping me?"

"Maybe they have good reasons to be slapping you."

"Well, they don't! And that hurt," he grumbled. "So much for feminine gentility; it's the greatest hoax of all time."

Cloeneth crouched up next to a flour sack at the opposite end of the room, and after a little while, they both fell fast asleep.

Chapter 25

The Blacksmith's Apprentice

Stories happen in their own time. To rush the details is to spoil half the excitement.

-The Journals of Bengolian

Percival's hosiery had worn holes in each of the knees, and the feather on his hat had become so badly misshapen that at last he decided to detach it and leave it behind one afternoon. This broke his poor, royal heart a little, as he had been growing very fond of that feather during the journey. It had been, after all, the most decorative element to the entire ensemble of travelers.

Oddly enough, however, Percival was starting to really quite enjoy this adventure. Each morning he would open his eyes, stretch himself out on the ground with a gloriously expansive yawn, rise, and follow his insane companions all day until nightfall. He didn't worry himself with the details. It was a delightful hiatus of princedom, excluding the occasional centipede or mosquito. And, of course, when he was to return home, his popularity would be insurmountable. To think in the years to come, his prestige would not only concern his wealth, handsomeness, intelligence, and poetic artistry, but also his adventuresome spirit. He was beginning to feel even more well-rounded and admirable than when he had left Rumandy.

And then there was the fact that they were heading to Lordale. Percival was looking forward to it. He would see Frayda, no doubt; that plain, strange, incorrigibly obsolete creature he had somehow been temporarily mad enough to choose as his betrothed. It seemed ages ago now. And she would see him, now an experienced adventurer. How regretful she would be that she had refused his hand! It gave Percival such delight to imagine the scene of their meeting.

Around suppertime one night, the companions were camped around a little fire. Percival sat a little ways apart from the rest of the group, cleaning off his shoes with a brush they used to scrub the pots and pans. He had never tried to clean anything before in his life, of course, so his process was somewhat clumsy.

"Hello there, princess," said Orion, sitting down next to him. He offered the prince a bowl of stew.

"Oh, bug off," Percival muttered, scrubbing vigorously.

"Bug off?" Orion smirked with disbelief. "Did you just tell me to...*bug off?*"

"What of it?"

"Oh, Percy! I could understand if you told me to desist from such tasteless apery or to refrain from impinging upon your much needed period of solace...but just to *bug off?* Wherever did you get such a phrase? This is terribly humorous! I think I might be rubbing off on you."

"Very well, I shall be most happy to retract my statement and replace it with one that would be more fitting. And who gave you permission to call me Percy?"

"I gave it to myself. I can't resist the adorableness of it. You want any?"

"Any what?"

"Supper."

"Supper?"

"Yes, you know? Chomp-chomp? Munchies?"

Percival set down his shoe and scrubber, took the bowl and spoon from Orion, smelled the stew, then took a bite.

"Look at this," Orion felt his stomach to assess his slimness. "I'm losing body weight. Everybody is. It's deplorable, isn't it?"

Ben, meanwhile, was crouched cross-legged on the other side of the fire. He sat calmly, wordlessly warming his hands as he stared through the flames.

"I swear," Orion continued, "I'm going to be such a gangling thing when this is through, I'll never be able to enamor a woman again. What about you, Brunwick?"

Brunwick did not have time to answer, for suddenly Ben silenced the company, putting a finger to his lips. "Shhh!"

"What is it?" Pavlock added.

"Listen."

"...I don't here anything," Percival said at length.

"The winds have changed again" said Ben. He broke the intensity of his stare and looked upward beyond the tangling boughs.

"Not this again," Orion whispered.

"I don't feel any wind," Percival put in.

"Of course not. It's not just a normal, everyday wind. And besides, this time it's only above the trees. Listen...The echoes from trickling streams and rocky pathways come with it. It's a mountain wind now, coming from the East and going to the West."

Orion raised his eyebrows with a doubting grin as he put another spoonful of stew into his mouth.

Ben reached his hand towards the base of the fire where the ashes were cooled and weightless. He put his finger into the ashes and drew some sort of foreign letter or symbol. He then immediately rose and took up his walking stick. "I'll be back!" he said, and he began to walk westward.

The rest of the travelers were quiet until Ben was out of sight.

"Well, that was odd." Orion said. "Or am I the only one who thought so?"

"Nothing Ben does seems odd to me anymore," Percival added.

"That's true..." Orion crushed bits of meat with his spoon then set the bowl aside. "It's getting dark. The horses should get water once more. There was a stream a half mile down the path. I don't understand why we didn't set up camp there."

"Ben chose this place," Pavlock answered matter-of-factly.

"Oh, well that makes sense. Must be something to do with his prophetic wisdom, or something. Do I have your permission to save the horses from dying of thirst, tonight? Or perhaps I should run and ask Ben."

"No one should leave the group by themselves. Brunwick will go with you."

"Yes, sir," Orion saluted, a bit sarcastically, and went to the horses. Brunwick followed him, and they eventually left Pavlock and Percival sitting alone at the camp.

Pavlock pulled out a knife from his boot. The blade caught the light of the fire as he began to sharpen an arrow-like stick. Percival chewed his food in exceptionally awkward silence.

"Have you known Ben long?" Pavlock inquired suddenly. It was the first time on the entire trip that Pavlock had spoken in anything like a conversational tone to Percival.

"No," the prince said. "Just a few days. Or one day, rather, before he met up with you. I was in the woods, and I. . .just sort of found him, I suppose."

Pavlock laughed quietly. "If there's one thing I know about Ben, it's that no one ever finds him. He always finds you. . .at exactly the time he wants to find you. And exactly the time you need to be found."

They returned to the sounds of the sharpening of the stick and the chewing of the food for another moment. Percival stirred the remainder of his stew a little. After a hesitant pause, he asked, "How do you know him?"

Pavlock looked surprised at the question. He paused as well before speaking again. "Where are you from?"

"Rumandy."

"And what sort of country is Rumandy?"

Percival's face lengthened, as though the question pained him slightly. "You've never heard of Rumandy before?"

"...No."

"It is arguably the center of civilization and culture in the entire world."

"...Still never heard of it."

"Well, I've never heard of your country either. Whatever it's called."

"Doesn't surprise me." Pavlock leaned forward to reposition the logs on the fire. The flames immediately flared, a shoot of sparks flying out and dying as they fell to the ground. In the sudden flash of light, Percival made out something which looked like a bandage tied tightly around Pavlock's left forearm. Once the flare of firelight faded, he lost sight of it. The little glimpse of the bandage made Percival wonder, however. Pavlock, who neither wasted words on boasting or sociability, seemed to carry much on him. Many thoughts seemed to constantly keep his mind focused on some concern which Percival knew nothing about. The prince wondered if Pavlock was in fact a fighter. What sorts of battles or brawls had he been engaged in recently? And Percival even began to ponder, very briefly of course, but it still counted as pondering: what sort of conflicts in the world were there to fight for? And were some worth fighting for and some not?

"Ben told you I am from Armidia, I believe," Pavlock began suddenly, surprising the prince a little. "But I was not born in that country. I am from a village called Heathwyn. My brother and I were apprentices to a blacksmith there."

"How did you become a...whatever you..."

"Knight of Armidia," Pavlock finished.

"Yes."

"Ben."

"Oh." Percival hesitated, then a strange sort of curiosity began to well up inside of him. This was a relatively knew feeling, or at least a new category of the feeling. Naturally, of course, Percival had been curious about some things in life before this moment. But the things he had been curious about had always orbited around himself in one way or another. This was a curiosity to know how a story might end. Or how that story had begun. What the details were which took a story from some beginning through to some ending. Percival tried to suppress this feeling for a moment or two, but then found himself clumsily stammering, "So..then...how did...you um..."

"Meet him?"

"Yes." The prince scratched his ear.

"...You want me to tell you the story?"

"Well, no. I mean, sort of. It doesn't have to be like a *story-time* or anything." Percival laughed awkwardly and felt very young all of the sudden.

"...Alright." Pavlock cleared his throat a little as he seemed to mentally prepare for story-telling. He looked just as awkward in telling it as Percival felt in asking for it to be told.

"Well," he began, "I was apprentice to a blacksmith, like I said. My brother and I were both apprentices under the master blacksmith named Kraeff. He was fairly well-known for his trade.

Or at least known to anybody who had ever heard of Heathwyn, which wasn't many people, I suppose."

Pavlock paused there, gathering his thoughts for the next section of the story. "Well, one morning this old man came into the shop, and it was fairly clear he was not from the village."

"Everyone in the village knew each other, then?"

"No. Not exactly. But he looked extraordinarily excited to be there, and most everyone who lived in Heathwyn knew it wasn't any place to get excited about. It wasn't a bad village, but nothing had happened of any significance there for the last hundred years."

"Ben seems like he'd be the type of person who would get excited about mud puddles," Percival interrupted.

Pavlock laughed a little. "I suppose that's true. Anyway, this stranger came to Master Kraeff with a small shield and asked that a symbol be embossed into it. It didn't seem like an overly difficult task, but it was beyond my skill level, so Master Kraeff gave it to my brother who had a great deal of practice with embossing. Ben tore out a page from a journal and drew the design for us to follow. He said he had some business in town that day and would return the following morning to pick up the shield."

"What was the design?" the prince asked.

Pavlock hesitated, but his eyes seemed to glisten as he answered the question. "It was a phoenix. A bird with feathers of fire." He paused again, and then continued slowly. "I watched my brother as he worked that night, like I always did. He traced the design with his stylus, then removed the paper from the metal.

But there was scarcely a trace of the design transferred, so my brother had to repeat the process. The same results came of that attempt, and again on the third. The metal, it seemed, would not take any mark or indention. At last, my brother cast it aside to work on another project, as it was growing late into the evening. I had forgotten about the shield until my brother had left. I had the chore of cleaning up the shop after work hours and so I stayed later than he did. And when he left, I studied the design of the phoenix. It was so beautiful. And strange.

"Suddenly, Ben appeared in the doorway. He found me poring over his drawing and asked if we had completed the task. I told him it was not finished yet, and he told me to make haste and have it done within the hour. He sat outside with a pipe and began to hum, I think. So, I had no choice. He was expecting me to finish it, without any question, so I figured I had to at least do something and fail in the attempt. I quickly redrew the design and began with the stylus to trace it onto the metal. This time, it copied easily. And I took the embossing tool and followed the etchings, finding the metal easy to configure. I finished just as the morning light began to glow softly on the horizon."

Pavlock stopped there. His words had been rather plain and void of affectation. He had even seemed a bit embarrassed when he was speaking about himself. And yet something in his story pricked Percival's curiosity about him. The prince found he was eagerly waiting to hear more.

"...So then what happened?" he asked.

"You only asked how I met Ben. That was it."

"Yes, but...what did you do after that?"

Suddenly they heard a call in the distance, which stopped any answer from Pavlock. The forest had become much darker now, and they could see only sparingly. Orion and Brunwick were approaching with the horses, but it appeared they came with another man. This man's hands were tied, and Orion held him, forcing him forward.

"What's going on?" Pavlock said, rising from the ground.

"We're about to figure that out," said Orion as he threw the man forward to the ground in front of the campfire.

"He tried to jump us back by the river," Brunwick added.

The man's bald head was soiled and dark, and his face was painted with horrific designs and pierced with metal. He looked up at Pavlock and smiled venomously, revealing his stained and fragmented teeth, then said something in a harsh, raucous language. "Auhn iya cronchim unfekas dem, ishal bayisa," he said, seeming to mock them.

"What is your name?" Pavlock asked, his voice placid.

"Legion thirty-four, row one, column nine," the savage man answered.

"And to whom is your allegiance, soldier?"

The man spoke again in his own language, grinning wickedly. "Unahc Hekashas fiyda hac ushesa." He spit at Pavlock's feet.

Pavlock walked closer to him, and the man seemed to cower more with every step Pavlock advanced. The expression of arrogance, however, still remained fixed on his painted face.

Pavlock lowered himself onto one knee, so that he and the

soldier were face to face. "Your lady fears defeat far more than she would have you know. There are reasons she tells her servants nothing"

"My lady can be a worthless whore for all I care," said the soldier. "But her promises are good and her payments are high."

Pavlock and he locked eyes. "Ben dovu chevahta ti uhndeset," Pavlock said, as if in reply. It shocked Percival to hear Pavlock speaking the same language as the savage-looking man before them. Pavlock's voice however, carried a nobility which was lacking in the way the soldier had spoken. The language sounded ancienter and less vulgar on Pavlock's lips, as if it had been his own, and not the soldier's primal tongue.

The soldier grinned sourly. He scanned the faces of the others standing around him. When his eyes rested on Percival, he sneered. "The Lady Lucira's armies are gathering from all corners of the earth, and her generals know death only from the hunter's side." He turned back to Pavlock, "And yet you bring boys to a man's battle. Is that your great wisdom, knight?"

Pavlock stood and pulled the soldier to his feet, appearing to dwarf him in size and strength. He untied the rope around the soldier's wrists. "Return to your general. Tell him Bengolian is returning to the North, and no word of the prophecy which Lucira Ravensong knows well will go unrealized."

The soldier grinned once more at this, a mocking grin, as though it was made to corrode whatever it was cast upon. He turned away, beginning to walk slowly in the direction towards Percival. Suddenly, as he passed by, a knife was drawn from somewhere in his vest, and he took hold of Percival, bringing the blade to the prince's throat.

Orion immediately tore across the camp, snatching a cooking knife from the fire. He attacked the soldier fiercely, plunging the knife into his chest. Pavlock ripped Orion away and threw him to the ground, but the soldier and Percival fell as well, and they lay in a heap in the confusion of shadow and firelight. Percival, after finding himself still alive and not hurt, kicked off the weight lying on top of him. He felt a warm, sickening wetness on his shirt, and hesitantly brought his eyes down to see the scarlet smears. He stood up quickly and looked back towards the soldier, who was heaving curses and writhing on the ground. Orion sat up beside him with a bloody knife in his hand.

"What's gotten into you?" Pavlock said harshly to Orion.

"Should I have stood by and let him kill Percival?" Orion replied. "Seems like that's all you were doing."

"Stand to your feet, boy!"

Orion did so, indignantly. The soldier stopped moving. His eyes were open wide, staring upward. But he saw nothing. Orion tossed the knife so that it bounced off the soldier's chest and fell to the ground beside him. He looked at Pavlock without regret.

Percival's heavy breathing was the only sound to break the silence. The prince felt the bloody shirt clinging in places to his stomach. Though he tried to prevent himself from shaking, his hands were jittery as he began to remove his shirt.

Across the camp, through the flames of the fire, he suddenly made out a figure standing at the edge of the glow of firelight.

Ben had returned. All of them turned towards him but no one dared to speak. Slowly, he walked to the soldier and squat down beside him, putting his hand to the lifeless face and lowering the dead man's eyelids. Ben breathed out a light stream of air, which became a flow of unrecognizable words beneath his breath, like the soft rustle of leaves in a summer breeze.

"We will not spend the night here," he said. "Brunwick and Percival, see that all is prepared to travel within the hour. Orion, you will bury the soldier. The earth is soft here. Make haste. When all is prepared, we will make our way westward."

"Westward?" Orion remarked. "That would lead us into the villages."

"What is it that brings us westward?" Pavlock added.

"The wind," Ben replied. He looked upward, beyond the boughs of the trees. "The wind. Though the forest is motionless, the wind wisps above the branches. It is a mountain wind. It carries the echoes of the streams and the running gazelle. It goes westward." Ben took the knife from the ground and handed it to Orion. He met the boy's eyes with grating silence for a moment, but as Orion took the knife he turned away.

"Pavlock," Ben began slowly, "the paladin are abroad."

Pavlock stood silent but his attention seemed to flare.

"What are you talking about?" Percival interrupted.

"They're here?" Pavlock asked, gravely.

Ben looked at Percival, "There's another shirt in one of the bags, lad. We will wash that one when we get the chance." Then he dropped his eyes. For the first time, Percival thought he saw something like fear in Ben's face. And seeing it frightened the prince. "The paladin are servants of Lady Lucira," Ben continued. "There is at least one of them in the forest."

"Who?" Percival repeated with distressed ignorance. "What's going on? Who is Lucira and why do you keep mentioning her all of the sudden? And who was this soldier? Is he one of the...paladin, or whatever you're talking about?"

Ben shook his head gently "No. He was a mercenary hired by Lucira. The paladin are her generals. I've seen one of them tonight; a rider, at the edge of the forest. There must be a reason for his presence here." Ben stood to his feet. "Come now, we must not tarry. All will be explained in time."

Chapter 26

The Raven and the Rider

There is usually always a moment in a young man's
life when he wakes up from a prolonged daydream
and realizes that life isn't quite as simple as he had
thought it would be.

-The Journals of Bengolian

Bromley was dreaming the type of dream which is nothing
but a compilation of non sequitur parts that make perfect sense
together only at the time one is dreaming it. He was in some kind
of ballroom, similar to one in Rumandy, but its floor was made of
mud and pebbles instead of marble tiles. Mourha was mumbling a
song as she sat on the ground, collecting some of the pebbles into
a small bucket. When he walked by her, she looked up and told
him his mother was very disappointed in him and he had better
do something productive with his life. Then, he decided to try a
cartwheel, but found his arms were so weak and his legs so
unstable that he couldn't even make it halfway through. After this,
he suddenly got the sensation of being tickled, so he began
laughing and rolling about.

"Bromley!"

"What? Haha...Hah. What?"

"Bromley!"

He started and awoke, quickly jumping a trail of thoughts consisting of ballrooms, pebbles, running away, flour sacks, and Cloeneth of Fairbourne. Once his thoughts solidified, he remembered his situation. He was still lying in between two flour sacks in the storage room above a bakery, and Cloeneth was kneeling beside him, her little, cold hands trying to stir him awake.

"Oh. Hullo, you. What is it?"

"Shh!"

Bromley closed his eyes again out of sleepiness and reduced the volume of his voice to a whisper. "What is it?" he repeated.

"The townspeople. I think something is happening."

"Is it morning, already?"

"No."

"What?" the boy croaked. "Oh, don't worry about it and go back to sleep."

"No, something is wrong. Please wake up."

Bromley grunted and stretched himself out as much as he could between the flour sacks.

"Bromley, look," Cloeneth quickly rose, disregarding his sluggishness, and scurried to the window of the storage room.

Bromley lugged himself after her, rubbing sleep from his eyes a few times before he could see anything outside. A crowd of villagers were gathered in the town square, some of them standing on the platform used during the slave trade. Torches were lit, allowing some sparse visibility on the scene.

"Look," Cloeneth pointed to the gateway. A dozen or so men scrambled around the gate, fortifying it with planks and nailing beams in Xs across the wall's doors and windows.

"Well," Bromley yawned, "That doesn't look particularly good."

"What's going on?"

"It looks like a siege."

"What? What do you mean?"

"I mean we probably picked the wrong town to spend the night in, my lady."

"What do we do?"

"I'm not sure. If I didn't wake up one minute ago, I could probably think of something."

"Bromley!"

"Cloeneth."

"You're not in the least bit worried about this?"

"Of course I'm worried about it, but I'm also very, very sleepy. In real life, dashing young gentlemen don't spring out of bed in the middle of the night endowed with superhuman energy and ideas. Would you just give me a second?"

Suddenly, there was a screeching caw sound outside the window, and Cloeneth jumped, putting her hand to her mouth to silence a shriek. A raven landed on the windowsill, its wings spread as in a predatory state. It looked at Cloeneth and made a hissing sound, then charged towards Bromley, who swung at it with his arm until it turned to fly away.

"What the hell was up with that thing?" Bromley grumbled, watching it fly over the town's walls into blackness. "Was it sick or something?"

"No. But its left eye was scarred. I've seen it before." Cloeneth's voice was grave, but her words seemed to be only a light foam on the surface of what she was thinking.

"What are you talking about, Cloeneth? Would you stop being so damn mysterious for one moment and tell me what the hell is going on right now!"

"I don't know what's going on right now."

Cloeneth had barely finished speaking when the village's warning bell tolled. Men were yelling orders, but it was hard to make out their words. They heard a scream, and a sudden volley of arrows rained down from somewhere out in the darkness.

"Shit," said Bromley.

Another volley of arrows.

"Shit. Damn it."

"Stop swearing. You're not helping."

"Sorry."

"Bromley, what's happening?"

"I don't know! You tell me!"

"Who would be attacking the town?"

"I don't know!"

"Should we stay here or try to go somewhere else?"

"Cloeneth, I don't know!"

The two did stay there for the next few minutes, however.

Not because they decided on it, but because of their indecisiveness. Several men were shot before them and dragged by other villagers into buildings, away from the deluge of arrows. Some villagers stood positioned on the ledges of the wall, firing arrows back into the darkness. It was impossible to tell the numbers of the army that assailed the town, however, for it seemed they made no noise but the wisping of their arrows. Suddenly there was a loud thump at the gate, followed by another. And with each thump the gate swayed and creaked, till at last it gave way and the head of a battering ram crashed through the opening, splinters of wood shooting out.

A group of men rushed in past the battering ram and the broken gate. They were large and dark skinned, their heads slick and hairless and their faces and bodies painted with symbols. Men of the East. The noises of screaming and slashing of swords grew loud, and arrows darted from every corner of the town square.

"Shit." Bromley took Cloeneth into his arms, and this time she did not complain. "It's alright. You're alright. We're going to stay here, Cloeneth. And whatever's happening will be over soon, alright?"

Cloeneth didn't make any answer.

"Alright, Cloeneth?" Bromley asked again, insistently. "Do you understand me?"

"I understand," she said finally, trembling in his arms.

"I'm going to take care of you."

They looked again out the window. Some of the dark soldiers who had entered the town were carrying large, heavy looking barrels. They overturned these, and a black liquid spilled out, creeping across the ground in streams. One soldier threw a lit torch into the stream, and a river of fire quickly swept across the town square.

"Bromley," Cloeneth whispered weakly.

"I know. It's alright, Cloeneth. It's alright." Bromley repeated these words in attempt to convince himself as well as Cloeneth. The fire spread directly beneath their window, and the smoke rose into their faces. The sound of the flames crackling grew louder and the smell of burning filled their nostrils. Within moments, the view of the street was lost entirely by the smoke, and they began to cough for want of air.

Bromley did not waste time with words but grabbed Cloeneth's hand and ran with her to the other end of the room. They rushed down the ladder and out of the building, fire and smoke rising all around them. The air was scant and they heaved for breath at every turn as they ran hand in hand through the allies. They passed villagers bleeding and screaming and tearing off their fiery clothes. A woman holding her bleeding eye, wailing in pain. A painted soldier rushing by with a torch, lighting more fires.

Bromley tried to think of a plan, but his mind was blank. He had no weapon. There was no shelter. Any house could be burnt, any street could be open to a volley of arrows. "It's alright," he repeated to Cloeneth, though he was trembling himself. The smoke and flame were both a terror and a protection, for many soldiers passed them by in the confusion without doing them harm.

Suddenly, as they turned a corner of a street, there was a loud neighing of a horse. Cloeneth screamed. The horse reared and its hoof struck Bromley's head. He fell back into the dirt, his forehead cracked and his vision blurred.

"Bromley!" Cloeneth knelt beside him and gently touched his face and his bleeding head. Bromley heard her voice only as a distant echo which rung through his ears with the sounds of burning and screaming. The blood began to drip into his eyes, but in the haze he saw the rider dismount. Behind him there was a line of fire, and his figure was a black silhouette. He grabbed Cloeneth and began to drag her away. Bromley lifted his head weakly from the ground and sat up. He took hold of the rider's forearm but found no strength to hold him. The rider struck Bromley, sending him to his back once more. Bromley felt a hand, cold as death, take hold of his neck. A sharpness penetrated his skin as though someone was digging a nail into the flesh below his ear. This sent a fire through him immediately and he lost all sensation but the burning. The images before him faded into black fog.

Then after a moment his vision returned. He saw Cloeneth and the rider before him. The rider grabbed Cloeneth by her arm again and dragged her to her feet. She struggled but could not free herself. Bromley tried with every ounce of his strength to rise up, but his body felt frozen, ice hard but scorching as though his skin crawled with flames. Suddenly, another horse and rider came into his view. This rider rode a grey horse like clouds. The dark rider turned towards him, throwing Cloeneth back to the ground.

But the colors before Bromley began to blur and the rest of the scene was lost. Red bled into blue and yellow blended with green; the light and darkness seemed to battle with each other until his vision became a wash of gray. Then he felt as though he was rising and leaving his body behind him. Suddenly there was no longer any sound, no vision, no feeling of warmth or chill. Only blackness.

Chapter 27

Reunions

Though hidden among the rocky turf, the pearl remains untouched. Till at last it will be found, and what was lost beyond hope will be restored.

-The Journals of Bengolian

It had been Percival's very first real battle. He was rather excited about it after the fact. He later remembered it with much greater resplendence than it probably actually held, and he deemed himself much more valiant a fighter than he probably actually was. This is how it occurred, to the prince's understanding:

On that previous night, Ben had taken the company in haste to a little town which was being overrun by some sort of army of savage mercenary soldiers from the North. Or East. Or something like that. They were being led, Percival gathered, by a man whom Ben and Pavlock called a paladin of Lucira. He hadn't yet figured out who Lucira was, but he figured that was a detail which could be easily overlooked in the grand scheme of things.

When the company arrived at the town, black smoke was

rising and flickers of fire could be seen here and there above the town's walls. Ben gave Percival and Orion each a sword (apparently he had them somewhere amidst the clutter he piled onto Padgett) and instructed them, as if it were as simple a task as making supper, to defend the village or die in the attempt.

They rushed into the town square, Pavlock on his horse and the others on foot, and were instantly immersed into the battle. It was certainly not the sort of swordplay Percival was accustomed to. These soldiers had neither elegance nor good form. The prince however, after almost being killed several times and being saved by either Pavlock, Orion, Ben, or Brunwick, decided that it would most likely be best to surrender some style for the sake of effectiveness.

Percival's heart was throbbing when at last he heard the cheering of the townsmen and the word spreading that what remained of the attacking army was retreating. He sighed heavily, took his sword in his left hand, and shook out the soreness from his right. From behind him, Orion sneaked up and threw his arm around him. Percival shrieked and broke loose, raising his sword.

"Woah, woah there! It's only me!" Orion said, panting as he wiped perspiration from his brow.

"Don't do that again unless you want me to inadvertently run you through," the prince replied.

"Oh now, I was just giving you a post victory embrace."

"I'd rather you didn't directly after I've been engaging in battle with savages."

"Don't be so skittish, Percy! You'll get premature age lines and gray streaks in your cherub hair."

"Orion!" came a call from ahead. It was Pavlock. "Orion! Percival! We need you."

The two boys made their way quickly towards Pavlock and Brunwick, who were standing in one corner of the town square.

"There are many villagers injured," Pavlock said, lifting up an elderly man whose leg had been burned. "We're taking them all to the inns to be cared for. Gather as many as can be found to help."

"Yes, sir," Orion said.

"Brunwick has some skill with healing. He will be helping Ben see to those with the most severe wounds, but we will need many other aids."

Suddenly, a small cry came out from behind them. "Sir!"

Percival turned to see a particularly frightened looking girl about his own age running towards them. "Sir!" she cried again, addressing Pavlock. Her face was pale and her eyes reddened and streaming with tears. "There's a boy over here; he needs help gravely," she stammered, her voice cracking as though she had been crying for a long while.

"We're doing everything we can," Pavlock replied.

"But sir, his heart is so faint and his hands are cold. He's stiff; I can't wake him, his head is bleeding badly."

Something about the girl seemed familiar to Percival, though the dirt on her face and her tussled hair hid her.

"Orion," Pavlock commanded. "Go with her."

Orion did so, and Percival stayed with Pavlock. For the next hour or so, they assembled the able-bodied villagers to help carry the injured civilians inside to be cared for. Percival even lifted a few people himself, though every time he had to touch someone, he flinched a little and afterwards spent a good deal of time cleaning his hands on his shirt.

He was proud to say that the only injury he had acquired throughout the entire night was a small gash on his left shoulder. He was at first sickened by the sight of it, but as the night wore on, he began to grow rather fond of it. He wondered if it might leave a faint little scar for him to boast about, proving his gallantry in battle.

Eventually, when all the injured were housed, the prince went himself to an inn to be bandaged. Since his was a rather small wound, however, he sat in waiting for a time. It was a rather disgusting experience to be around so many commoners who stunk of sweat and were bleeding and burned, but he wasn't entirely miserable. If anything, he felt braced for another round of adventuresome fun. Perhaps the next battle would be on a grander scale. He might even get another injury. A larger injury. On his back, or his leg, or his stomach, or across his eye...Of course, he reconsidered that last idea. Having a scar across his eye would be simply unbearable. He couldn't live with himself if his face was tainted from its perfection.

Pavlock entered the inn and, after speaking to some of the nursemaids, sat down next to Percival. "Seventy-four injured," he said, grimly. "Eleven dead. But the good news is everyone seems to be accounted for."

"That's good," Percival replied.

"You fought well."

Percival noticed again, as he did the previous night, that Pavlock's left forearm was bandaged. He decided to take advantage of the circumstances to test Pavlock. "Did you injure your arm last night?" he asked nonchalantly.

Pavlock hesitated. "No," he replied. And though it seemed he was not going to continue in an explanation, he added, "The paladin. Did you see him?"

"Uh. The..."

"The rider. He was masked in black. No heavy armor."

"Oh, yes. I did see him. You fought with him, but I didn't see the end of it. Did you kill him?"

"No. He and what was left of his army will not return to this same town. But I owe my injury to the one who sent him. His mistress, Lucira."

"Oh." Percival was surprised at the mention of the name again. He hesitated. "Who...who is that, exactly?"

"There are only a few who know. Ben is one of them. I suppose you could say they were brother and sister."

"Brother and sister?"

"In a fashion."

"...And she's trying to kill everyone?"

"Well, we're not entirely sure what she's after. Or why she would have sent one of her paladin to this town. She has many armies but only seven of her riders. And these she only sends out with great reserve."

"Pavlock!" came a voice. Percival turned to see Brunwick

approaching. He was wearing an apron stained red and a pair of round, thin spectacles on his nose. "You might want to see this," he said.

Pavlock rose from his seat, and Percival, not sure whether or not it was the proper thing to do, rose and followed. Brunwick led them into a separate room with only a few beds, all occupied with severely injured men. They came to one of these beds, beside which sat a girl leaning over a sleeping patient. Percival recognized her as the girl who had approached Pavlock earlier. Her eyes were wide with fear. "What's wrong with him? Why aren't you telling me?" she said, looking at Brunwick.

"In time, lass," Brunwick said, gently but with some anxiety. "Look," he turned to Pavlock, showing him a wound on the boy's neck.

Percival had to peep between their shoulders to get a look at the wound. It was swollen and black. Not a burn, but not a gash from a sword. Brunwick nimbly touched the wound with a metal instrument and extracted a few crumbs of a green powder.

"I originally was seeing to him because of his head injury," Brunwick began. "The lass says he was hit by the hoof of a horse."

"The paladin." Pavlock said grimly.

"Aye. And look at this. The boy was paralyzed. One of Lucira's tricks, no doubt."

"Have you shown Ben?"

"Not yet."

"What's going on?" the girl repeated. "Tell me what's happening."

"Don't worry, my dear," Brunwick said, "He'll be alright. You stay by him."

"Of course."

"Percival," Pavlock added, "You stay here as well. Keep both of them company."

"Yes, sir," said the prince as Pavlock and Brunwick left the room again.

There was an empty chair beside the bed, and Percival pulled it towards himself. He didn't sit down immediately, however, because at that moment, he caught a better glimpse of the boy's face.

"Bromley," he muttered quietly in disbelief.

The girl beside the bed looked up. "What did you say?"

The prince stared speechlessly. Bromley's head was badly broken, the wound from the horse's hoof still open but the bleeding dying down. His eyes were bruised and swollen, and of course there was the gruesome injury on his neck. But he was still recognizable.

"Did you just say his name?" the girl beside him asked again, astonished.

"I..." Percival sat down. "You look familiar; who are you?"

The girl hesitated. "You almost look familiar as well." Her eyes widened suddenly in amazement. "Prince Percival!" she exclaimed.

"How do you know me?"

"I'm Cloeneth of Fairbourne."

"Who? Oh! Yes! I remember you! You were at my birthday

party!"

"So were you! I mean—well. You were..."

"What are you doing here?" asked the prince.

"What are you doing here?" asked the princess.

"And what is Bromley doing here?"

"It's...sort of a long story."

"Well, mine is too, I suppose."

Percival looked back at Bromley, laying almost lifelessly on the bed. He found there was nothing he could say, so he just sat. And Cloeneth sat as well, her eyes intent on Bromley's face. She softly covered his hand with hers.

It is difficult to say what the prince was feeling exactly at this moment. He wasn't entirely unhappy to see him. Then again, he wasn't entirely unhappy to see him in a state close to death, either. He, of course, remembered he was inexpressibly angry with Bromley. But he couldn't quite remember why. He tried to unfold the reasons in his mind, but the more he unfolded things, the more he began to kick them aside. He was certain there was a substantial conflict between the two of them. Whatever this deeply planted conflict was, he had plenty of time to remember, but in the meantime, he was glad that Bromley was alive and here. And unconscious.

"This is where he is, is it?" said a voice behind him. He turned to see Ben, Pavlock, and Brunwick. They approached Bromley's bed, and Percival quickly rose and stood aside.

Ben laid his hand gently on Bromley's brow, then began to examine the neck wound.

"Do you still have a sample of the poison?" he asked.

"Yes, sir," said Brunwick. "I've saved what I could in a bottle for you."

"Good. See to it that the bottle is airtight. There's not much left around the boy's wound. Most of it has been absorbed into his bloodstream already. He'll be out for a while, but he'll awaken." Ben looked at Cloeneth, "You know him?"

"Yes, sir."

"Friend? Brother?"

"My friend."

"And where are the two of you from? Not from this village, I trust. You have a different sort of look about you."

"Oh. Yes, sir." Cloeneth looked at Percival briefly then returned her attention to Ben. "He and I are from different countries. But we were traveling together."

"Ah..." Ben squint his eyes at Cloeneth. He studied her for a moment, a faint smile growing on his face. "He did well in protecting you. That necklace you're holding, is it yours?"

Percival had not previously noticed, but the girl was clasping a golden necklace in her hand, rested on the bed.

"Oh. Yes," she said, startled. She brought it towards herself protectively.

"May I see it?"

She hesitated, but slowly raised it up and handed it across the bed to Ben. The old man hummed softly as he examined it. Returning it to its owner, he grinned gently at one corner of his mouth. "Thank you," he said, letting his smile widen as his gaze fell upon the girl. His eyes seemed exceptionally bright, nearly glistening. "I better go now. It's wonderful to see you again, my dear."

"...I'm sorry?"

Ben rose from his seat. "The boy will survive, but he needs a great deal of care. I will inspect the poison; there may be other effects besides the paralysis. Will you stay beside him, lady?"

"Yes. Of course I will," Cloeneth answered, a little dazed. "I'm sorry, sir, but have we met before?"

Ben laughed. "Oh, no. I'm sure we haven't. That's one thing I most definitely would have remembered. If you'd excuse me, my dear," Ben bowed, "there are others who need my attention. Oh, and Percival—"

The prince looked up.

"Stay with the redhead as well, will you?"

"...Yes sir," the prince replied.

Simple Language Translations
(The ancient tongue of Diyric)

"Auhn iya cronchim unfekas dem, ishal bayisa."
"If these are the enemies of my master, she has already won."

"Unahc Hekashas fiyda hac ushesa."
"Lady Crow sends her love."

"Ben dovu chevahta ti uhndeset."
"May you find mercy in defeat."

auhn - if the circumstances are, if it is so
iya - these are
croncha(im) – enemy(ies)
unfek(as) — (of the) master
dem – my
ishal - she has won
bayisa - already, has already happened

unahc – lady
hekash(as) - of the crow
fiyda - she sends
hac - her
ushesa – love

ben – may, I hope, a bestowal of blessing

dovu – you receive

chevahta – mercy, absolution

ti – in

uhndeset – defeat

ACKNOWLEDGEMENTS

A few people must be thanked by name...

Kathleen Rea, my dear friend and voice of reason. I would surely have set these characters aside long ago had you not insisted I finish the story. Thank you for your friendship and love through the years as we've grown from awkward girls into even more awkward young women.

Michael Herman. Words cannot express how much you continue to inspire me. Thank you for the years of grueling competition, friendship, and love. Surely the bards shall sing of our glorious rivalry for years to come.

All teachers who have inspired and encouraged me, especially Kim Pavlock who set a spark, Edmund Miller who fanned the flame, and Joseph Zettelmaier, who caused an explosion. You have helped me more than you know!

And of course, my incredible family: Mom, Dad, Phil, Pete, Gen, Paul, Mary, and Roni. Home is where there's plenty of good food and bad puns.

JOSEPHINE ELI

ABOUT THE AUTHOR

Josie's love of all things artistic has led her to pursue a variety of fanciful endeavors in addition to writing. She has studied drawing and painting, graduated from Eastern Michigan University in Theatre Arts (2014), and owns her own small photography business. Outside of her day job, she dabbles in film projects, costume design, graphic design, music, and cosplay, and is the proud owner of a growing assortment of fantasy weapons. She currently lives in Michigan, and can be reached for comment at josephineeliwriter@gmail.com.